Strobe lights  silhouettes. Bodie.
I eyed the dance floor, eager to sway like that with Andrew.

He leaned over, speaking directly into my ear. "Can I buy you a drink?"

"Vodka tonic," I requested. "Make it a double."

Andrew nodded and led me toward the bar. We maneuvered around strangers as though navigating a crowded New York subway.

From behind, Zack squeezed my shoulder. I glanced back as he disappeared into the throngs of people, grinning mischievously.

Music vibrated off the walls, forceful and upbeat. Despite having flown around the country all day, I felt alert and excited. I was keenly aware of Andrew's trembling, eager body…as well as my own.

As we approached the bar, Andrew's hands wandered. His fingers moved so quickly I could hardly tell if they were on my shoulders, waist, or hips. We placed our order and watched the bartender pour two identical drinks. Unwilling to wait any longer, I planted Andrew's hand on the neckline of my dress, so his middle finger dipped into my cleavage. Thanks to the dim lighting in the club, nobody seemed to notice. Or, if they did, they clearly didn't care. His fingertips swept across my chest eagerly. I bit his ear, softly, to show him I wanted to play.

Flight Path

by

Lisa Wilkes

Flight Path

Cover Art by *Tina Lynn Stout*

The Wild Rose Press, Inc.
PO Box 708
Adams Basin, NY 14410-0708
Visit us at www.thewildrosepress.com

Publishing History
First Champagne Rose Edition, 2019
Print ISBN 978-1-5092-2946-8
Digital ISBN 978-1-5092-2947-5

Published in the United States of America

Dedication

To the adventurers and the risk-takers,
the free spirits and the stargazers,
this book is for you.
Your boldness is your strength.

Part One: Windshear Ahead

Chapter One

December 21, 2019

"You *smell* pregnant," I tell Mackenzie.

"What, exactly, does pregnancy smell like?" she asks while shoving a month's supply of tomatoes in the fridge. Her back is toward me. The angled red and green stripes on her Christmas sweater make her look like a festive zebra.

Although Mackenzie is turned away from me, her tone indicates she is smiling her signature lopsided grin. I've loved that grin since day one. Four years ago. When she sat next to me on the 38-Geary Bus and proceeded to offer me a partly smashed granola bar. Which I accepted, of course.

"Pregnancy smells like…like a lifetime of boredom and early bedtimes," I inform her. I pop a tortilla chip into my mouth, then reach for another one. "Like the death of all things fun. You know the stench on Post Street, by Webster? The dumpster where drunk dudes take a shit sometimes? It smells like that."

Mack closes the fridge and leans against it. She folds her arms across her chest, covering the giant reindeer on her sweater. "I smell like a toilet?"

I shrug. "Not you. The pregnancy."

Mackenzie shakes her head. "I love your imagination, Callie…even when it's gross and twisted.

This is why your books are fabulous."

Yet still unpublished, I muse.

"But it's too soon to make any predictions," she continues, flipping her long brown hair over one shoulder. It sparkles beneath the kitchen lights, a mass of silky strands against her olive skin. "We don't know for sure if I'm preggers. At this point, it's just a hunch."

"Your back hurts and your boobs are sore," I say. "Plus, you missed not one, not two, but three periods. So I vote yes."

"That happens all the time, though," she reminds me. "My body isn't exactly predictable."

"I know, love," I murmur. "Endometriosis is a royal bitch. However, three periods is a lot, and I think it's because there's a tiny creature invading your belly."

"Shoot, I guess I'd have to buy a different wedding dress," Mackenzie reflects, glancing out the window. "By June, I might be enormous. Ugh."

"Aww, you'll have a cute little baby bump," I say with a laugh. "Just think how much money I'll save on alcohol. As your maid of honor, I will only have to buy you sparkling grape juice at the bridal shower and bachelorette party."

Mack chuckles. "Glad this works out well for you."

"Me, too."

We are silent for a moment, listening to the cars as they whip past Mack's apartment. It's a familiar sound, the inner-city equivalent of screeching cicadas. This side of Geary always gets loud at rush hour, buzzing with excitement as the streetlights flicker on.

I pull a pregnancy test from an overflowing grocery bag. Small and light, the box fits neatly in my hand. A few years ago, after a long night of cheap vodka, I'd bought a similar drugstore kit. It seemed much more daunting back then. In comparison, this one looks harmless.

"Time's up, Mackie. Get in the bathroom," I instruct my best friend.

She glances at the device in my fingers. "Maybe we should bake cookies first."

"Nope," I say. "Test first, cookies later. I'm not even hungry. I will, however, drink all the wine in your apartment. Since you won't need it anytime soon."

She inhales sharply. "I'm not ready. What if my suspicions are wrong…or, crap, what if they're right? It's a lot of pressure either way."

I place a hand on her shoulder. "Mack, you've been ready to have a kid since I met you, before David even entered the picture. He loves you like crazy, and he can't wait to be a daddy. This scenario is basically as good as it gets. Right?"

She nods. "Every detail of our lives will change. But, like you said, we've been ready for a long time. Know something, Callie? You are an okay best friend."

"Thanks," I respond with a grin. "I'll take a compliment wherever I can get one."

"Can we at least put the cookies in the oven, so they'll cook while we wait?"

"Sure. Hope you plan to eat all of them. Liquid diet for me tonight." I nod toward the bottles of cabernet lining the kitchen counter.

Mack greases a baking pan and tosses pre-cut holiday cookies on top. Seconds after she slides the treats into the oven, the scent of melted chocolate fills her apartment. I hop up from the kitchen table.

"All right, get in there," I instruct, pointing to the

bathroom.

Mackie stares at the hallway and frowns. "Come with me?"

"To the bathroom? Sure. I've seen you pee before."

"No, I want you to take a test, too," she clarifies. "I bought a bunch of them, since Dr. Hemani said it might be hard for me to get pregnant."

"I don't think so, Mackie. Those things are expensive. Why waste one?"

"I have tons of extras. Please, Callie. I don't want to do this alone." Mackie reaches into the grocery bag and retrieves another pregnancy test.

We walk into the bathroom with our arms linked. Considering how small this apartment is, the master bathroom is quite spacious. Shiny white tiles separate an old-fashioned tub from the toilet, which has its own door. A mirror stretches across the marble sink, framed by miniature oval lightbulbs. One glance into the glass reveals big, dark circles under my eyes.

"Mackie, why didn't you tell me I look half-dead?" I groan, tugging at my eye sockets as though this can somehow alleviate the unsightly bags beneath them.

She wraps a skinny arm around my neck. "Shut up. You're gorgeous. I'd have sex with you."

I turn toward her, our noses practically touching. We have been best friends for four years, but it might as well be four decades. She's practically the sister I never had.

"First of all, your fiancé would murder me if we didn't film the whole thing, and my phone battery is too low," I inform her with a smile. "Secondly, that phase ended for me right after college. Sorry, Mack, I bat for the other team now."

She shrugs and releases her grip on my neck. "Fair enough. In five years, when you're married or CEO of SkyLine Airways or a famous novelist, promise me you'll still hang out with my boring ass. Even if I have a couple toddlers hanging off my arm."

"Meh. If you get a babysitter and drink absurd amounts of wine with me, then *maybe*," I joke, grabbing her hand. "Now go piss on a stick, please."

While Mackie pees, I inspect the fine lines on my face. The lighting in here is unforgiving; every single groove is visible. All those years I spent roasting in the Florida sunshine have finally caught up with me.

"Twenty-eight going on ninety," I murmur.

"Huh?" Mackie asks, placing her test on the counter.

"Nothing. My turn?"

"Yep."

I march toward the toilet and successfully soak the soft end of the pregnancy test. Then I cover it up, place the stick beside Mackie's, and wash my hands. "You think the cookies are done?"

She smiles at me and heads back to the kitchen. I follow closely behind, enjoying the smell of freshly baked pastries. It's a satisfying aroma which, surprisingly, complements the pine scent emanating from the Christmas tree.

With pink mitts on both hands, Mackie reaches into the oven. She retrieves the sheet pan and sets it on the counter, then lifts one cookie onto a spatula. Steam rises from the sugary treat. I shake my head to indicate I don't want a bite, but Mackie shoves part of the cookie in my mouth anyway.

As I chew, I bask in the warmth of this cozy

kitchen. Colorful Christmas lights outline the windowpane. They shine fiercely, as though attempting to offset the dim haze outside.

My best friend winks at me while devouring her half of the cookie. She hums a holiday tune, then begins addressing a stack of Christmas cards on the kitchen table. Her pen glides across each envelope easily. Gracefully.

I find myself wondering if there's ever been a more deserving mother in the whole world. Mackenzie is always brainstorming ways to brighten everyone's day. She's the kind of person who never forgets to call on your birthday. She drops everything to offer a hug or a reassuring word in a moment of need. Mack is the type who eats dinner only after making sure everyone else is well fed and happy.

"You're my hero. Even though I make fun of you all the time," I tell her once I've swallowed my cookie. "Just saying, the potential bun in your oven is one lucky kiddo."

She glances up from her holiday cards. "I'm your hero?"

I pop the cork from a bottle of cab and reach for a wine glass. "Yes. This world needs more people like you. Dave made a smart move, picking you for his future wifey. Although everyone knows you're really *my* wife."

"Duh."

I point to the digital clock on top of the stove. "Did we set a timer for the pregnancy test? How long is it supposed to take, five minutes?"

Mackenzie nods. Her phone vibrates from the marble countertop, startling both of us. "It's Dave. Hey,

Cal, go check in the bathroom? It should be ready by now."

While Mackie answers the phone call, I stroll down the hallway. Spotify is on in Mack and David's bedroom, music seeping through speakers on either side of their dresser. I hum along with the melody, trying to remember the lyrics.

Briefly, I wonder whether I'll have time to write a new song before next month's open mic night. With my hectic flying schedule around the holidays, it seems unlikely. Then again, in the past I've managed to compose something in an hour or two, the same day as open mic...so it's definitely possible.

Music continues to wash over me as I step into the bathroom. This time, I intentionally avoid the mirror.

"My face looked much better in Denver yesterday," I think aloud as I approach the sink.

While the background music fades into a commercial, I glance at the countertop. A digital red plus sign stares up at me. Excitedly, I grab the dry end of the sticks and run back to the kitchen.

"Oh, no. Don't say it!" Mackie exclaims when I approach her. "Shit. This is surreal."

"Tell us, Callie. What's the verdict?" Dave echoes from the kitchen table, where Mackie's cell phone is on speaker. He sounds so hopeful.

"David and Mackenzie, you're having a baaaaaaa-by," I declare, tossing both pregnancy tests on the table. "Bam! There's a kiddo on the way. Welcome to planet Earth, tiny human."

Mackie inhales deeply. Tears fill her eyes.

"This is amazing." Dave's voice floats up from the table. "Wow. I can't believe it."

"Dave…" Mackie responds, trailing off. "Is this really happening?"

"Sure is, babe," he says.

"Congrats on your super-sperm, Dave. Those feisty little swimmers did the job." I laugh.

"Thanks, Cal," Dave says. "Listen, Mack, I'm heading home in a second. We need to celebrate. I love you so much."

"Love you, too," Mackenzie echoes. As she ends the call, I wrap her in a giant hug.

"Are you certain?" she asks into my hair. "Not a false positive or something?"

I shake my head. "Doubt it. Look for yourself, Mack. The plus sign is so bright, I bet it glows in the dark."

Mack wriggles out of my arms and places her palms on the kitchen table. She inspects the pregnancy tests for a minute.

"Uh, Callie…"

I reach for my wine glass and take another swig. "Yeah?"

"Callie."

"What is it, love?" I repeat, swirling the wine around in my glass.

"Cal."

The gravity in Mackenzie's voice catches me off guard. Her tone seems wildly out of place, considering the circumstances. I whirl around to face my best friend. Her eyes indicate something is very wrong.

"Mackenzie, what's going on?"

With trembling fingers, she points at the tests on the table. Silence hangs thick in the air, wrapping itself around us. I creep forward.

Staring at the pregnancy tests, I realize they are identical. Red plus signs illuminate each rectangular stick. I can't tell which test is Mackenzie's, because mine has the same exact result as hers.

"What the hell? Yours must've contaminated mine," I say.

"Take it again," Mackie suggests, pointing at the grocery bag.

I hurry to the bathroom and pee on a second stick. Barely breathing, I carry it to the living room and set it on the coffee table, a wad of paper towels below it. Then I stare. And stare, and stare.

Every passing second feels like a year.

Mackie holds my hand while we wait for little lines to appear on the screen. Slowly, a plus sign forms inside the digital box.

"Is it possible?" Mackie asks, looking up at me with wide eyes.

Technically, yes, I think. *But I'm not* that *girl.*

In an instant, the atmosphere shifts dramatically. Mackenzie curls up on the couch with me while I attempt to process everything. Resting my head on her shoulder, I close my eyes. Mackenzie tells me she loves me, she always has, and I will be fine even though things feel heavy right now.

Her words jumble together. All I hear is my own heartbeat. It's so damn loud.

"Tell me how it happened," Mackenzie finally says.

"Huh?"

"Who was it? When? The whole story. It's okay, Callie. I'm here for you."

"It was right before Thanksgiving," I say.

"Remember the West Palm overnight I had?"

Mackie nods. "Sure. You were so excited to travel to South Florida. Isn't Palm Beach your favorite layover?"

"One of them, yes. I was just trying to enjoy myself. Have a good time, soak up the heat, savor the tropical vibe. I'd been flying to so many cold, bleak cities…"

"Tell me everything, honey," Mackenzie says softly. "The whole story."

I clear my throat and start at the beginning.

Chapter Two

November 20, 2019

"You've been doing this four years, right?" Zack asked. He leaned against the galley sink, his black hair nearly grazing the airplane ceiling.

"Four and a half. You?" I peeked down the aisle. Shawna, the girl flying in the back of the plane, hadn't even begun her trek toward the front galley. Which was fine; we had plenty of time to complete our service. The flight from San Francisco to West Palm Beach was blocked at nearly six hours, thanks to a massive headwind.

"Six years, so far."

I retrieved an oversized bag of pretzels from the cabinet. "Isn't it the best?"

"Girl, you're not kidding." Zack grabbed my elbow, pulling my face toward his. I was close enough to see every long, perfect eyelash. He grinned, mischief dancing in his chocolate eyes. "This job is a constant adrenaline rush, which I love."

"Same here. They pay us to fly across the country and spend twenty-one hours in gorgeous cities like West Palm."

"Mmhmm. We're spoiled…"

"Spoiled rotten."

Zack reached for his apron. "I fell into this career

by accident, but I plan to stay as long as possible. Can you imagine anything more fun and random? You never know what to expect...or who you'll cross paths with. In my six years at SkyLine, I've met politicians, actors, and athletes. My friends are jealous because I always have the best stories."

"Never a dull moment, right?" I chuckled.

Shawna grazed my side, startling me. I hadn't noticed her approaching the galley. Luxurious blond hair tumbled over her shoulders, every strand perfectly in place.

"Hey, y'all," Shawna said in a thick Texas accent. She grabbed a stack of napkins from the cabinet, her bracelets jingling as they collided with each other. "Shoot, it's only day one and I'm already tired."

"Me, too," I reflected. "The neighbors threw a party last night, and my roommates convinced me to go. I stayed up way past my bedtime."

Zack shook his head. "You did the right thing, girlfriend. You live in San Francisco. Might as well enjoy it."

"I agree," Shawna said with a laugh. "Okay, let's get this done quickly so we can relax. There's an empty row in the back of the plane. And I found a few magazines in the cubby."

I grabbed the drink cart and headed into the aisle.

****

"You coming to the back with me, honey?" Shawna asked once we finished our beverage service.

I glanced at the galley, where Zack had scattered liquor minis and half-empty soda cans. "Maybe in a couple minutes. I'll help Zack clean up first."

"Sounds good," Shawna said as she headed toward

the back of the plane. "I'll be in the last row."

While Zack was reorganizing the liquor kit, I grabbed a few soda cans and emptied them in the garbage.

"Thanks for helping," he said, rearranging the minis so they lined up in neat little rows.

I nodded. "No problem."

"Hey, I think we've flown together before," Zack commented, shuffling two bottles of gin. "Or maybe we've seen each other in the crew room? I can't place it."

"We worked a trip together when I was brand new at the airline. Shoot, I was so nervous, I almost threw up. You told filthy jokes until I laughed. Truly disgusting. One was about a Dirty Sanchez, which I had to look up online."

Zack chuckled. "Sounds like something I would say. Where did we fly?"

"Double JFK layovers. They were short but fun."

Zack zipped up the liquor kit and returned it to the proper cabinet. "Good. So tell me about yourself, Miss Callie."

"What would you like to know?" I asked while emptying a soda can. A tiny spray of liquid shot out of the garbage bin, splashing across the floor. I threw down a paper towel to soak up the spill.

"Everything. Have you been in San Francisco a long time?" he asked.

I tilted my head to the side. "Coming up on four years, actually. I was living in Central Florida, but I moved to SF after I got this job."

"You like California, then?"

"Love it. Where do you live?"

"Portland," Zack said with a frown. "I plan to relocate soon, though. Maybe Los Angeles? I'm tired of commuting."

"I bet. Commuting is for the birds," I noted, scrunching up my face. "I commuted for a few months when I first started at SkyLine, then I swore I would *never* do it again."

"Do you miss Florida?"

"Yes, sometimes. But I'm happy in the Bay Area. There's this artistic, whimsical side to the city. San Francisco is so vibrant."

"Definitely. Are you from Florida?"

"Boston, actually. I grew up in Massachusetts, but I went to the University of Florida and then hopped all over the country. I tried everything, Zack. Taught high school for a year in Austin. Wrote poetry and short stories in Denver while waiting tables to pay rent. Ended up back in Florida, in Orlando. I was bartending and trying to get my books published...which never happened. And then I got hired here."

"You have such a gypsy heart, Cal," Zack said, his eyes shining brightly. "It's refreshing."

He plopped down on the jumpseat and crossed his legs.

"Mmm. Maybe I'm just impulsive. Or indecisive."

"More like brave," Zack insisted, sitting up a little straighter. "Most people don't have the balls to uproot their whole lives, even if they're unhappy. They just stay in the same town, working the same job, surrounded by the same people. And they become more miserable every day."

"There's some truth to that," I reflected. "You know, people always told me I was a dreamer. I couldn't figure out if it was a compliment or not. But you make it sound like a good thing."

"It is, I promise. Hey, are you dating anyone?" Zack asked, shifting gears rather abruptly.

"Nope," I said. "To be honest, I'm glad I'm not tied down. Most of my friends from back home are married and it feels like a prison sentence. They talk about water heaters and new curtains. It's the stupidest shit, Zack. I couldn't care less."

"But being in love is the best…" Zack murmured. "My ex and I were together for five years. I was sure I'd marry him."

"Shoot. What happened?" I asked. The airplane took a sudden dip, and the seatbelt sign lit up. I grabbed a seat beside Zack in anticipation of turbulence.

"Oh, you know. *Life* happened," Zack said.

"I'm sorry."

"It's okay. I love him like crazy. But it's a big world. And there are lots of other boys out there," Zack said with a shrug. "Maybe I'll find one in West Palm Beach tonight. Who knows? Anything's possible."

"True."

"You're coming downtown with me tonight, right? Please don't be a slam-clicker. I might need a wing-woman," Zack told me.

I nodded. "Sure, I'll go downtown with you. Why not? What have we got to lose?"

Zack grinned. "Exactly."

Later, after we had touched down in West Palm, excitement stirred in my core. Palm trees flashed by the jumpseat window as we cruised toward the gate. Even before opening the main cabin door, I could practically taste the saltwater breeze.

"Meet in the hotel lobby in an hour?" Zack asked as the last few passengers shuffled off the airplane.

I nodded vigorously, unable to contain my enthusiasm.

"You think Shawna will come with us?"

"Not sure. She seems nice. Do Texas girls hang out with California crews, though?" I asked, nodding toward her as she wheeled her suitcase up the aisle. A Texas flag decal was affixed to the back of her roller bag.

Zack shrugged. "She said she was exhausted, so I predict it'll just be me and you tonight." He lifted my suitcase from the overhead bin and set it on the floor.

I grabbed the handle. "Thanks."

"No problem."

We followed our pilots through West Palm Beach Airport. It had been several months since I'd traveled there; I'd forgotten how cute the airport was. The moving walkway was lined with miniature palm trees, red-and-white garland wrapped around their trunks to make them look like sparkly candy canes.

"This airport is so festive," Shawna murmured as we walked through the exit.

I nodded in agreement, thankful for the blast of pleasantly warm air which enveloped us as soon as we stepped outside.

****

My hotel phone erupted, a jarring ringtone that sounded like an alarm clock. I gasped and slid my finger one inch to the left, smudging my eyeliner.

"Shoot," I groaned while reaching for a washcloth.

The phone rang again. I leaped across the king-sized bed, diving for the receiver.

"Hello?" I said. With my free hand, I wiped eyeliner off my cheek.

"Callie, I'm waiting for you in the lobby," Zack said. "By the way, why don't I have your cell number? Are we following each other on Instagram?"

"Not yet. But we can."

"Okay. I'm searching for you on IG right now. Umm, are you ready to go, girl? We've got lots to do tonight. I'm not going to look this young forever."

"You're too much," I told him, a smile spreading across my lips.

Zack coughed. "Thanks. Now get downstairs…"

"On my way."

I sucked in my stomach and slithered into the black dress I'd tucked in a corner of my suitcase. Glancing in the mirror, I nodded in approval. My makeup was dramatic and my dress was tight, but not obscene.

Zack was grinning like a fool when I spotted him in the lobby. His cheeks were flushed. It wasn't hard to guess why; a flask protruded from the pocket of his jeans.

"You made it," he noted happily.

"I did."

"Excellent," he declared, opening his arms wide. I sank into them. The scent of bourbon oozed from his skin. "Callie, you gotta try this…"

He reached for his flask. I took a swig, the metal surface cool against my lips. After a brief pause, I took another gulp. Zack folded his arms across his chest, impressed by my determination.

"Now we're ready to party." He laughed as I returned the flask to his pocket. "Actually, I need your number. In case I decide to go home with a hot stranger tonight. Safety first, right?"

I smiled as Zack handed me his phone. After sending myself a text, I placed the slim cell phone in his open palm.

"Done. Uber or walk?" I asked.

"Walk," Zack replied without hesitation. We marched through the hotel's double doors together. "Let's find you a sexy man. Someone to have fun with."

"Oh, that's okay!" I shouted as we darted across a small intersection. Clematis Street stood before us, a beacon of light against a pitch-black Florida sky. "Let's just dance and drink. And then dance some more. God, this place is beautiful. I could stay here forever."

"Yeah, the weather is ideal," Zack said, hopping a curb. "This beats the Portland snow, for sure."

Music poured from a bar to our left, some pop song with a lively beat. Beside the bar, there was an alley with crisscrossed staircases leading up to apartments.

Five guys stumbled toward us, a cloud of polo shirts, chinos, and open containers. In a pitiful attempt to conceal their booze, they'd placed their beer in brown bags. The smell was unmistakable, though.

I moved a couple inches closer to Zack instinctively. One of the boys, a tall guy in the front of the pack, nodded at me. He was handsome, by far the cutest person in the group. His big brown eyes stood out.

I could get lost in them, I reflected, surprised by the peculiar thought.

While I watched, those brown eyes moved up and down my dress. Slowly. Deliberately.

"Hey," I said to the tall stranger. Wind rustled

through my skirt, shifting it an inch higher. The dress was short to begin with. By that point, it was basically a tank top.

"Hey," the guy echoed. His friends sipped their drinks, less hurriedly than before. We stood clustered together in an asymmetrical semi-circle, halfway between the alley and the street.

"Where are you guys heading?" I asked, nodding down the road. Lights flashed from a marquee a few blocks away, advertising a local band and no cover charge.

"Anywhere but Matchpoint," the brown-eyed boy informed me.

"Where, then?" I asked. The rest of his crew glanced at each other, a sure sign that they had no specific plan.

"Let's go to Reston's," Zack suggested to the entire group. "I was there a few weeks ago. It was fun."

"Reston's sounds good," the tall guy said. He stepped closer, allowing me to absorb his scent. I'd smelled that cologne before, strong and earthy. But I couldn't remember where.

Without missing a beat, I grabbed his beer can, nestled inside a flimsy paper bag. Then I threw my head back and chugged.

"I'm Callie," I said, returning the mostly empty can.

"Andrew," he told me with a smile.

Zack introduced himself, as did the other four guys. None of their names stuck. I couldn't pay much attention to the others. Andrew's gorgeous eyes were fixed on mine and his lips looked so inviting.

We walked toward Reston's, with Zack leading the

charge. Andrew and I stayed a few steps behind everyone else. Stars shimmered above us, proud and almost defiant in their luminescence.

Without much warning, something inside me stirred. Suddenly, I wanted Andrew. The desire grew stronger as we trekked toward Reston's. My heartbeat, previously calm and consistent, became erratic.

"What are you and your friend doing tonight? Any special occasion?" Andrew asked. He grabbed my hand as we darted across the street.

I bit my lip, in no rush to untangle our fingers. "Oh, we're just in town for twenty-one hours."

"Just one night? Really?"

"Yes. We're SkyLine flight attendants," I explained. "For us, that's plenty of time."

"Wow. Do you like your job?"

"Of course," I told him. "What's not to love? The airline pays me to visit new cities. Actually, I'm on the clock right now."

Andrew's eyes widened. "You are?"

"No." I laughed. "No, I'm not. Which is why I can do this."

Right there, in the middle of the sidewalk, I grabbed his face and kissed him. He tasted like beer and peppermint gum.

Moments earlier, I'd told Zack I wasn't interested in getting any action tonight. Yet with this stranger's tongue in my mouth and his fingers grazing my side, I craved more. My panties dampened in anticipation of things to come.

I opened my eyes, searching for signs that Andrew's lust matched mine. He cleared his throat and shifted slightly, his hips brushing against me. Through his jeans, I could feel him getting hard. This was all the proof I needed.

Suddenly, I knew how the night would end. And it wouldn't be alone.

****

"Do they charge cover at this club?" Zack asked, reaching into his pocket. "I can't remember."

"Nah, Reston's is free before ten," Andrew informed us.

The walls were lined with TVs, all of them replaying some college football game. A massive bar stretched across one side of the club. Bartenders poured colorful drinks at record speed while ear-shattering music poured through speakers. Every seat at the bar was taken, with people spilling onto the dance floor.

Behind me, the boys told jokes and slapped each other on the back. Andrew stood at my side. His fingers traced my panty line, flirtatious and teasing.

Strobe lights flashed, illuminating hundreds of silhouettes. Bodies pressed against each other hungrily. I eyed the dance floor, eager to sway like that with Andrew.

He leaned over, speaking directly into my ear. "Can I buy you a drink?"

"Vodka tonic," I requested. "Make it a double."

Andrew nodded and led me toward the bar. We maneuvered around strangers as though navigating a crowded New York subway.

From behind, Zack squeezed my shoulder. I glanced back as he disappeared into the throngs of people, grinning mischievously.

Music vibrated off the walls, forceful and upbeat. Despite having flown around the country all day, I felt alert and excited. I was keenly aware of Andrew's trembling, eager body…as well as my own.

As we approached the bar, Andrew's hands wandered. His fingers moved so quickly I could hardly tell if they were on my shoulders, waist, or hips. We placed our order and watched the bartender pour two identical drinks. Unwilling to wait any longer, I planted Andrew's hand on the neckline of my dress, so his middle finger dipped into my cleavage. Thanks to the dim lighting in the club, nobody seemed to notice. Or, if they did, they clearly didn't care. His fingertips swept across my chest eagerly. I bit his ear, softly, to show him I wanted to play.

We grabbed our drinks and gulped them down, then ordered another round. While the bartender refilled our cups, Andrew's hands moved down my back, resting on the curve of my ass.

"Let's get out of here," I suggested after we had chugged our second round of drinks. Andrew nodded. He placed our empty glasses on the bar and slid a few bills toward the bartender.

"Sounds good. Another club?" Andrew asked.

I shook my head. My plans for the night required privacy. "How about your place."

He paused. "You sure? We just met—"

"Shhh," I instructed, placing my finger on his lips mid-sentence. "I trust you. Let me tell Zack I'm leaving."

I searched the room for my coworker, but there were too many people. Everything looked misshapen beneath the strobe lights; bodies blended into each other. It was impossible to distinguish faces.

"Text Zack. I'll get my friend to tell him, too,"

Andrew promised. He flagged down one of his buddies and asked him to deliver the message.

I sent Zack a text, grateful we'd exchanged numbers earlier. —*Where are you? Is it cool if I leave with Andrew?*—

Zack's response lit up my phone immediately. —*Go get bent, Callie. I want details tomorrow*—

I ran outside with Andrew. Seconds later, our Uber arrived. We crawled on top of each other in the backseat, oblivious to everything except our intertwined bodies.

"This feels so good," Andrew breathed into my ear. His hand rested on my neck, gently cradling my face.

I grabbed his hand and pushed it down, below the plunging neckline of my dress. He rubbed my nipple between his thumb and forefinger, causing me to groan softly.

"You're so…" Andrew swallowed. "So beautiful."

I didn't respond, just leaned over and kissed his ear.

As soon as the Uber stopped, we rushed out of the car. Andrew's apartment complex was an off-white shade. Aside from the tall pillars out front, it lacked adornment. I had no idea where we were, but I sensed we were no longer downtown. This area looked residential and quiet. Compared to the flashing lights and blaring music at the club, the silence felt empty.

So we created our own excitement. The elevator ride was a frenzy of wet kisses and wandering hands.

By this point, Andrew had explored nearly every part of my body. Desperate to feel his fingers inside me, I placed his hand under my dress. It stayed there, caressing my thigh, until the elevator doors flung open on the sixth floor.

Andrew was being respectful and cautious, but I wanted reckless abandon.

I held my breath while he slid his key into the door of his apartment. Once inside, I leaned against the wall and guided his fingers under my panties. He kept them where I had placed them until I moved his hand further up. The higher his fingers traveled, the wetter I became. My nipples hardened as he traced circles inside of me.

I bit my lip, surprised by the ecstasy spreading through my body. It had been so long. I'd nearly forgotten this sensation.

We wasted no time. Together, we made a beeline for his bedroom, located on the righthand side of the apartment. I unbuckled Andrew's belt, tossing his pants in a messy heap on the floor. Then I climbed onto the bed and pressed my chest to his.

"Are you thirsty?" he asked. "I can get some water."

"I'm good," I assured him.

"Oh. Um, okay," Andrew said as he toyed with the hem of my dress. "I'm glad we met tonight."

"So am I," I said.

He leaned into my face. "God, you're gorgeous."

I smiled. "Thanks."

"Are you all right, Callie?" he asked. "Do you need some time to sober up?"

"I'm not even tipsy," I lied, trying not to slur my words.

"We can take a nap, if you want…"

"Shh," I instructed, pulling him onto the bed. I climbed on top of him and licked his bottom lip.

He reached under my dress, running his fingertips

along my thigh. Then he slid two fingers inside me. As he rubbed, I sighed happily. My head was spinning, yet somehow all my senses were heightened. Each stroke felt divine.

With adrenaline coursing through my veins, I was struck by the urge to wrap my lips around his cock. I helped Andrew shift positions, leading him up the bed until his back touched the headboard. Then I grabbed the waistband of his boxers and pulled them off. Andrew was hard as a rock. I slid my mouth down his shaft until I could taste him deep inside my throat.

Andrew's fingers grazed my neck, just below my hairline. He guided my head up and down. Gently, I moved his hand to my shoulder, letting him know I would set the pace.

Starting at the base, I licked and sucked while making my way toward the tip. Once I reached the head, I swirled my tongue around it. Small circles first, followed by larger circles.

I glanced up at Andrew, leaning comfortably against the pillows. With his eyes fixed on mine, I smiled. Then I lifted my dress over my head, tossing it halfway across the room. He reached behind my back and unclipped each latch of my bra. It tumbled onto the sheets, disappearing in folds of white. Andrew's hands cupped my bare breasts.

Moonlight seeped in through the window, illuminating his lean waist and sculpted arms. My heart thudded against my ribcage as I slid out of my panties.

Andrew placed his hands on my shoulders, looking me squarely in the eye. "Are you sure, Callie?"

"You ask a lot of questions." I smirked. "I know what I want, Andrew."

"Good. Me, too."

As I advanced toward him, headlights swept across the blinds, shining in my eyes. Instantly, my vision blurred. It seemed all the alcohol rushed to my brain at once. Blinking away the dizziness, I crawled closer to Andrew.

He was hunched over, fumbling in the top drawer of his nightstand.

I smiled through clenched teeth while waiting for the wave of vertigo to pass. Fortunately, Andrew didn't notice my drunken state. While he retrieved an item from the nightstand, I straddled him.

"I like being on top," I declared.

I grabbed his firm penis and slid it inside of me. Andrew placed one hand on my thigh while the other hand caressed my chest. We rocked back and forth, the bed creaking ever so slightly.

I sighed, amazed at how well we fit together. Determined to savor the impossibly perfect moment, I closed my eyes and took a deep breath.

But my head refused to cooperate.

Opening my eyes, I grabbed the headboard for support. The disoriented feeling persisted, despite my best attempts to diminish it.

Andrew raised his head to kiss me. I kissed him back with as much passion as I could summon. Then I waited, patiently, for the room to stop spinning.

****

Even though my ringtone was on the lowest volume setting, the sound sliced through Andrew's bedroom like a wailing siren. I thought my eardrums were going to burst.

"Shit," I muttered, reaching across the nightstand.

"Cal-leeee," Zack sang into the receiver.

"What the hell?" I asked with a yawn. "What time is it?"

Andrew stirred next to me. He murmured something unintelligible as his arm grazed my hip.

"Time for breakfast," Zack informed me cheerfully. "Come get food with us."

"Okay, okay," I agreed. Tufts of hair fell over my eyes. Quickly, I glanced at Andrew's naked body. He was on his side, one foot casually dangling off the bed. He appeared to be fast asleep.

"Sweet Pancakery in fifteen minutes. It's on Northlake Boulevard," Zack said. "See you there, girlfriend."

I tossed my phone back on the nightstand and stood up. Andrew's chest rose and fell methodically while I put on my dress. His eyelids fluttered a bit, like he was lost in some magnificent dream.

You were really fun, I thought.

Then I shoved my phone into my purse and hurried toward the door.

Outside, I had to shield my eyes from the blinding sun. I ducked into an Uber, thankful for some relief from the bright sky overhead.

Every table at Sweet Pancakery was occupied. Chatter echoed throughout the restaurant, periodically marked by the clinking of a glass. Zack had chosen a table all the way in the back. To my surprise, he wasn't alone; two of Andrew's buddies were with him. One of them had long, wavy hair and the other was wearing a faded hipster T-shirt.

"Hey, guys," I greeted the trio.

"Morning, angel," Zack beamed. He piled a couple

layers of pancakes onto his fork. "Want some food? I'm sure you need it, after last night's workout session."

I slid into the booth, shuffling toward my crazy coworker. He smelled like rum and maple syrup. I liked Zack sober, but I *loved* him drunk.

"Coffee is my top priority right now. And water. Oh, and a pair of sunglasses and earplugs probably wouldn't hurt," I admitted with a laugh. "So, what did you guys do? Did you go to another club after Reston's?"

"We went to several bars," one of the guys informed me.

"And ended up doing *everything*," Zack bragged, lifting his fork above his head. "If you know what I mean."

"Zack," I hissed. "Have you been converting straight boys?"

"Nah," the guy with the long hair smirked. "Daryl goes both ways."

"Yes. I just unleashed what was already there," Zack declared proudly. "He thanked me afterward. Seriously, I blew his mind."

"Among other body parts, I'm sure. Where's the lucky guy now?" I asked as I made eye contact with our waitress. I ordered coffee and orange juice.

"He's...*recovering*," Zack informed me, raising an eyebrow.

"Like Andrew, right?" the boy across from me guessed.

"Oh, no. We didn't do much. Just watched TV until we dozed off," I said with a flick of my wrist.

"Right," Zack smirked. "Your dress is on backwards, Cal."

I gasped and glanced down at the wrinkled fabric. "No, it's not."

"But it could have been," the guy in the vintage T-shirt said. "Because it was in a pile on the floor all night."

Smiling, I sipped Zack's water. Then I rested my head on his shoulder while the boys talked about last night's escapades.

****

"Well, you had a good time, eh?" Zack surmised as we walked into the hotel lobby. "I'm proud of you, California."

"Mmm. I love when people call me that."

Zack wrapped an arm around my shoulders. "You're living the Cali dream. It's a fitting name."

"Thank you." I yawned while waiting for the elevator. "Man, this hangover is vicious. I need a nap."

"Same here. We'll feel better once we get some rest," he promised me. "Let's go to my room."

"You sure? I can head back to mine…"

"Nah. Come snuggle with me," Zack insisted. "I am not interested in any of your parts, Callie. Gross. We can cuddle and sleep and wake up refreshed for our flights tonight."

I shrugged. "Sure. Why not?"

"Great," Zack said, pushing a button. When we reached his floor, I lost my balance, teetering forward slightly. Zack held my arm as we walked down the hall. His grip on my elbow was a steady, reassuring presence.

Once inside his room, I marched toward the curtains and tugged them closed, eager to crawl into bed. Zack handed me a bottle of water, mercifully. I gulped it down and tossed it in the recycle bin. "Thanks. Last night was fantastic, right?"

"Yes. So random and exciting," Zack declared, helping me onto his bed. I leaned against the headboard and shut my eyes. I didn't bother pulling the blankets over me; the room was warm enough, a comfortable temperature which needed no adjustment.

Zack curled up next to me, fully clothed, and wrapped his arms around my side. I could feel his heartbeat, strong and steady. His breathing slowed. Instantly, I felt safe.

"Here's to us," Zack murmured. "The free spirits. I hope you catch all your dreams, Callie."

"You, too," I whispered as I drifted off.

****

Zack woke me up at four o'clock, tapping my shoulder lightly. I blinked and inspected my surroundings. The black dress clinging to my skin told me everything I needed to know.

West Palm, I remembered. *Late night out.*

"One hour until showtime," Zack announced. "Two flights today."

"Where are we flying?" I asked with a yawn.

"Baltimore and then Nashville. Medium-long day."

I stretched. "Ugh. I need coffee."

Zack stepped into the bathroom but left the door open. Water splashed in the sink as he began shaving his face. "You and me both, girlfriend. I'm gonna crash so hard when we get to Nashville."

I stood up, collecting my purse and shoes. "Same here. I plan to sleep the entire layover. I might wake up to eat, and then go back to sleep."

"Sounds like a great plan. Recovery mode."

"Right? Okay, see you in the lobby at five."

"Don't go," Zack insisted. He set his razor on the countertop and turned to face me. "Get ready here. With me."

A flash of color caught my eye. Three little toothpaste containers were stacked neatly, and there was a surplus of tiny facial soaps. In addition, a couple mini deodorants rested against the mirror, next to a toothbrush wrapped in plastic.

"Zack, did you request those special? For me?"

He grinned while picking up his razor. "I did, while you were napping. The cleaning staff must've thought I was a huge ladies' man."

"I'm sure you broke a few female hearts, years ago…" I snickered.

"All broken hearts in my past belonged to dudes," he assured me. "I still have my gold star, Callie. Never had that weird phase where I needed to sleep with a chick. Yuck."

"I see. Well, thanks for getting me extra supplies," I said as I selected a shrink-wrapped toothbrush. "All right, I guess we can get ready together."

"And then power through the workday together, too," he said as he took out the ironing board.

Chapter Three

December 21, 2019

"Cal," Mackenzie murmurs, leaning into the couch cushions. "You'll be fine, I promise. You have options. Don't be scared."

"Mackie, I can't have a kid. I just can't," I say, my voice cracking.

Mackenzie bites her lip. "Okay. What about Andrew? Do you have his number? He can help you pay for an abortion."

"I never got his number. Didn't ask."

"Oh. Find him online, maybe?"

"I don't even know his last name." I stand up, grabbing my coat as I approach the door. "Sorry, girl. I have to go."

"Don't leave, Callie. Stay here tonight; we will take care of you."

"I love you," I say, avoiding her gaze because I'm on the verge of tears. "But I need to be alone right now. Clear my head."

She hops to her feet. "I'll order an Uber. You shouldn't walk home if you're upset or distracted. Plus, it's getting dark."

"I'm fine," I say with a wave of my hand. "I need the fresh air. I'll text you when I'm home safe. Deal?"

Mackenzie places a hand on her hip. She stares at

me for a second, eyes full of worry. "Okay. But if you don't text me within fifteen minutes, I'm calling the cops."

"I promise I will," I say while swinging the door open. "Mack, I'm so sorry this happened on your special day. You should be planning your baby announcement shit that everyone always posts on Facebook. You should *not* be worrying about my crazy life. I'm sorry."

She throws her arms around my neck. "Don't apologize. Never apologize, Callie. You're my best friend and whatever we get into, we get into together. I'm by your side through it all."

"Thank you," I say with a deep sigh. "Love you. I'll text later."

I step through the door and into the chilly night.

****

My apartment is a block away. A "Quick-Stop Travel" sign flashes directly below my bedroom window. The wrought iron gate creaks as ice-cold wind whips through it. I hurry past my apartment building, enveloped by darkness. There's only one streetlight on this block, and it's been out for weeks. I am alone in the blackness.

I text Mackenzie. —*Got home safely. Goodnight, love*—

Up ahead, twinkling lights from bars, clubs, and restaurants beckon me toward Polk Street. It's always busy, and tonight is no exception. Music blares from Lucille's, while several people linger outside of FrostBar. The sweet smell of whisky hangs in the air. A line has formed in front of Cordial House. Hurriedly, I weave around well-dressed men and women, avoiding eye contact.

I couldn't stay in SF, I reflect as I pass countless strangers. *Not with a child. I can hardly afford this town on my own, let alone with another human being.*

"Where would I possibly go? Fuck," I say aloud, mad at myself for thinking about keeping the baby. Even for a split second.

As I dart across the intersection of Sutter and Polk, I resolve to destroy the thing growing inside of me. Mackie made it seem like I have choices, but there's only one realistic option. This isn't the life I want. Having a baby is someone else's dream, not mine. Especially under these circumstances.

My phone rings from inside my pocket. I retrieve it, staring at the screen with an exaggerated sigh. It's my dad, calling from Boston.

I bite my lip and shove the phone back into my coat. Then I advance toward Sacramento Street. A homeless man staggers past, nearly knocking me to the ground. I step aside just in time to avoid a collision. Staring through glassy eyes, the man teeters toward the building, leaning against the bricks for support. He reeks of booze and skunk weed.

My phone buzzes again, this time with a text from Mackenzie.

—Hey, lady. You'll figure this out, and I'll support you every step of the way. You should try to find Andrew. He can help with any costs. Maybe you can fly back to West Palm if needed. Love you. Goodnight, Cal—

Chapter Four

December 23, 2019

"Callie!" Teresa yells from across the crew room.

I glance up from my computer and wave to her. Then I hurriedly click a few keys, completing my check-in. Teresa meanders through the sea of airline-approved suitcases and lunch bags until she's standing directly beside me. We walk to the printer together.

"Hey, girl." She smiles. Her vest looks freshly ironed. Her shoes are impeccably clean and shiny, unlike my scuffed heels. "Where are you flying today?"

Pulling my trip sheet from the printer, I read my pairing aloud. "Let's see, San Francisco to St. Louis to Pittsburgh."

"Pitt? Bummer," Teresa says, grabbing the paper from my hand. "How about tomorrow night? Oh, you're in Orlando. Not bad. I have double Austin layovers."

I gasp. "The hotel on Congress Street is one of SkyLine's best overnights. I'm jealous."

Teresa hands my sheet back to me. Then she glances in the mirror beside the computers and reaches up, fluffing her blonde hair with her fingers. "You still living in Pac Heights? With those two girls who work downtown?"

"Yes, Tammy and Linda. They're in finance."

Teresa's green eyes sparkle. "You're really enjoying the good life, huh? Must be nice to have an apartment in that part of the city."

I nod. "We snagged a great deal, rent-controlled and all. It's incredible. Our building is central to everything."

"Sounds perfect."

"It really is. How's Spokane? Is it cold there? Snowing?"

Teresa nods and pulls a pair of polka-dot earmuffs from her oversized purse. "Don't laugh. I have to wear these when I commute home. Spokane has been freezing lately."

"Shoot, I didn't even know earmuffs were still a thing. Well, if you must wear 'em, at least yours are really cute," I note. "I like the colors."

"Zack bought them for me, can you believe it? That clown actually has a matching pair. In fact, he was wearing them this morning, when he commuted in," Teresa says.

I pause, an idea forming in my mind. "Zack Friedman? He's flying today?"

Teresa nods emphatically. "He was in the crew room a minute ago. I think he just left."

"You know where he's heading?"

She bites her lip. "Uhh…I think he said Phoenix then Denver. Or maybe Denver first, then Phoenix?"

I reach for my suitcase and sprint toward the exit. "Thanks. Have a good trip, Teresa. See you around."

It's noisy in the terminal today. Christmas music blares through speakers, the lyrics to "White Christmas" circulating in my head as I scan the departure screen. Holiday travelers spill onto every walkway. Kids run and play, oblivious to the world around them.

"Phoenix leaves from Gate 14, Denver from Gate 11," I note aloud.

I reach Gate 11 first. The flight crew is waiting by the podium, their uniforms crisp and clean. There are two older ladies and a younger one with stunning blue eyes. No sign of Zack, though.

Gate 14 is crowded, with passengers packed in like sardines. It takes me a minute to spot the flight attendants. Zack leans against a window, playing on his phone while waiting for the airplane to arrive. I sidestep several toddlers and a giant poodle to get to him.

"Zack," I say breathlessly.

He turns toward me. "Hey, girl. Merry almost-Christmas."

I wheel my suitcase beside his. "You, too. Teresa told me you were in the airport today."

"Yep. Starting a three-day trip," he says with a nod. "You?"

"Same. Pittsburgh and Orlando," I tell him. "Hey, uh, I have a weird question. Did you get any of those boys' numbers when we were in West Palm?"

Zack winks at me. "I sure did. You trying to get in touch with Andrew? One round wasn't enough?"

A flashback enters my mind, Andrew's hands on my waist as I straddle him, our hips grinding together.

Blinking, I scold myself for reviving the memory.

"Not exactly," I say. "I think I left something in his apartment."

"Oh, right," Zack says, snorting. He scrolls through his phone. "Like what? Your back-door virginity?"

"Zack," I groan, punching his arm playfully. "You

really think I haven't tried anal? What is this, amateur hour?"

He grinned. "True, my mistake. Okay, California, you're in luck: I'm airdropping you Daryl's contact info. I bet he'd be thrilled to give you Andrew's number."

Within seconds, Daryl's number illuminates my screen. "Thanks, Zack. I owe you."

"Hope you find the item you lost in Andrew's apartment," he says with a wink. "Know what, Cal? We should pick up a trip together next month. Something with cool layovers."

I nod. "Definitely. And if you ever get stuck in SF before or after a trip, feel free to crash at my place."

The buzzing of an aircraft grows louder, signaling Zack's plane has arrived. I glance outside. This particular plane has been painted for the holidays; snowflakes cover the fuselage.

"Check it out: I got the Christmas plane for my Christmas trip," Zack says. He strolls toward the jet bridge. "You could've just texted me to ask for Daryl's digits. I'm glad you stopped by in person, though. Much more dramatic this way."

I shrug, a smile tugging at my lips. "Just wanted to add some healthy excitement to your workday."

"Well, you succeeded. Have a good one, Cal."

As Zack disappears from sight, I shoot Daryl a quick text. *—Hey, this is Callie, the SkyLine flight attendant who visited West Palm with Zack Friedman. Just wondering if you could send me Andrew's number. I never got a chance to write it down—*

Daryl's response arrives before I even reach my departure gate. *—Sure. Andrew talks about you a lot.*

He'd love to hear from you—

I scoff at the text. Andrew talks about me "a lot"? He hardly knows me. We spent eight hours together. We pawed at each other like a couple of horned-up teenagers half the time and slept the other half.

Daryl must be thinking of somebody else, I reflect.

****

When we land in Pittsburgh, it's dark outside. I check my cell phone. 10:16 p.m.

Vera, a tall girl with a gorgeous complexion, is flying the lead position. I've seen her around the base before, but this is our first trip together.

She completes her closing announcement as we taxi into the gate. "On behalf of this entire crew and all of SkyLine Airways, thanks for flying with us today. Welcome to Pittsburgh, and happy holidays."

I hop out of my jumpseat as the airplane screeches to a halt.

"Cal, are you coming downstairs for a drink tonight?" Vera asks while disarming her door.

I lift the girt bar on my door, then turn to face Vera. "Nah. I'm exhausted. Plus, it's a short layover."

Vera smiles understandingly. "True. Thankfully, our Orlando layover will be much longer."

The shuttle ride to our hotel is fairly quiet. Both pilots are playing on their phones and the flight attendants are comparing notes on our new crew hotel in Boston. It's snowing outside. Big, fluffy snowflakes cover the streets in a blanket of white.

Once inside my hotel room, I collapse on the bed. For about thirty seconds, I stare at my phone screen. Then I slip out of my flight attendant dress and throw on an oversized T-shirt. I sit at the wooden desk, biting my nails.

Before I can second-guess myself, I dial Andrew's number.

"Hello?" Andrew's voice explodes in my eardrum on the second ring.

I swallow. "Hi, Andrew. This is Callie, the flight attendant who was in town right before Thanksgiving. Sorry to call so late."

"Hey, Callie. It's great to hear from you. Daryl told me you texted him today. I would've reached out to you sooner, but you left in such a rush that morning, I never even got your number."

That was on purpose, I note internally. My face grows hot as the image of Andrew, tangled blissfully in the sheets, floods my mind. I shake my head to dissolve the enticing vision.

"How's everything going?" he continues. "How are you?"

"Pretty good," I lie. "Just traveling and trying to stay warm. It's snowing in Pittsburgh tonight. You doing okay, Andrew?"

"Yes. But I'd be better with you here."

"Hmm. It was just one night," I remind him. One steamy evening meant to release pent-up sexual energy. With zero strings attached.

"Exactly. Just one night. Which is why I'd love more time with you," he clarifies.

I frown. "Listen, Andrew, there's something I really need to talk to you about—"

"Over dinner, maybe?" he interrupts. "Are you flying back to West Palm anytime soon?"

Putting my phone on speaker, I scroll through my SkyLine app to find my monthly schedule. "Let's see.

Well, I don't have any PBI layovers in December or January. I have an overnight in Miami on New Year's Day."

"Okay. A week from now," Andrew notes. "What layovers do you have before then?"

"I'm in Pennsylvania right now. Tomorrow we work three flights to Orlando."

"Hmm. Orlando isn't too far. What time do you arrive?"

"6 p.m.," I say.

"I'll pick you up at the airport. There are some great restaurants in Winter Park, which is only about twenty minutes away. We can get something to eat."

"Are you sure? Tomorrow's Christmas Eve, Andrew."

"No problem. Restaurants should be open."

I pause. "What about your family; won't you be celebrating? And isn't it a long drive for you?"

"We are Jewish, so we won't be going to church, if that's what you're asking," he explains. "And I don't mind the drive. See you tomorrow at six."

As soon as I close out the call, I search the distance from West Palm to Orlando, only to discover it's a two-and-a-half-hour drive. Without traffic.

"Andrew, you're a nutcase..." I mutter as I drift off to sleep.

Chapter Five

December 24, 2019

"Your friend is picking you up at the airport? On Christmas Eve?" Vera asks as we descend into Orlando.

I fasten my seatbelt and cross my legs. "Yep."

"Wow. Such dedication," she notes.

"Right? I told him he didn't have to come, but he insisted."

"At least you get to do something special for the holiday. I'll be eating Christmas Eve dinner inside the hotel." Vera pouts. "My holiday meal will probably be some kind of chicken sandwich."

"You should order steak and lobster. We get paid double-time today and tomorrow," I remind her as we touch down. "Treat yourself."

After Vera recites her closing announcement, people begin to deplane. It's a painful, drawn-out process, thanks to all the babies and toddlers on this aircraft. We stand in the galley for at least twenty minutes, waving goodbye to the slow trickle of passengers.

When I finally make it to the airport exit, Andrew is outside, waiting patiently in a blue Mazda.

I wheel my suitcase to the back of the vehicle, expecting him to pop the trunk. Instead, he sprints from the car and hoists my bags for me. Then he wraps me in a buoyant hug, lifting my toes off the ground.

"Happy holidays to you, too," I say once I've landed safely on my feet.

He smiles. "Merry Christmas Eve, Callie. There's a restaurant in Winter Park we can eat at, if you like seafood."

"Sure. Fish sounds good."

"Perfect." Andrew walks to the passenger side and opens the door for me.

I watch him hurry back to the driver's side. He seems taller than I remember. A little thinner, too, although my vision was somewhat blurry that night. His hair looks thick and soft, shining beneath each passing streetlight. His eyes are a deep, delicate brown. That's one feature I recall with total clarity.

"How was your flight?" Andrew asks as we leave the airport.

"It was okay," I tell him. "Vera, the girl flying up front with me, is amazing. She lives in the Bay Area, up in Berkeley."

"Is that far away?" Andrew asks.

"Forty minutes. Maybe closer to an hour, with traffic. Have you ever been to SF?"

He shakes his head. "Not yet. It's on my list."

"You should go. There's no place on earth like San Francisco," I inform him. "Anyway, Vera is funny and smart. I like flying with her. The third flight attendant is also pretty cool. We have a good dynamic."

"You didn't freeze in Pittsburgh last night?" Andrew inquires with a half-smile.

We zip through an intersection, then drive under the Beeline Expressway. I roll down my window. Tepid air wafts toward me, hints of citrus and saltwater embedded in the breeze. I inhale deeply, welcoming the fragrant air into my lungs.

"Pitt was brutal," I admit. "I'm happy to be in Florida now."

Andrew turns toward me for a split second. "You and me both."

****

The restaurant is a cross between an old-fashioned diner and a trippy Vegas club. Neon walls are covered with oversized paintings and photographs. Intentionally mismatched chandeliers dangle above our heads, emitting light that ranges from chalk-white to pastel pink. Andrew selects a corner booth, nestled between a fluorescent green wall and a purple one. I'm wearing my flight attendant uniform with my sweater zipped all the way up, covering my airline wings.

"Let's split a bottle of wine," Andrew suggests while browsing the menu.

I toy with the idea. "No drinking allowed in uniform. Think anyone will notice?"

"Not a chance," he says with a smile. "Looks like a normal black dress to me. You could've bought it anywhere."

Much like the restaurant's décor, its menus are a cheerful array of non sequitur items. Seemingly random pictures and song lyrics adorn each page. On the back cover, the restaurant owners, originally from New Orleans, explain how they wound up in Central Florida.

"Ever been to New Orleans, Andrew?" I inquire, flipping through the menu.

"Yes. I was there for a short-term work project a few years ago. Spent about four months in the French Quarter."

"What do you do?"

"I'm a civil engineer. Boring, right?"

I laugh. "It's not as fast-paced as jet-setting around the country, but it's a great career. Definitely more sustainable than my job…and I bet you have better benefits, retirement, the whole nine yards."

The waiter approaches our table. "Can I get you started with something to drink?"

"How about a bottle of pinot," Andrew says.

"And we're ready to order," I announce. "I'll take the salmon."

The waiter scribbles on his pad. "And for you, sir?"

"Seafood gumbo, please," Andrew says, closing his menu.

As the waiter leaves, I glance at Andrew. His eyes are filled with wonder usually reserved for small kids. Yet he exudes maturity, too. The freshly-ironed shirt, the confidence in his gestures and facial expressions. He appears to be young at heart but also an old soul.

"How old are you?" I ask out of nowhere.

"Thirty," he responds. "You?"

"Twenty-eight."

"I liked my twenties, but thirty seems great so far, too," he reflects, leaning back against the booth. The cushions, bright red and fluffy, provide a lively backdrop for a conversation that will be anything but pleasant.

I inhale sharply, my heart pounding in my ears.

"Listen, Andrew, I need to tell you something," I say softly. "We screwed up that night in November. We forgot to use protection."

His expression immediately changes. "Cal, we *did* use protection. But the condom broke. Remember?"

I tilt my head to the side, trying to recall the sound of latex tearing. Or the moment when Andrew had unwrapped a condom. My mind is blank, though.

"Honestly, I don't remember," I confess. "I drank too much."

"Really? I thought you only had a couple drinks."

I swallow. "Yeah, about that…I lied."

"You did?"

"Yep. I was straight-up wasted."

Andrew scratches his head. "Okay. I got tested a few months back. I'm clean, if that's what you're worried about. I would've told you the next morning, but you were gone by the time I woke up."

"Sorry. I was in a rush," I say. "I figured you wouldn't want me there when you woke up anyway."

He lifts an eyebrow. "Are you kidding? I could've made coffee and breakfast. It would've been fun."

I glance down at my shoes and exhale slowly. "Andrew, we had a wild night. It was a good time, reckless and spur-of-the-moment and carefree. Here's the thing, though…"

I trail off, unsure how to break the news. Across the restaurant, somebody laughs. The noise sounds obnoxious and wildly inappropriate.

"Are you okay?" Andrew asks gently, leaning forward.

"No."

"What's wrong, Callie?"

I suck in a huge gulp of air. "I'm pregnant. You're the only person I've slept with in a while, so it's absolutely, most definitely yours."

I hold my breath while waiting for Andrew to say something. He blinks a few times. The color drains from his face. For a second, he looks like he might faint.

"You're…you're sure?" he stammers.

I nod. "I took two pregnancy tests, because I didn't believe it."

"Damn. What are the odds? It's like winning the lottery or being struck by lightning."

"Much more like being struck by lightning," I note. "And then dying of electric shock."

He stares off into space. "I don't tell a lot of people, but I was married in my early twenties. Right after college. We tried to get pregnant for a while, but it never happened."

"Really?" I ask. "How long have you been divorced?"

"Four years," he responds. "Sara and I weren't compatible in the end. I was ready for a child, way back then. I still am. Shit, every time I see my nephew, I mean…it's the highlight of my week. I wouldn't mind being a dad."

I lift a hand, baffled by his optimism. "Andrew, I'm not following. What are you saying?"

"I'm saying I am ready," he informs me. "If you choose to keep the baby."

"Have you lost your mind? I don't know anything about you, Andrew. I just learned your age two minutes ago."

"We have plenty of time to get to know each other," he suggests with a hopeful smile. "I'd love to learn all about you, Miss Callie."

"Come on. We're strangers, Andrew. Did you know I have an older brother? No, because we never talked about it. My last name's Schneider, by the way.

Another thing we never discussed, because we've spent a grand total of eight hours together."

"That's not a problem. It just means we have a lot of catching up to do."

"We live on opposite coasts," I remind him. "This isn't a fairytale. It's literally my biggest nightmare. I can't imagine anything worse."

He makes eye contact with me. "Nothing, Cal? It's that bad?"

"I don't want kids, Andrew. Not now. Maybe not ever."

"Is there a chance you haven't spent much time around children or haven't figured it out yet?" he asks. "Do you have nieces or nephews?"

"I have two nephews. They're hyper as hell," I tell him. Then I shake my head. "Wait, why are we talking about this? I can't handle a kid right now. I prefer pets. Or plants."

"Do you see yourself changing your mind someday?" he asks.

I shrug. "No idea. At this point in my life, I'm happy traveling the world *without* a screaming toddler at home. My dream is to rescue a cat, not make a baby."

Andrew pauses for a moment. "We can make it work, Callie. We don't have to, if you are against it. But I'm just saying we could figure this thing out, if you happen to change your mind. Actually, the timing's great; I was planning to buy a house soon."

"But I live in San Francisco. What am I supposed to do? Uproot my whole life and move to Florida? Also, let's not forget, I'm the one who would have to carry this thing inside my body for the next nine months. God, I don't understand why we are discussing this."

"Maybe I could transfer to California," Andrew reflects. "My company has an office in Mountain View."

"I'd never ask you to do something so drastic."

"You wouldn't have to."

I throw my hands in the air. I can feel my face turning beet red. "Are you listening? I can't keep this baby. What the hell would I do with a kid? I can barely pay rent on time. I'm telling you because…shit, I don't know…because my best friend said I should. She said you might help pay for the abortion."

"I'm sorry, Callie," he says quietly. "Didn't mean to upset you. This is your call and I respect your decision."

His voice is so apologetic that I soften my tone. "Look, I'm just really terrified."

"Don't be," he says, reaching for my hand. "It's your choice. You'll get through this, Callie, and I'll pay for everything. Don't worry about the abortion costs."

"Thank you."

"I wasn't trying to pressure you. Just wanted you to know you are supported, no matter what you choose."

"I appreciate that. My mind is made up, though," I assure him. "I'm getting an abortion."

****

We're both quiet during the drive back to the hotel. A bag of leftovers rests on my lap, warming my legs. We pass Colonial Drive, and I-4, and Curry Ford. There are only a few cars on the street tonight. After all, it's Christmas Eve.

We pull into the parking lot of the Marriott Airport Hotel.

Andrew clears his throat. "Should I drive back to West Palm right away, or do you want to maybe get drinks at the hotel?"

"I'm pregnant," I remind him.

He kills the ignition. "Since you're not keeping it, you're free to drink. Right?"

I tilt my head to the side. I'd sipped a glass of wine at the restaurant, but it made my mouth dry. "Guess so. But I'm kind of tired."

He runs a hand through his hair. "Okay. Well, have a nice night, Callie. Thanks for coming to dinner with me."

"Thanks for driving all this way on a holiday," I tell him. I pause, staring out the window for a moment. The moon hangs low in the sky tonight. Birds are silent and there's no wind at all.

Andrew will have a boring drive home, I reflect. *For two and a half hours.*

I glance at him. His head is tilted down, like he's studying the steering wheel or maybe the dashboard.

I sigh. "Hey, you can come in with me for a little while. We don't have to get a drink. We can just hang out."

"Sure," he says, unbuckling his seatbelt.

We walk inside the lobby. Colorful wreaths adorn the wall above the receptionist's desk. To our left, a Christmas tree displays shiny gold ornaments. Fireplace embers reflect off each metallic sphere, casting a warm glow on the walls.

"I like that tree," Andrew comments as we walk toward the elevator.

"Me, too," I say.

We are quiet as we ride the elevator up to my

room, which is located at the end of a short hallway. It's nothing fancy; there's a loveseat on one end and a king-sized bed near the window. A television sits on a modern black stand.

I glance up at Andrew, his brown irises filled with the same genuine kindness I've often seen in Mackie's eyes. There's something undeniably warm about him, in sharp contrast to my current mood.

"Andrew," I murmur.

"Yes?"

"Are you mad at me for getting an abortion? I assumed you'd feel the exact same way I do. In my mind, it was a no-brainer," I tell him.

He sighs and laces his fingers through mine. Unexpectedly, the sweet gesture sends shivers down my spine.

"Of course I'm not angry, Callie," Andrew replies. "Do I want to be a dad? Sure, I'm not against it. Will I do everything in my power to make this work, if you decide to keep the child? Absolutely. But I don't *need* a kid; I've gone this long without one. More importantly, you are entitled to your own opinions and decisions. I respect your choices."

"Thank you," I say. "The situation feels so heavy. I can't quite wrap my head around everything."

"Understandable. It's big news. Completely normal for you to feel overwhelmed," Andrew responds, pulling me toward him. We stand like this for a while, leaning into each other as though we would both crumble if either one of us backed away.

"I'm tired," I whisper.

He helps me onto the bed. I curl up against him, on top of the sheets, and close my eyes. Andrew runs his hands through my hair. "I'll head out, Callie. You should rest."

"Stay," I instruct him, my eyes still closed. His fingers feel so good along my scalp. "Please."

He wraps an arm around me as I drift off to sleep.

****

My cell phone erupts, echoing off the walls of this quiet hotel room. I roll over and grab the phone before the second ring.

"Cal?" a female asks tentatively.

"Mmhmm," I respond with a yawn. Andrew is lying next to me, fast asleep. Tufts of hair stick out in every direction.

"Hey, it's Vera. Oh gosh, were you sleeping?"

"Yep, but it's fine. I needed to get up anyway."

"You're still on California time," she tells me with a chuckle. "I'm sorry. Didn't mean to wake you."

"No worries. What's up, Vera?"

"Just curious if you'd like to come to the pool with me? It's gorgeous outside. I'm determined to enjoy this Florida heat while I can," she says.

"Thanks for the invite. You go ahead. I might meet you there in a while," I say. "What time's our report?"

"Airport van is scheduled for four o'clock," she says. "We have plenty of time."

The digital clock on the desk informs me it's almost noon. "Thanks. I'll try to come join you."

"Sounds good. I have extra sunscreen if you need some."

"I definitely will." I laugh, looking at my pale skin. Closing out the call, I sink back into the bed. Andrew stirs as I snuggle against his chest.

"Morning," he says, eyes still closed. He wraps his

arms around me. "Mmm. You smell nice."

"Um, thanks? I need a shower," I say, glancing down. "Holy crap, I'm still in my uniform."

His eyelids open slowly. "Shit. Is it wrinkled? We fell asleep so fast…"

"I packed an extra uniform in my suitcase."

"Which is still in the trunk of my car," he reflects. "I'll go get it."

"Thanks," I say. I roll over as he stands up and searches for his shoes. "Vera asked me to join her at the pool soon. You up for a swim, Andrew?"

He shrugs and bends over to kiss me. "I didn't bring my swim trunks."

"No worries, I have an extra bikini," I tell him with a smile.

"Great plan. Hey…"

"Hmm?"

He pauses in the doorway. "Merry Christmas, Callie."

"You, too," I tell him. "I mean, Happy Hanukkah? Is it already over?"

"Yes. But thanks anyway. Okay, I'll be right back," he promises, darting into the hallway.

As I peel off my airline dress, I glance in the full-length mirror on the wall. My stomach looks flat. Even when I turn to the side, there's no visible bump. I place a hand on my navel. The fact that a tiny human is forming in there just doesn't seem possible.

I don't feel pregnant, I reflect. *And I certainly don't look it. Guess that will take a few months.*

"I'm sorry," I whisper to my still, silent belly.

****

As soon as Andrew returns, I change into my

swimsuit. I turn away from him, my back visible while I fasten the bikini top. He's already seen everything, of course, yet it doesn't feel right to bare my skin. Not in this moment, anyway.

Once my bikini's on, I whirl around to face him.

"Wow," he says, leaning against the television stand. "You look like a Florida girl now."

"Minus the pasty white complexion," I remind him.

Andrew shrugs. "I live in a beach town, and I'm not much darker than you."

"False," I argue, holding my arm against his. "No comparison, sir."

Andrew is quiet for a moment. "Thanks for letting me stay overnight, Cal."

I tilt my head to the side. "It was nice to have some company. Hey, know what? You should come to the pool. Who cares if you don't have swim trunks. Just lay on the lounge chairs."

"Sure," Andrew agrees, no trace of hesitation.

Fierce sunlight washes over us as soon as we step outside. Vera is the only person at the pool. She's in the shallow end, near the steps. When she spots us, she doggy paddles toward our side of the deck, a smile planted on her lips.

"You must be Andrew," she guesses. "Callie mentioned you were taking her to dinner. Nice to meet you. I'm Vera."

"Merry Christmas, Vera," Andrew says.

"Thank you. The water feels great. You guys should get in," Vera suggests before diving below the surface.

I slip out of my sandals and dangle my toes over the edge.

"Go ahead," Andrew tells me, nodding at the blue water. "I'll be on the lounge chair by the towel rack. Might take a quick nap."

"Okay." I step into the water. Tiny blue waves emanate from my feet as I immerse them.

Vera swims toward me, splashing furiously. I linger in one spot. I'm happy remaining perfectly still and letting the sunshine warm my skin. Birds chirp in the trees behind us. A few clouds punctuate the brilliant blue sky.

"He's cute," Vera comments.

"Huh?"

"Andrew. You didn't tell me he was so handsome."

I glance over at Andrew, asleep in his lounge chair. His chest is exposed, sharp lines intersecting to form his pecs and abs. He's gorgeous, but I can't allow myself to wander down that rabbit hole with Vera. "Guess so. He's all right."

Chapter Six

December 26, 2019

Even though it's nine in the morning, our Christmas tree glows fiercely. Tiny globes twinkle and shimmer, illuminating our apartment. I sit at the kitchen table, admiring the décor. Water creaks through the pipes, a telltale sign my roommate Linda is taking a shower.

Tammy pours me a cup of coffee. "I bought a dark roast at Albertson's. You'll love it. This one's hazelnut flavored."

I stare into my ceramic mug. Dark liquid grazes the brim, warm and inviting. Tentatively, I take a sip. I quickly decide something must be wrong with my taste buds, because the coffee tastes like dirt.

"How was your trip?" Tammy asks. "I heard you come home last night, but I was already in bed."

"The trip was good. I had layovers in Pitt and Orlando."

"Was it warm and sunny in Orlando?" Tammy guesses. "Did you make it to the beach?"

"There wasn't enough time to drive to Cocoa. After eating dinner in Winter Park, I slept like a baby. Then I hung out at the pool on Christmas morning."

"Gotcha. Did you eat with your crew?"

"Umm, not exactly. Remember the guy I

mentioned a while ago, the one in West Palm Beach? He drove in to see me."

Tammy drums her fingers on the table as though trying to recall. "Hang on, the dude at the club? What's his name, Alex?"

"Andrew," I correct her.

"Wow, I didn't realize you two kept in touch after your drunken escapade. You must really like this guy, huh?" Tammy surmises. As she crosses her legs, her gray slippers brush against my ankles.

I swirl my coffee inside the mug. "Not sure, actually…"

"Damn, he drove so far to see you. He stayed overnight, right?"

I nod.

"Well, did you have fun?" Tammy presses. "I think you described that dude as the best roll in the hay—"

"It was amazing, our night together in November. What I remember, anyway; I was shitfaced," I reflect. "I hadn't gotten laid in a while, and he's super fucking hot. We went at it like rabbits."

"Sounds like relationship goals."

I try to smile, but it feels forced.

"Hmm. I know that look. What's the problem, Callie? And do you have a photo, by the way? I'm curious."

"No photos, sorry," I tell her. "Andrew's tall. Brown hair. He's Jewish but he looks Greek or something. He has olive skin and big, dark eyes. Slim but muscular."

"Yummy. What does he do for a living?"

"He's an engineer."

"Civil, mechanical, aeronautical?"

I finish the cup of coffee, despite its rancid aftertaste. "Civil, maybe? I didn't ask too many questions. It's a weird dynamic; I can't explain it. He's a good guy, but I'm not sure I'm interested."

Tammy lifts an eyebrow. "In him? Or commitment?"

I frown. "Very funny. What's that supposed to mean?"

"C'mon," she says, tying her curly hair into a bun. "You're a total commitment-phobe. You've alluded to it before."

"I have?"

"Yes. Dan was obsessed with you last year. Javier practically stalked you over the summer. Cory and Charles *both* asked you to the military ball in Berkeley…and every girl in NorCal would kill for a date with either of those guys. But you turned them down."

"How is that fear of commitment? I'm just bored by these California dudes. I'm tired of their façade. They are all the same, Tammy. They talk about money and the startup they created at age fifteen. Oh, and the school they built in India. While graduating in the top of their class at Stanford. None of it is real. It's all bullshit."

"Wait, so building a school in India sounds like bullshit to you? And creating a startup at age fifteen? Maybe some of us are fine with that so-called bullshit."

"Well, you can keep it." I laugh, setting my empty cup in the sink. "I'm not interested in the giant pissing contest these guys are determined to win. Everything feels fake. Sure, they've accomplished a lot. But mostly to feed their own egos."

"You sound a little jaded, Callie," Tammy says, placing her elbows on the kitchen table.

"Just observant," I say with a smile.

"Whatever," Tammy responds, chuckling. "Well, I wish you'd been here yesterday. I had a big Christmas dinner with my parents in Santa Clara, then a bunch of girls met up for wine and dessert at Candice's place."

"Sounds fun," I note with a frown. "Sorry I missed it. Damn, I haven't seen Candice in a month. Maybe longer."

"The girls were asking about you," Tammy says. Her black eyes bore holes in mine. "Everyone misses you. You've been flying so much lately. Seems like Mackie is the only person you spend time with when you're home."

I nod. "Sorry I've been absent recently. January should be slower; the holiday rush will calm down."

"Good," Tammy says. "Our apartment's not the same without you, girl."

"Yeah?"

"No, I'm just kidding. We love the peace and quiet when you're gone."

"Thanks," I respond, laughing. "The best part about living with a flight attendant—"

"Is putting her room on Airbnb when she's out of town," Tammy supplies, wrapping her arm around me. "And eating all her snacks. You're out of chips and salsa, by the way…"

****

Tammy heads downtown for a networking event, and Linda meets one of her girlfriends for lunch in Nob Hill. Which means I have the apartment to myself.

It's cold today, even with the heat cranked up high.

Shivering, I grab a fluffy blanket. Then I hop onto the blue couch our neighbors gave us for free. It isn't the most comfortable piece of furniture, but with a blanket as padding, it feels fine. I prop my feet up on the coffee table. Directly in front of me, the Christmas tree shimmers against a murky sky.

Every television network is playing a holiday movie. I flip through a billion channels, but nothing catches my eye.

—*You home, love?*— I text Mackie.

—*Nope. Spending time with the in-laws. But you should come over tomorrow. Let's do some crafting*—

I smile at her text. I was never a big fan of creative projects until I met Mack. Then something shifted inside of me and I grew to appreciate artsy endeavors, especially ones involving hot glue guns and glitter.

—*Sure. Call me in the morning*— I reply.

Muting the TV, I pull my guitar from its resting place behind the gray ottoman. I strum a few chords, absently sliding my fingers across the strings. It's been weeks since I played. My fingers remember what to do, though. They switch from one chord to the next, creating a sweet melody.

"*I never chose this,*" I sing. "*Never chose you for a minute...*"

The words seem to cascade from my mouth before my brain even has a chance to assemble them.

"*But you chose me...*
I never voiced these angry
Strong opinions,
Until last week.
See you're my downfall
My biggest fear,

A downward spiral
And yet you're here..."

I sing to the child I don't want, the tiny creature who couldn't have chosen a more inconvenient time to make a cameo appearance in my life.

Unexpectedly, my hands begin to tremble. I lean my guitar against the couch.

"Those girls I grew up with, the ones who picked all their baby names by middle school? That was never me," I murmur aloud. I try to picture the mass of cells in my tummy, but it doesn't feel like a human. If anything, it's a cyst. A tumor.

I was always the kid writing stories and running around the playground, I reflect, one hand resting on my stomach. *I was a free bird.*

Rain smashes against the window, rhythmic and persistent.

An ambulance speeds past my apartment with sirens blaring. The noise echoes off the living room walls. I exhale, wishing I weren't alone in this apartment right now.

****

Andrew calls at seven o'clock.

"Hi, Callie," he says. "I wanted to make sure you got home safely."

"Yep," I tell him, sprawled across my bed. "We landed late last night; I crashed as soon as I got to my apartment. Slept about ten hours."

"Glad you got some rest," he says. "I go back to work tomorrow, but I had today off. I haven't really accomplished anything."

I smile. "Join the club. I didn't leave the house today. Hung out with my roommates, took a nap, and

61

did some writing."

"Writing? What do you write?"

"Everything. Short stories, novels, songs. Really bad poetry."

"You write books?"

"Well, they're not published. It's a tough industry. Cutthroat, actually."

"I'm impressed that you finished a book. Whether it's published or not. The longest thing I've ever written was a five-page essay for some literature class in college."

"Makes sense. After all, you're a math guy," I reflect. "Hey, where'd you go to college, anyway?"

"Florida State. You?"

"University of Florida. You went to FSU? Dammit. How did I end up in bed with a Seminole?"

Andrew chuckles. "By the way, my football team has been kicking your team's ass this year. In case you're wondering."

I sit up, leaning against my headrest. "Nobody cares. It's basketball season now, Andrew."

"We're ranked higher in basketball, too," he declares triumphantly.

The front door creaks open, and Tammy's voice fills the hallway. She's talking into her phone, giving work instructions to one of her colleagues.

"My roommate just got home," I inform Andrew. "We'll probably cook dinner together. I should get going..."

"Sounds fun," he says. "Enjoy your night, Cal."

"You, too. Hey, Andrew? I'm not going to keep asking, I promise...but I just want to clarify something. Are you sure you're okay with my decision to get an abortion?"

"Callie, I'm behind you one hundred percent. And I will cover the cost," he promises.

"Thanks, Andrew."

"You're welcome. Have a good night, Cal."

****

"Toss in some of those," Tammy instructs.

I do as I'm told. The tomatoes sizzle when they hit the pan. Steam clouds rise toward the ceiling, warming my neck and face as they ascend.

"You're not the terrible cook you claim to be." Tammy laughs, reaching into the fridge for a green pepper.

"I'm *worse*," I say. When I place my spatula on the counter, it awkwardly tilts to one side and then tumbles to the ground. "See? I can't even keep the utensils clean."

Linda marches into the room holding her laptop. "Don't mind me, I'm just here for the tacos. I'll be doing some work in this quiet corner of the kitchen."

"Me, too," I joke as Linda sits on the stool closest to the living room. "Everything I do on my laptop is super professional."

Tammy snorts. "I've seen your browser history. Mostly porn."

"Wouldn't surprise me," Linda quips.

I place both hands firmly on the kitchen table. "First of all, I don't watch porn. I'm a flight attendant; I get enough sex in real life."

"Must be nice," Linda muses. She clicks a few buttons, gaze fixed on the laptop screen.

"You should tell us all about it, so we can live vicariously," Tammy suggests as she adds green pepper to the half-cooked beef. "Kinky stuff? Chains and whips? I'd imagine it's annoying to carry so much shit in your suitcase. Although butt plugs don't take up a lot of space."

"Look, I have a couple videos saved on my phone," I quip. "But the sound quality is much better in person."

"Obviously." Tammy chuckles while keeping a close eye on the ground beef. "Hey…didn't you say it had been a while since you got laid, before Andrew?"

"Yeah, but for good reason," I inform her. "I was trying to focus on my writing."

"That seems counterproductive. As far as I know, sex is the best inspiration out there," Tammy reflects.

I smile. "True. It gets the creative juices flowing. Among other juices."

"Eww." Linda laughs, closing her laptop. "Is the food ready yet? I'm starving."

"Ditto," I agree.

"It's just about done," Tammy says. "Linda, grab the corn tortillas from the cabinet? And Callie, there's shredded cheese on the second shelf in the fridge."

We arrange each item neatly on the table, then dive in.

"Please tell me more about this Florida dude who broke your dry spell," Linda notes with her mouth full of food.

I shrug. "What's there to say? He lives in Florida. We spent a night together in November because I was hammered and horny."

Linda reaches for the hot sauce. "Go on…"

"He seems cool. The sex was amazing, but I don't know much about him. We hung out in Orlando yesterday. It was pretty good."

"Just 'pretty good?' " Linda asks, disappointment coating each word.

I shrug. "Yeah."

"And there's the noncommittal Callie we all know and love," Tammy declares, flinging a stir-fried pepper my direction. "First sign of something potentially long-term, and she hops a flight to the moon."

I swat the pepper away from my plate. By some miracle, it lands in the garbage can. Surprised, I raise both hands in the air. "Did you see that? I'm super coordinated, bitches."

"Lucky shot." Linda chuckles. She makes herself another taco, this time with extra cheese.

"Look, Cal, we're just suggesting *maybe* you should give this guy a chance," Tammy says.

Linda smiles. "Yes. What's the worst that could happen?"

Tammy raises her hand above her head, like she's answering a question in elementary school. "Oh, I know: you could get knocked up! Ha. *That's* the worst that could happen."

Linda sets her taco down for a second. "Or an STD."

I clear my throat. "Umm, we had sex once. Literally one time. You two are getting ahead of yourselves."

I crack open the window, letting frigid air fill the kitchen. Then I fan my face with my hand. Blood rushes to my cheeks and my fingers tremble slightly.

"Is the beef too spicy, Cal?" Tammy asks.

"Yep," I say, even though the tacos were mild. "Yeah, I just need a minute."

Chapter Seven

December 27, 2019

Mackie texts me around noon. —*I'm sorry, girl. Today won't work; I'm not feeling so great. Hate to cancel on you like this—*

—*Shoot. You okay?—*

—*Yeah, I just need some rest. Thanks for understanding—*

I sigh and flip open my laptop. My screen shows a trip tomorrow, a relatively easy two-day with a long layover in New York City.

The open time grid displays tons of awesome trips up for grabs. I spot layovers in Austin, Vegas, Boston, Atlanta. Nearly every trip pays better than my original pairing.

After a moment's deliberation, I select a trip with overnights in San Diego and Fort Myers.

Since the trip checks in at seven o'clock, I hurriedly start a load of laundry. Then I hop in the shower and spend twenty minutes blow-drying my hair. My attempt to flat-iron the frizz is only moderately successful.

"Eh, this will suffice," I tell my reflection, combing my messy mane one last time.

As I'm packing my lunch bag for the next three days, my phone rings from the kitchen table. Andrew's name flashes across the screen.

"Hey," I say. I rest the phone on my shoulder while tossing food into my insulated cooler.

"Hi, Callie. How's your day? I'm just getting off work."

"Was it rough going back after the holidays?" I ask.

"Nah," he reflects. "It was quiet around the office today. I actually got a lot done. You flying tomorrow?"

"Tonight, actually," I inform him. "I traded my two-day trip for a three-day that starts in a few hours. Since my best friend canceled our plans today, I figured I might as well fly."

"Makes sense. Where are your layovers?"

"San Diego and Fort Myers. Two warm destinations, thankfully."

He lets out a whistle. "Okay, you know I'm gonna come see you in Fort Myers, right?"

"Come on, Andrew. Don't be crazy. You're driving all over the state for me."

"I'm happy to do it. Maybe one of these days you'll get another West Palm trip. Until then, I'll meet you wherever you are."

"It's not even a very long layover," I inform him.

"Fine by me. What time do you land?"

"Seven o'clock tomorrow night."

"Perfect. See you then."

"Okay, Andrew. Damn, you are off your rocker..." I laugh as I close out the call.

****

Linda rushes into the apartment as the sun is setting.

"Hi! You're home early," I call from my bedroom.

I slide into my flight attendant dress. It feels a little loose today because I haven't eaten much this week. I sigh as I reach for the zipper in the back.

Linda appears in my doorway with windblown hair and smeared mascara. She meets my gaze, then looks out the window.

"Is something wrong, girl?" I ask.

She bites her lip. "Uh, Dave was fine at work all day today. Nothing out of the ordinary, you know? Then he left suddenly, around three o'clock. I was heading into the break room for another cup of coffee. I swear I didn't mean to eavesdrop. When I passed Johnny's office, Dave was in there explaining he had to leave because Mackie was experiencing complications with her pregnancy. It sounded serious."

"Oh my God," I murmur, my dress still half-zipped.

"Callie, I don't even know if I should be telling you this," Linda says with a sigh. "I thought about it the whole way home. You're her best friend and I figured if anyone could help her through these tough moments, it's you."

"I'm confused. Are you sure you heard Dave correctly?" I ask, dumbfounded that Mackie would keep this information from me. "When Mack texted me earlier, she made it sound like she had a slight cold."

Linda tucks her hands into the pockets of her trousers. "Oh, you know Mackie. Always trying to be upbeat, even in the worst circumstances. I bet she didn't want to worry you."

I shake my head. "She's my best friend, Linda. She should've told me, so I could help."

"Are you flying today?" Linda asks, nodding at my

uniform. "I thought your trip started tomorrow."

"I switched it to tonight. Shoot, if I'd known Mackie was having problems, I would've kept the original trip. I can't believe this," I reflect, zipping my dress all the way up.

"Cal, don't worry. We will take care of her," Linda says. Her green eyes seem to pierce my heart directly. "Just focus on your flights and don't stress about Mackenzie. She has Dave and about a billion friends to rely on for support. You can help once you're back in town."

"Right," I murmur, grabbing my suitcase as I fly out the door.

****

I call Mackie the instant I get to the airport. Her phone clicks over to voicemail.

"Hey, Mack," I say as I head downstairs to the crew room. It's quiet today, just a few reserve flight attendants occupying the couches and chairs. Hurriedly, I check in for my trip using one of the SkyLine computers. "I need to talk to you ASAP. Linda overheard Dave telling the boss about your pregnancy complications. I'm sorry you're going through this, Mackie. You're my best friend in the whole world and I am here for you. Call me back. Flying now, but I'll be free later tonight. Or text me anytime. I'll buy airplane Wi-Fi today."

I close out the call and shove my phone into my pocket. While my schedule prints, I release an exasperated sigh.

"Stressed, Callie?" a male voice asks from behind me.

I whirl around, coming face-to-face with Zack

Friedman. "Well, isn't this ironic? We don't cross paths for four years, then suddenly I see you everywhere I go."

He hugs me tightly enough to rearrange my ribcage. "Lucky you."

"Yep. I hit the jackpot."

"How's Andrew?"

"He's good. Umm, how's Portland?"

Zack shakes his head. "Not as interesting as your love life. Details, please."

I grab my trip sheet from the printer. "There's not much to say, honestly. He's a nice guy. We hung out last week and we've been talking on the phone."

Zack scrunches up his nose. "Did you bang again?"

"*Again?* We fell asleep watching Netflix the first time," I say, but I can't stop a smile from spreading across my lips.

"Oh, right. I forgot." Zack laughs. "Netflix and chill. Emphasis on the 'chill.' Well, I'd like to point out I was your Cupid, since I had Daryl's number. You're welcome, Callie."

"Umm, thanks? Have a good trip, Zack. We'll be in touch," I promise. Then I make a beeline for the door.

Mackie texts me just before I reach my gate. —*I wanted to tell you everything. I just couldn't, Callie. You are going through a lot right now. I don't want to burden you with my own problems—*

—*You're never a burden*— I text her before walking down the jet bridge. —*What a crazy thing to suggest. I'm here for the good, the bad, the ugly, and the absurd. All of it. Don't you remember giving me the same speech just a few days ago?*—

—True. Hey, I love you—

—Ditto. I'll call you from San Diego tonight, Mack—

—Thanks, Cal—

Smoothing my dress, I step onto the airplane. The other two flight attendants are already onboard, checking equipment. I slap a smile on my face and introduce myself.

****

The ocean pulses below my balcony. Small boats line the harbor, dancing in the breeze. There must be a hundred ships docked at this port. They're anchored in neat little rows, practically touching each other. Beneath the dark sky, they all look similar. Yet I know their distinct personalities will emerge tomorrow, when morning light hits the harbor.

I turn my phone on speaker and set it on the small, round table. Wind whistles through the trees.

"Hey, Cal," Mackie says.

I lean against the railing. "Mackenzie, I'm so sorry you got sick."

"I'm fine," she assures me. "Dave went to pick up my prescription. It's been a hell of a day, but we're all right."

"What happened? Linda mentioned it as I was running out the front door. She said there were complications," I explain.

"Yeah," Mackie says. "I went to the doctor this morning. Late last night, I had sharp pains in the pit of my stomach. I was terrified the baby was gone, Callie. With endometriosis, there's a high risk of losing the child."

I sit down in the patio chair and cross my legs at

the ankles. The chair is plastic, yet surprisingly comfortable. An ocean breeze flows through my hair, tossing it around my face. "But you didn't lose the baby, right?"

"No. I broke out in hives, though. And my stomach was killing me. My doctor told me to expect significant pain while my body adjusts to new hormone levels," Mackenzie tells me. "It won't be easy. I can't do anything strenuous until the baby is born."

"Thank goodness you work from home," I reflect.

"Right. If I had an office job, I'd be forced to take medical leave," she notes. "But, luckily, I can work a few hours on my laptop, then lie down for a nap if needed."

"Exactly. Are you still hurting?"

"Not as much. It eased up over time," she assures me. "The pain was awful this morning, but throughout the day I felt better."

"Good."

"How about you, Cal? I wish I could've seen you today."

"Same here. Umm, I'm okay. Andrew's going to help me pay for an abortion. I'm still in shock this happened."

Mackenzie is quiet for a minute. "How did Andrew react when you told him?"

I gasp. "Shoot, with all the madness of the holidays, I forgot to tell you. Andrew took me to dinner during my Christmas Eve layover. He drove to Orlando."

"Whoa. How sweet of him. Was the conversation okay?"

I stand up. A plane roars overhead, then descends

toward the runway across the harbor. Lights flash as wheels meet pavement. "He actually wants a baby, Mack. He even said he would move to California. But I hardly know him. If he moved cross-country for me, packed his bags and came to San Francisco…well, I'd feel guilty forever. And, eventually, he would resent me. I'm sure of it."

"Hmm. Maybe, maybe not. I'm surprised he welcomes the idea of keeping the baby, Cal. I didn't see that coming. Would you be willing to raise a child with this guy? Does he make enough money to help with expenses?"

"He's an engineer. Money doesn't seem to be a problem for him. But it's complicated," I tell her, searching for words to explain my feelings. Stars dot the night sky like shimmery golden confetti. I marvel at them as I attempt to string together a coherent thought. "See, Mack, you were made to be a mom. You're selfless and giving. I'm different. I love traveling wherever I want, whenever I want. Also, I cherish my alone time. When someone gives me an agenda, I feel trapped. I'm too damn selfish to have a kid right now."

"But what if this is your defining moment?"

I tug on a strand of hair. "Huh?"

"An abortion is definitely a viable option, and I'm not trying to change your mind. But I'm just thinking aloud: what if this is your chance to grow and evolve? You're cut from a different mold, Callie. Personally, I love that about you. You're a free spirit; anyone who's spent five minutes with you knows that. But life involves change. What if this is your big chance to shine?"

"Mackie, you make it sound so positive. But being

forced into this kind of responsibility is toxic," I say. "Right? It's disastrous to raise a child out of obligation. I have to get an abortion."

"Absolutely. I get it," she assures me. "Just a reminder: I support you through this and whatever other stuff life throws your way. Like everything else you've been through, this experience will mold and shape you for the better. I'm sure of it."

I stare out at the boats. They are motionless; the breeze has calmed down. "I'm still really angry at myself for being so reckless."

"Cal," she murmurs. "You're human. Things happen. Don't beat yourself up."

"Thanks, Mack," I say. "How did we start talking about me, anyway? This is about you. You're having some health problems and I wanted to remind you I'm here for you, girl. I am so sorry your pregnancy is not starting off smoothly."

"Thank you, Callie. Don't worry, I can handle a little discomfort," Mackie says. "The baby is doing great and I'll pull through. Promise."

"You better stay healthy," I demand. "You're my best friend, Mackenzie. I need you."

She laughs. "Okay, deal."

****

A wisp of moonlight floats in through the curtains. I push them open. Thunderous waves crash against the rocky shore. With a sigh, I step onto the balcony. I've been awake for hours, tossing and turning like the ocean below me.

A military ship drifts past, far enough to be noiseless but close enough for me to see the water splashing behind it. There's a row of palm trees to the right of my balcony. They sway with the melody of the wind, their synchronized movements slow and steady. Branches cascade through the breeze like slim, delicate fingers etching an invisible masterpiece.

I take a seat on the patio chair and dangle my toes over the ledge. The air is perfectly warm, even though it's well past midnight. As much as I love the Bay Area, it never gets this balmy. Not even close. Sitting outside in a tank top in the middle of the night wouldn't be an option in SF.

Bathed in moonlight, I begin to hum. The next thing I know, I'm composing song lyrics by accident.

Once upon a broken dream
You wandered in the dark with me
And I was never strong enough
But you believed in me, in love.
Once upon a lonely night
We stumbled home, turned out the light
Not knowing what would happen next
Or how to clean this tragic mess

There is neither applause nor uproarious laughter; the universe responds to my creative outpouring with disinterested silence.

Stupid, I think after singing the words. They're incredibly cliché, a compilation of pathetic wistfulness and agony. Yet deep down I am aware that, cheesy or not, those lyrics contain some truth. Andrew was supposed to be a one-night escapade, but now he's intricately woven into the scariest, most regrettable incident I can remember.

Out of nowhere, sadness seeps into my veins. I rise to my feet, waiting for the melancholy feeling to pass. Something about this beautiful night feels utterly hopeless.

Freaking pregnancy hormones, I think, tying my unruly hair into a ponytail. I place my hands on the balcony, peeking over the edge. My arms look frail. Bones intersect with bones at sharp right angles, perhaps because I haven't been eating much lately. I also haven't been drinking much. Alcohol has lost its appeal; everything tastes rancid.

Will Andrew come with me to the abortion clinic? I wonder, turning my face toward the star-studded sky. *That might be too painful for him, since he actually wants a kid.*

Tension builds in my chest. Andrew would accompany me if I asked, I'm certain of it. He'd put on a brave face and hold my hand and pretend he was fine with everything. But his heart would shatter. Silently.

He has waited years for this opportunity. The same opportunity which feels like a torture chamber to me.

I am suddenly tempted to call Mack. She would make me feel better. She always does.

It's late at night, though, and she's fast asleep by now. Briefly, I contemplate dialing my parents in Boston. I haven't heard their voices in a while, and I could use some comfort. But they both work tomorrow. The last thing they need is to be woken up at three o'clock by a daughter who has kept the truth from them for weeks.

I unlock my phone, desperate for a distraction. Anything to pry myself away from the thoughts running circles in my head. The Facebook icon catches my eye, with a notification highlighted in bright red.

I open the app to find a friend request from Andrew David Goldberg. I can't help but smile at his persistence. There must be a dozen Callie Schneiders on Facebook, yet he found me.

"Let's learn a little about Mr. Andrew David Goldberg," I murmur aloud. His profile lists Florida State as his alma mater and indicates he's a civil engineer. Both of which I already knew. I flip through his photos absently, hoping they might provide some insight into this stranger who has recently become a central part of my life.

Andrew has lots of pictures with his friends, the ones I met at Reston's in West Palm Beach as well as a bunch of unfamiliar faces. The photos depict their adventures on a local kickball league, wearing matching T-shirts and drinking beer on a faded baseball diamond.

There are also pictures of his parents, who appear older than mine. His mother has a slim, elegant face and striking eyes. Scrolling back a little further in time, I reach a cluster of pictures containing Andrew's sister. She's pretty. Her hair is a few shades lighter than Andrew's, but her eyes are the same deep brown hue.

I spot an entire photo album dedicated to his nephew, who looks approximately five years old. The boy is adorable, laughing in every picture. *Andrew's sister must have married an Asian guy*, I reflect as I skim the photos. Although the nephew looks nothing like Andrew, they have the same mannerisms. One photo shows the boys fast asleep on the couch, their arms propped up in similar positions.

Andrew tosses a ball to the kid in one picture and eats a burger with him in another. There's a snapshot of Andrew hoisting his nephew onto his shoulders. The images look incredibly sincere. Andrew's smile is big, far too big to be fake. His eyes are filled with pride.

They're luminous, practically.

Andrew's nephew must mean a lot to him, I conclude.

The next photo is captioned HAPPY GOTCHA DAY. The little boy, dressed in a miniature suit, is holding a bunch of balloons. He's grinning from ear to ear, chin tilted up toward Andrew's sister. She kneels beside the toddler, joy emanating from her face.

That explains how there's an Asian kid in a Jewish family, I reflect. I had guessed Andrew's sister was married. However, she's alone in the adoption-day photo, which indicates otherwise. I linger on the photo for a second, then close out of Facebook.

A thought occurs to me. It's so farfetched and insane, I actually laugh out loud.

My voice carries, dissipating into the breeze. I am utterly alone on this balcony. The isolation feels thick and heavy, an unbearable weight on my shoulders.

How would that scenario even work? I muse, returning to the unrealistic idea that has invaded my brain. *How the hell would I make it happen? Is it a suicide mission?*

Briefly, I envision a world where I am selfless enough to sacrifice a few months of freedom. I've never been in a position to do so before, but everything has changed recently. As much as I hate the thought, I am also intrigued by the opportunity to do something out of character.

Maybe this experience really will change me for the better. Like Mackie predicted.

The night sky wraps itself around me. I close my eyes, listening to the ocean. Waves toss and turn.

"Tell me what to do," I murmur aloud, a desperate

plea with no recipient. The sky silently denies my request. I place one hand on my belly, on the space which used to be empty and now contains the biggest mistake of my life. Coincidentally, also the biggest opportunity to help someone other than myself.

It's always just been me, taking care of myself, looking out for number one, I think, tears forming out of confusion more than sadness. *What happens if I shake things up? Will my whole life unravel?*

I recall a song I composed months ago, planning to sing it at open mic night with my friend Trevor. I'd written the lyrics, revised them endlessly, and ultimately decided they weren't authentic enough. Coming from my lips, the song felt fraudulent. Eerily inaccurate and stale.

From the ash of despair,
Opportunities rise.
Ascend through the air,
And light up the skies.
From burning disaster
The flames of regret
There comes a hereafter
The best I've seen yet…

A ship blares its horn somewhere in the distance. It's a strange sound, a tale of caution issued to an empty sea.

There will be no sleep tonight, I realize. Which is perfectly fine because I have a billion thoughts to sort out. And a plan to devise.

Part Two: Repositioning

Chapter Eight

December 28, 2019

Andrew calls me the minute I land in Fort Myers. As passengers exit the aircraft, I duck into the airplane bathroom to take his call.

"Hi, Cal. I tracked your flight," he says.

"Nice. We're still deplaning, but I should be ready in ten minutes. Are you waiting at baggage claim?"

"Yep. Were your flights okay? Do you have a good crew?"

"Flights were…long," I tell him. "My crew is decent. The girls aren't super friendly, but they seem nice enough."

"Not as good as your last trip, huh?"

"Nah. Vera sets the bar high. Listen, I think we are almost done deplaning. I'll grab my bags and meet you outside."

I toss my phone back in my pocket and peek out of the bathroom door. The plane is empty, except for the crew members. Ground-up pretzels and crumpled napkins litter the aisle. This airplane has flown across the country today. Twice. The disastrous cabin reflects that mileage.

"Callie, you're meeting a friend, right?" Devonne, the flight attendant in the back, asks me. She takes off her lanyard and tucks it into her purse.

"Yes."

"Hot date tonight?" the captain guesses. He's a short, middle-aged white guy with a bald spot in the center of his head. He blocks the aisle, puffing his chest out. His epaulets shine under the airplane's fluorescent lights.

I slide past him without batting an eye.

"Just spending time with a buddy," I reply while wrestling my suitcase out of the overhead bin.

"Sure. That's what they all say." He chuckles.

I roll my eyes. Then I hurry off the plane, sprinting up the jet bridge at full speed. This terminal feels longer than I remember. Windows line the moving walkway, giving me a clear view of the setting sun. A pink haze lingers over the horizon.

I wade through tons of passengers to reach the exit. It's the typical Florida clientele: women with big, floppy hats and men dressed in colorful shirts. I smile at one elderly lady with a flowered fanny pack.

Humid air smacks me as soon as I step through the sliding doors.

Andrew's blue Mazda is parked directly in front of the exit. He hoists my suitcases into the trunk, then smothers me in a huge hug. "Welcome back to Florida."

"Thanks. Nice and toasty here," I reflect.

"Perfect for a beach day," Andrew says. "It's supposed to be in the low nineties tomorrow."

"Our crew hotel is right on the water. My layover is pretty short, but hopefully I can at least dip my toes in the ocean."

Andrew smiles. "I brought swim trunks this time. Just in case." He helps me into the passenger seat before sprinting to the driver side.

"How was the drive?" I ask as we leave the airport. Andrew turns onto a ramp. Suddenly, we are speeding down a four-lane highway. There's a river on one side and the last traces of a Florida sunset on the other side.

"Traffic was light; I made it here in two and a half hours," he explains.

I gasp. "Holy crap, Andrew. You shouldn't drive five hours roundtrip just to see me."

He glances at me for a moment, then returns his gaze to the road. "I wanted to."

"Andrew, are you hoping I'll change my mind about the baby?" I ask quietly. "It's okay. You can be honest."

He shakes his head. "No. I mean...maybe? I wouldn't mind being a parent, and maybe in some parallel universe you'd want the same thing. But that's not why I came to see you. I would've driven here if this whole pregnancy incident had never happened. I just want to get to know you, Cal."

I stare at him for a moment, observing the angles of his face. Then I shift my gaze to his grip on the steering wheel. Confident and controlled.

"What if you kept it?" I blurt out before I can stop myself.

"Huh?"

"I'm so confused, Andrew. One thing is crystal clear: I'm not ready to raise a child. But you've been ready for years. I had this crazy thought...it's probably stupid. I couldn't sleep last night, and I began to wonder if you'd want to be a single dad. If so, I could carry the baby and then sign away my parental rights."

Andrew pulls over, parking on the side of the road.

He turns to face me. "Cal, I can absolutely raise a child alone. I saved a bunch of money and I was planning to buy a house soon. My parents live in Boca, less than twenty minutes away. You should see them with my nephew; they love watching him while my sister's at work."

"It sounds feasible. But I need you to understand I do not want the responsibility," I insist, my tone gentle but my words firm. "I'm not going to warm up to the idea of being a happy family, in case you're thinking that will happen. I *wish* I wanted that right now. But I don't. I'm sorry."

"Callie, it's fine," he assures me, starting the engine again. "I will gladly take sole custody. You can carry the child for nine months, give birth, and then never see him or her again. You never have to see *me* again. Unless you want to."

"Andrew, I have no idea how I'll feel in the future. I'm trying to take things one day at a time," I say.

"As you should, Callie. I will never pressure you into anything. I just enjoy hanging out with you."

"You, too," I admit.

He smiles and merges into the righthand lane. "That's a good start, then."

"So how would all this work?" I wonder aloud. "The custody stuff, I mean."

"I'm not sure. Maybe you'd surrender full parental rights before the baby is born," Andrew says. "My lawyer can figure out all the legalities. You won't have to worry about any of it, Cal."

"Thanks, Andrew."

"I can transfer to California during the pregnancy. Take you to doctor's appointments and bring you ice cream when you get cravings."

I smile. "That's nice of you to offer, but not necessary. Here's the tentative plan I devised last night, during my sleepless delirium: I'll sublet my apartment for the next nine months and switch to the Fort Lauderdale base."

He pauses. "Really? You love California."

"Yes, but I don't want everyone in The Bay to see me pregnant. It would be a piece of cake to rent out my apartment, and I'd prefer to be in Florida for the pregnancy. The thought of answering everybody's questions, or dealing with their judgment…well, it seems awful. I could transfer to a different base and avoid the bullshit. Start with a clean slate, you know?"

He nods, keeping his eyes on the road. "Makes sense to me. How do you feel about leaving SF?"

I sigh. "Actually, it might be a good change. Life is expensive and fast-paced out there. Although I love it, I miss Florida sometimes. Things are calmer here. This move will force me to slow down and evaluate my goals. I'd love to do some writing, maybe pick up a new hobby."

"I'm really glad you're comfortable relocating. But if you change your mind, I promise I'll be on the next flight to the West Coast."

"Noted. And thanks."

We veer off the highway. Within minutes, we pull into the parking lot of a small, eclectic restaurant with an oversized pink door.

"You know it's usually the girl who's dying to have a baby, right? At least, in every cheesy movie," I muse as Andrew parks the car. "The guy is always terrified at the prospect of being a parent."

"Well, that's Hollywood for you," Andrew says. "Or maybe we both defy the norm. Think so?"

I tilt my head to the side. "Yes. Sounds about right."

****

I slide closer to him. This hotel room is warm; we've tossed the blanket on the floor, leaving one thin sheet on the bed.

Andrew runs his fingers through my hair. My waves are thick and messy, but he manages to avoid getting stuck in them. His hands glide through with ease.

"Don't you work tomorrow?" I ask.

"I stayed late last night, so tomorrow's just a half-day," he tells me, kissing my forehead. "They're not expecting me at the office until after lunch."

"Gotcha. Andrew?"

"Yes?"

"I'm really glad you came tonight," I say quietly. My head rests on his chest and my arm stretches across his waist. It's narrow and firm; Andrew doesn't have an ounce of fat.

"Me, too," he says.

"You don't have to keep driving so far to see me," I murmur. "I haven't made this whole thing easy on you. And I reached every decision on my own, which was selfish. I'm sorry."

He lifts my face toward his. "Don't apologize. This is a lot to handle, Callie. I fully respect your choices because, ultimately, it's your life."

"Thanks."

"Besides, I love coming to see you," he reflects. "It's a great excuse to get out of town and do something

85

different."

I nestle my chin into his neck. He reaches across the nightstand and turns off the lamp. Moonlight seeps into the room, coating the bed and dresser and carpet. "Where do you live? I was so tipsy when we Ubered there..."

"I'm in Palm Beach Gardens. Just a couple blocks from the breakfast spot where you had brunch with Zack."

I gasp. "You know about that? When I snuck out of your apartment to meet the boys at Sweet Pancakery?"

Andrew chuckles. "Obviously. My buddies were there with you, Callie. They told me you claimed we watched Netflix all night."

"I didn't know what else to say. Shoot, if binge-watching a TV show could do *this* to a girl," I muse, pointing at my belly, "we would all be in big trouble."

Andrew wraps his arm over my side, pulling me closer. I sink into him. The grooves of our bodies line up perfectly. I think of all the nights I spent in San Francisco, tossing and turning in my pint-sized twin bed. And the mornings I woke up in strangers' apartments, careful to sneak out before sunrise. There were tech boys, finance boys, start-up entrepreneurs hoping to be the next big thing.

There were awkward first dates, painful second dates, and by our third dinner together, things usually fizzled out.

Nothing felt this authentic and effortless. Nothing.

I am tempted to roll over and start kissing Andrew. I want to make love to this handsome man. My thighs ache with the desire to be touched.

Stop, I instruct myself. *Those thoughts will only get*

you in trouble.

Andrew's breathing becomes slow and methodical. His grip loosens as he falls asleep. Pressing my palms to his chest, I lift my head just enough to see his face. His eyelashes are longer than mine. His hair, thick and soft, cascades over his left eye. He is truly, undeniably stunning.

I stand up as quietly as possible. Stepping into the bathroom, I drink water from the sink with my hands. My throat is on fire.

As I'm returning to bed, a piece of paper catches my eye. It hangs out of my suitcase, a flash of white in this dim room.

Thanks for another great night, Callie, the note reads. The handwriting is small and precise. Andrew must've stuck it in my bag when I wasn't looking.

I lay down again, resting on his chest. Somewhere in the distance, a bird sings to nobody. Its tragic song floats into the room and echoes off the walls.

Chapter Nine

December 29, 2019

I submit my bid for the Fort Lauderdale base while riding the hotel shuttle back to the airport. Immediately, a pop-up box illuminates my phone, confirming my submission. *Your base bid has been recorded. Results will post on December 31st. Thank you.*

I stuff my phone inside my purse. Devonne and Susan are sitting in the row behind me, not saying much. There are two pilots in the back seat. They introduced themselves to us in the hotel lobby, briefly, but I already forgot both of their names.

Air-conditioning blasts through the vents above me. Outside my window, the sun burns fiercely. *It must be ninety degrees by now*, I reflect. When Andrew and I walked along the shore earlier today, there was a warm breeze. We'd gotten sweaty, coated in midmorning sunshine, and showered as soon as we returned to the hotel.

I close my eyes for a second, envisioning clouds of steam rising from the shower while Andrew washed off the remnants of our trek along the beach. I'd wanted to join him. Badly. Somehow, I had resisted. Although every fiber of my being protested, I showered separately. It seemed like the safer choice.

Someone taps my shoulder, pulling me back into

the moment. I turn around just as the van cruises to a stop in front of a red light.

"We're delayed," Devonne informs me, holding up her iPad for me to see our schedule. "Our inbound aircraft won't land for another hour."

I shrug. "Shoot. Guess we can grab food and hide in a corner someplace…"

Once we're through security, the crew scatters. Devonne heads to get soup while the pilots venture off in search of coffee. Susan takes a bathroom break. The smell of burgers lures me toward a chain restaurant at the end of the terminal. I lean my suitcase against the wall and scan the menu.

"I love the milkshakes here," someone says from behind me.

I turn around to face a girl who's about half my size, dressed in full SkyLine attire. Her brown hair is pulled back into a ponytail. Heavy eyeliner accentuates big, hazel eyes.

"You've eaten here before?" I ask the flight attendant. "I forgot to eat today; I'm starving. At this point, everything sounds great."

She laughs. "I never forget to eat. Where are you guys headed?"

I check the schedule on my phone. "New Orleans, then back to San Francisco."

"Long day, huh?" she reflects.

"Yep. And we're delayed an hour," I say. "Where are you flying?"

She reaches into her purse and pulls out her wallet. "Deadheading to Atlanta. Then Orlando and done."

I pause. "You live in Orlando?"

She shakes her head. "No. I'm in Vero Beach, an

hour and a half southeast of the airport. I'm basically right in between Orlando and Fort Lauderdale."

I lean against the condiment counter. "Wow. Were you based in FLL at any point?"

"Yes," she says. "I was in Fort Lauderdale for four years before transferring to Orlando. They're both good bases. The trips are actually better out of FLL; you get more international layovers. But I was sick of fighting South Florida traffic. The drive to Orlando is much calmer."

"How crazy. I submitted my bid for the Fort Lauderdale base literally ten minutes ago," I tell her.

She grabs my arm gently. "You did? You'll love it. Let's get food and find someplace to sit. I'll tell you about my experience in South Florida."

We order at the counter, then claim the last empty table. It's in a corner, quiet and secluded. I stab a plastic fork into my salad.

"I'm Felicity, by the way," the girl tells me. "Felicity Daniels."

I smile. "Nice to meet you, Felicity. I'm Callie Schneider."

"What's your employee number?"

"Thirty-two fifty. I've been here just over four years," I tell her. "Based in San Francisco the whole time. I live in SF right now, but I plan to relocate to Florida for nine months or so. If I can get into the Fort Lauderdale base."

"Oh, you'll definitely get in," she assures me, dipping her fries in ketchup. "I know girls who have only been flying two years, and they got in without a problem. This is exciting. Welcome to Florida, girl. I hear SFO is a nice base, but Fort Lauderdale is smaller and much more intimate. In all my time there, I never had a bad crew. Not once. Everyone is really friendly."

"Sounds perfect," I say.

"It is. You know, Callie, you're more than welcome to stay with me while you search for housing. If you want."

I pause. "That's awfully nice of you. Especially since we just met."

She waves her hand and a flash of gold sparkles beneath the neon airport lights. "I've got a spare room I was looking to fill anyway. It's a cute beach house. Nothing big, but it's cozy and close to the ocean. The guest bedroom has a separate entrance."

"You're married?" I ask, nodding at the rock on her finger.

She smiles. "Yep. I married young. Jared's great; he's really understanding about my crazy lifestyle. You know how hectic this stewardess gig can be…"

"Yes, but I don't have a significant other to consider."

"You're a free bird."

"Exactly," I agree, sipping my seltzer. "Gypsy heart. I've been accused of being a daydreamer."

Felicity smiles. "What kind of dreams?"

"I want my books published someday. And I wouldn't mind if my song lyrics got picked up, too."

"You're a writer? What a coincidence," she muses, reaching into the pocket of her dress. "My website and email are listed here. I have a blog; it's nothing fancy, but I try to post travel stories every week."

"Wow. Can't wait to check it out," I tell her, eyeing the decorative business card in my hands.

****

The flight from New Orleans to San Francisco is exceptionally long and boring.

After I've delivered drinks to business class, I dart into the galley. Devonne and Susan are still maneuvering the cart through the cabin. I peek up the aisle, to make sure nobody's watching. Then I shut the curtain and connect my phone to the wireless signal. My fingers fly across the screen as I navigate to Felicity's blog.

The backdrop is a simple pattern, light blue lines intersecting with dark blue ones. I read the first few posts. They take place in Raleigh, Santa Fe, and Nashville.

Felicity's descriptions are extremely vivid; she notes everything, down to the traffic patterns of each particular city. Photographs and memes accompany each post. It's a visual feast, as well as an emotional one.

Someone slams the bathroom door, startling me. The cart rattles toward the galley, a sure sign Devonne and Susan are done servicing the main cabin. Quickly, I open the curtain and help them pour out half-empty soda cans.

"There's an open row in the back," Devonne announces. "Wanna take a break?"

"We still have three hours left," Susan groans. "Ugh. Good thing I brought a book."

"I'm fine up here," I tell the girls. "Devonne, feel free to head back there and relax. I'm just going to do some journaling. I'll keep an eye on the cabin."

My leather-bound journal rests in the front pocket of my backpack. I love the way this small book feels in my hands. Although I bought it last month, it's already more than half full. There are song lyrics, poems, and random thoughts scrawled across each page.

I collapse on my jumpseat and thumb through the first few pages. They look like the diary of a madwoman. Chuckling, I flip to a blank page.

Felicity's writings were good, I reflect, tapping my pen against the paper. *I should do something similar. Something with a recurring theme.*

Of course, one specific topic has consumed most of my thoughts lately.

I sigh and lean against the jumpseat. The person who's always on my mind is also the exact person I'd prefer to avoid.

But I write anyway, initiating a one-sided conversation with an elusive recipient.

Dear small human, I begin. *Someday you'll hate me. A lot.*

I don't blame you. But there are some things you should know, details which will help explain why I am giving you to your daddy in seven and a half months.

I'm scared, kiddo. I don't know how to take care of someone else. I don't know how to be stable for long periods of time. My life is scattered; I fly by the seat of my pants, unsure where I'll end up.

But your dad...well, he's a whole different story.

The moment I told him you existed, his face lit up. He loved you right then. Crazy, huh? Without seeing you, he adored every piece of you.

I wish I had Andrew's mindset. You deserve that love from me. After all, I'm your mother. I owe you that much, and a whole lot more.

But I can't offer it. I cannot provide the affection, attention, and care you deserve. This has nothing to do with you. As perfect as you are, I am not ready to be a mother. I'm still discovering myself. Someone who isn't whole yet can't wholly love another. Right?

If you feel any kind of abandonment in the future, rest assured you are not unwanted; conversely, your daddy loves you more than either one of us can imagine. You mean a hell of a lot to him, small human. He will make you the center of his world.

As for me, I am thankful you exist. Even though I never envisioned myself carrying you in my tummy for nine months, I'll try to make it a comfortable and pleasant ride.

In the end, I will hand you to a man who waited years for your arrival. He is so excited to meet you and help you grow into the amazing person you are meant to be. I look forward to the moment Andrew gets to hold you in his arms.

Sincerely,

Your mom

Someone in the third row rings the call button. I shut my journal and tuck it inside my backpack. Then I march up the aisle and attend to the passenger.

****

Mackie's text lights up my phone as I'm wheeling my suitcase toward my car. The employee parking lot is dark and empty, except for a few scattered vehicles. Mine has a thin, translucent layer of frost on the windows. It's freezing tonight, colder than usual.

I shiver while glancing at the message.

—Can't sleep, ugh. Hope you had a great trip, Cal. How was your visit with Andrew? Want to hang out tomorrow?—

I slide my key into the ignition and connect to

Bluetooth, dialing Mackenzie.

"Hello, night owl," I say when she answers the call. "Sorry you're wide awake. I just got back to SFO. Damn, it's cold tonight. Driving home now…"

Mackie yawns. "Yep. I've got the space heater turned all the way up. I'm exhausted, Cal, but my mind won't shut off. What time is it, anyway?"

I glance at the digital clock on my dashboard, neon red numbers glowing in the darkness. "Just after midnight. Do you have to be up early tomorrow?"

"Not really," she says. "I'm in the middle of a work project, but I have a couple days' flexibility. I'll try to ignore Dave's alarm and sleep in."

"Good idea. What time do you want to meet up?" I tell her, cruising up the 101, past Daly City. "Oh, shit. I have a lot to tell you, Mack. This trip was crazy. To say the least."

Mackie gasps. "What happened? I'm guessing it involves Andrew."

"Yep."

"Are you guys together? Is it official?" Mackie asks.

"No, no, nothing along those lines. It has to do with my plans for the next few months," I clarify. "Okay, I had this absurd idea. I was sleepless and delirious, and I just started thinking, what if I didn't get an abortion? I don't want a child, especially not in this phase of my life. But Andrew does. Badly. I could sign away all the rights; he said he would pay for any lawyer fees. I could just carry the baby for the next eight months, like a surrogate or something. Is my plan completely idiotic?"

Mackie is quiet for a moment. "It's not idiotic, Cal. It's very generous. I'm surprised by the idea, but I like it. I bet Andrew was thrilled."

"Yes. Ecstatic."

"Have you told your parents? Your brother? You and I will have matching baby bumps soon. This is wild, Callie."

"Actually, I don't plan to tell my family," I inform her. "Mom and Dad would try to talk me out of giving away all my rights, but I need to reach this decision on my own. Without people influencing me, you know? I don't want any involvement in the baby's life. I am not ready for that kind of responsibility."

"I understand," Mackenzie says. "Your parents would definitely try to sway you, perhaps unintentionally. But you know what you want."

"Yes. And there's one more piece of news to share. I think I'm going to transfer to Florida, just for a little while. I want a clean slate during the pregnancy. It would suck to repeatedly explain to everyone, all my friends here, how I got knocked up and I'm not keeping it. They'd judge me. Or, even if not, I just don't want to repeat the story to every person I see. Am I being selfish?"

"Not at all. You're being realistic," Mackie assures me. "God, I'm going to miss you so much. How long will you be in Florida?"

"Not long. Probably nine months total. I submitted my bid for the Fort Lauderdale base. If I get it, I'll transfer there on February first."

"Are you going to sublet your apartment?"

"Yes," I say, turning onto Pine Street. My apartment comes into view. "Figured it'd be easy enough to find someone to rent my room, since the demand for housing is so high."

"Giovanna is desperate to get her own place. She's sick of living with her parents," Mackie reflects. "I'll text her first thing in the morning. I can basically guarantee she will want your apartment."

There's an open parking space in front of my building, which is a rare and exceptional treat. I glide into the spot and kill the engine. "Perfect. Thanks, Mack. Just got home."

"Okay, Callie. Can't wait to see you tomorrow."

"Same here. Get some rest," I say. Then I grab my suitcase and climb the narrow stairs to my apartment door.

Chapter Ten

December 30, 2019

"Don't drink that," Mackie warns, swatting my hand away from the container of almond milk.

"Huh? Why?" I ask, placing my empty glass on the countertop.

"Dave bought it months ago, when I was trying to give up dairy. It's probably curdled."

I scan the label for a date. "According to this, it expired last Friday. I bet it's still good."

"You're risking your life," Mackenzie warns as I pour the mostly unexpired almond milk into my glass.

"What time is Giovanna coming over?" I ask.

Mackie glances at her watch. "Any minute now. I'm sure she's on her way."

"Hmm. Do you think she'll flake? I keep wondering if my impulsive plan is going to fall apart."

"She won't flake. Not a chance. Giovanna's been apartment hunting for a while, but nothing is within her price range. Your place is unbeatable. Prime real estate, without the price tag of most other apartments."

"True," I note.

Mackie's phone buzzes from the kitchen counter. She hurries toward it, reading a text. "Okay, Giovanna says she's ten minutes away."

I inhale sharply. "I guess this is really happening,

huh?"

"Yes, girl. Are you nervous?"

I gulp down the rest of my almond milk. "Kinda. I mean, the crazy-ass plan I conjured in the middle of the night…it's not just an idea anymore. If Giovanna takes the apartment, then I'm one step closer to temporarily moving to Florida. And giving birth to a child I will never see again. And making Andrew a daddy. It's fucking weird."

Mackie wraps an arm around my shoulder. "One step at a time. You'll make this work, Cal. You are so good at carving your own path and doing things *your* way. It's inspiring."

I lean into her shoulder, speaking to her neck. "Thanks, Mack. My dad always says there's a fine line between brave and crazy. I cross that line a lot. But this time I've really outdone myself."

The doorbell rings. Mackie kisses my cheek and runs to open the door. Giovanna walks inside, looking gorgeous as ever. Her black hair is nearly down to her waist, wavy and shiny. Her cheeks are a perfect pink shade from walking through the city.

"Hey, ladies," she greets us. "It's been way too long."

"I agree," Mackie smiles, hanging Giovanna's jacket on the coat rack. "I think the last time we talked was at Frank's house on Thanksgiving, right?"

"Nothing's changed," I assure Giovanna, placing my cup in the sink. "Oh, except Mackie is with child…"

"Yep, I heard the news. Mackenzie will be a fun mommy," Giovanna predicts. She grabs a seat at the kitchen table. "She'll still sing karaoke in Japantown.

And eat Mexican food in the Mission at two in the morning, when we are starving after a night of heavy drinking."

"Sorry, I missed everything you said," I admit with a laugh. "On account of daydreaming about karaoke in Japantown."

"Oh my God, that's right. You're the singer/songwriter," Giovanna notes. "I remember now. You do open mic nights, don't you? And write your own lyrics."

I roll my eyes. "Yeah, but they suck. I'm probably the comic relief for those gigs."

Mackie frowns. "I call bullshit. Your songs are great, Callie. All right, girls, let's focus. We've got important business to discuss."

She pulls us into the living room. We all collapse onto separate couches. I claim the brown one, which has the most comfortable cushions. Tying my hair into a messy bun, I sink into the couch and glance toward the balcony. The sun's just beginning to set.

"So what's up, Mack?" Giovanna asks. "You told me there was something important but didn't really specify."

"Yep. I figured Callie should be the one to explain," Mackie says.

"Hmm. Well, I haven't officially talked to my roommates yet," I begin. "But I am most likely transferring to SkyLine's Fort Lauderdale hub in the beginning of February. I'll find out my base assignment tomorrow. I don't plan to stay more than ten months. Just need a change of scenery. And my seniority is better in Florida."

Giovanna gasps. "You're leaving, Cal?"

"Just for a little while," I assure her. "C'mon, Giovanna. You know me. I'm a California girl at heart. But this is an opportunity I can't pass up. I've been desperate to get my books published for years. I plan to work on my writing in the Sunshine State. It'll be a chance to slow down. A breath of fresh air, where I can relax and write and re-center myself."

"Wow. I'll miss you, girl. Everyone will."

"Thanks, Giovanna," I say. "That means a lot to me."

"SF won't be the same without you, Callie. Not even close..." Mackie trails off. She's lying flat on the black couch, her legs dangling over the side. One hand rests on her belly, as though shielding her child from the mixed emotions clouding the air.

"We'll FaceTime," I suggest. "And maybe I can snag a few Bay Area layovers. Don't forget, I travel for a living. I'll be around."

"Good," Giovanna notes.

"Anyway, this means I'll be subletting my apartment. Of course, I have to talk to my roommates about it, once I'm officially approved for the FLL base. But they know how crazy my job is and they will understand," I say. "Giovanna, they adore you. I am certain they'd be thrilled to welcome you to our cozy little Pac Heights apartment."

Giovanna shrieks and jumps up from her seat. "*What?*"

"Yep, there will be an empty room with your name on it," I confirm. "If you want."

Giovanna tackles me in a hug, pinning me to the couch. "Callie, I've been looking for housing forever, and your place is in the coolest part of the city. Plus,

Tammy and Linda are so much fun."

"Sounds like a perfect arrangement," I say. "You'd be a great fit."

"Remind me again…when will you know for sure?" she asks.

"Base assignments come out tomorrow. I figure I'll get Fort Lauderdale," I tell her. "The odds are high. And I'm going to discuss the situation with my roommates tonight. Actually, they'll be home from work soon. I'd better head back to my apartment."

"You'll keep me updated?" Giovanna begs.

"Absolutely," I promise.

****

Linda is cradling a cup of tea while Tammy absently places her spoon in a pint of ice cream, the metal arm sticking straight up like a spike. Our kitchen, loud and energetic a few moments before, is now eerily silent.

I clear my throat.

"It's not forever," I explain. "Just nine or ten months. I'll probably return to the city before our lease renews in December."

Linda stares into her cup, as though searching for something she misplaced inside the green tea. "It feels so sudden…"

Tammy nods. She pulls her spoon from the half-melted ice cream and sets it on a napkin. "We know you have a really, um, *different* lifestyle and sometimes plans change, Cal. Things come up. We get it. I think we're just in shock. We weren't expecting this news."

"It is sort of impulsive," I admit. "But I had an epiphany. I'm almost thirty, you know? And I am still unpublished, coasting through life as though I'm going to be twenty-one forever. Seems like a chunk of time in Florida, focusing on my writings, would serve me well. Does that make sense? Change of pace. Reset button."

"I guess everyone wants that," Linda muses.

"Yes." I nod. "But most people don't have the luxury of being able to relocate for the better part of a year. Since I do, I should probably take advantage of it, right? It's now or never. Next thing I know, I'll be forty-five years old, walking up Van Ness to Union Street for another round of drinks, and wondering where the hell the time went."

Tammy raises an eyebrow and stabs her spoon back into the ice cream container. "That's oddly specific."

"It's exactly how I see my life playing out," I declare. Neither girl protests.

"We will miss you," Linda says.

I sigh. "It's mutual; I'll miss the shit outta both of you. Giovanna is certain she can cover my lease, if you're okay with that. She will keep you two laughing so hard you'll forget you ever knew a free-spirited weirdo named Callie Schneider."

Tammy tilts her head to the side. "Giovanna is awesome. Thanks for setting that up."

"Yeah," Linda agrees. "She's really cool. She's been Mackie's friend for years, right?"

"They've known each other since college," I tell my roommates. "Giovanna was one of the first friends Mackie ever introduced me to. They go way back."

"She's not you," Tammy points out. "But if this is where you feel compelled to go, then we support it. Florida? Really?"

I rise from my seat at the kitchen table and walk

over to Tammy, placing a hand on her shoulder. "I have roots there. It's not busy or eccentric like the Bay, but it has its own charm."

"Don't get addicted to meth," Linda quips from across the table.

I roll my eyes. "Very funny."

"It's a serious matter," Tammy says, grabbing my hand and squeezing lightly. "Meth is Florida's number one export. They sell it at every gas station."

"Hilarious. Look, you idiots: it's Florida or nothing." I laugh. "I'm gonna do some writing, get a tan, and clear my mind. It'll be great. We can Facetime each other. I'll be back in SF before you know it."

****

Dad calls me as I'm heading out the door. It's a typical brisk night, icy wind weaving through my zip-up fleece. I shiver and unlock my phone.

"Hey, Dad," I say. "How are you and Mom?"

"We're fine," he tells me. "Haven't heard from you in a while. How was your Christmas?"

"Busy. I worked straight through the holiday and I'll be flying tomorrow, too. For New Year's," I inform him. "Missed you guys. Aunt Carla sent a bunch of photos to the group thread. Everyone looked progressively more drunk throughout the day. Uncle Dan was passed out in the last few photos."

Dad chuckles. "He nodded off at the dinner table. The problem is, we were drinking early in the day. And the food took so long. Paul didn't time it right. He started cooking too late."

"It's probably a good thing I was working," I reflect, darting across Steiner Street. "I would've been hammered."

"Are you coming to Boston anytime soon? Your mom's hoping to see you in January, since you missed the holidays..."

"Is Mom awake? What time is it?" I ask, glancing down at my watch. "Shoot, it's still early. I thought it was eight or nine."

"She's already sleeping. She is wiped out," Dad says. "Your brother asked us to watch the kids, so we were chasing after two rambunctious toddlers all day."

I smile at the thought of my parents trying to keep up with Kevin and Jacob. "I bet you're both pretty tired."

"Yes." Dad yawns, as if on cue. "Do you think you'll come home sometime in January?"

I pause, contemplating whether I can realistically schedule a Boston visit. "I'll try, but I might be busy packing for Florida."

"Florida?" Dad echoes.

"Crap, did I forget to tell you? I'm transferring to the Fort Lauderdale base for the rest of the year. It'll help me focus on my writing." I have reiterated this backstory so many times I can't even remember if it's true or not. "Plus, I'll save a ton of money."

"Wow, this is a pretty drastic change. Is your housing all set up?"

"I'm working on it. Tomorrow I officially find out if I got the FLL base."

"Think you'll get in?"

"Yes," I say, pausing in front of my favorite Vietnamese restaurant. The windows are covered with oversized handwritten descriptions of menu items. *Shrimp spring rolls! Spicy chicken clay pot! Honey BBQ spare ribs!* "I'm sure I will get in, actually. I have a strong feeling. It's a junior base, so there shouldn't be any issues."

"Your mom will be surprised," Dad predicts.

I stare at my reflection in the window of the restaurant. My hair falls in loose waves around my shoulders. This is the longest it's grown in years. "How about you? Are you shocked?"

"Nah. Your brother always walked the straight and narrow. We knew what to expect with him, because he did things by the book," Dad surmises. "But you? You're different. You make your own rules, Cal."

"Is that a good thing?" I ask, not really expecting an answer. The door jingles as a group of girls enter the restaurant. I linger near the curb with my phone cradled against my ear. I can see my breath, tiny wisps of air circling my face. Cars fly past the intersection, lights flashing and horns honking.

"Well, you're not afraid to be who you are," Dad reflects. "So yes, I think it's a good thing."

"Thanks, Daddy," I say. My voice sounds frail.

"I'm off to bed. I'll tell your mother about the big move to Florida. Night, Callie," Dad says before ending the call.

I shove my phone into my coat pocket. Inhaling sharply, I walk into the restaurant. It's a hole-in-the-wall, a tiny place with every seat occupied. The pho here is the best I've found in the whole Bay Area. I sit at the bar and order my meal to go, avoiding eye contact with everyone.

My phone buzzes from inside my pocket, but I don't bother to check it. Mackie's probably texting me. Or maybe one of my roommates, or even Andrew. I don't want to talk to anyone right now; I've met my quota of lies for the night.

If only Dad knew the truth, I think, staring at the bottles of liquor lining the wall. *Half the truth, even. Just a sliver of the real reason behind my Florida relocation.*

A girl sitting to my left breaks out into raucous laughter, pulling my attention toward that side of the bar. Her lipstick is blood red, and she's got an arm draped around one of the guys in the group. Everyone in her squad is smiling like they've discovered some fantastic secret. I stare at the strangers for a fleeting second, then return my gaze to a large, sparkly bottle of vodka on the wall.

Dear small human, I think, mentally composing another letter to the unnamed being inside of me. *Your grandparents don't know about you. I doubt I'll ever have the guts to tell them.*

You have two cousins on my side of the family, energetic boys who snuggle as often as they fight. My older brother is a good dad. He's attentive and patient. His wife is obsessed with babies; she would've spoiled you rotten.

I hate lying to my father, your granddad...but he wouldn't understand the situation. He would beg me to reconsider signing away all my parental rights.

And I might even do it, just to see him happy.

But that would be a disaster. You deserve better than a mom who doesn't know how to be a mother. You deserve better than me, little one.

Andrew's family is going to shower you with love. You have a cousin on his side, a sweet little boy Andrew's sister adopted a few years ago. I bet he teaches you to play sports. And teases you, and builds pillow forts with you, and helps you with homework. All the best parts of having a cousin close in age.

Maybe you'll have a sibling someday. Andrew loves kids; I bet he plans to eventually give you a little brother or sister. Siblings are a pain in the ass, but they're also pretty amazing. My brother was always the calm to my storm, the voice of reason during my wacky, harebrained schemes. You'll be a good older sibling. Somehow, I'm sure of it.

A waitress sets a brown paper bag in front of me, stirring me from my thoughts. I grab the food, which feels much heavier than I expected. Then I head home, eager to finish composing the letter while devouring pho.

Chapter Eleven

December 31, 2019

—Where are you flying today? I hope you have a great New Year's—

I glance at the text from Andrew, then place my phone facedown on the kitchen table. My laptop rests in the center of the table, but I can't quite bring myself to reach for it.

"Jesus, you look pale," Linda comments as she enters the kitchen. She opens the refrigerator and grabs a cardboard box of leftovers. "Everything okay, Callie?"

I nod. "Yeah. Just nervous to check the base bids. I mean, I think I got Fort Lauderdale. But it's still intimidating."

Linda sets her lunch on the counter and grabs a seat next to me at the table. "Want me to do it?" she asks, nodding at my laptop.

"I don't want to make you late for work…"

"Not a problem," she says, waving her hand. She glances at the clock on the wall. It's just after nine a.m. "Around the holidays, most people either show up late or don't come into the office at all. I'd rather check your bid, to be honest. I'm curious to see if Giovanna will be my new roommate in a month."

"Okay. God, why am I so nervous? This is what I

wanted, right? I've been mentally prepping to move to Florida. And I thrive off random, spontaneous adventures. So why the hell does it feel so *terrifying?*"

Linda grabs my laptop and presses a few keys. "What's the internal site for SkyLine? Is it easy to find the base assignments?"

"Super easy. It's like four clicks, total," I inform her, burying my face in my hands. My voice comes out muffled. "MySkyLineLink.com, and the login is CSchneider. Password is 'Amber.' "

"Girl crush?" Linda guesses, her eyes fixed on the laptop screen.

I laugh and peek at my roommate through my fingers. "No, you loser. Amber was my childhood kittycat."

"Mmmm," she murmurs. "All right, I'm in. What next?"

"Toolbar, all the way to the right, there should be a drop-down box labeled 'base assignment list' or something along those lines."

"Got it."

I sigh and lower my hands. "See the link for the updated assignments? Click on it. You'll have to scroll through and find my seniority number, thirty-two fifty."

Linda pauses for a second. "Okay, I found it. Number thirty-two fifty. Interesting…it says your new base is New York City."

"*What?*"

"Just kidding." She smiles, handing me the laptop so I can see for myself. "You got FLL. Dammit, Callie. You're really leaving us?"

I nod, unable to form words.

Linda sighs heavily. "We will miss you, girl. You

better return to San Francisco as soon as you find yourself, or recover from writer's block, or reconnect with your inner child. Whatever crazy-ass reason you're moving to Florida. I've already forgotten…"

"Change of pace," I remind her, fixated on the three-letter airport code next to my name. "Holy hell. This is it, huh? Switching coasts in one month."

Linda rises from the table. "Happy New Year, Callie Schneider. I'm pissed you're moving, but also happy for you. I know this is what you want."

I look up at her. "You'll hardly notice I'm gone, Linda. I plan to return before the end of the year."

Tammy marches into the kitchen in her pajamas. "Wait, what?"

"Callie officially got the Fort Lauderdale base. She's leaving us in February," Linda announces. "I guess we will have to throw a going-away party."

"I'm not leaving forever," I remind them both. "More like, I don't know…a temporary-break-from-CA party."

Tammy nods. "Hmm. Not your typical party theme, but I could work with it. 'Tacos and Tequila and Taking a Break.' "

****

"When will you move?" Andrew asks, his voice echoing off the walls of my bedroom. I placed him on speakerphone while getting ready for work.

"I'm not sure yet. My base assignment starts February first, so it would make sense to arrive in Florida a few days before then. I'd like some time to settle in."

"Do you have days off at the end of January? It'll take, what, four days to complete the drive? You're literally going from one side of the country to the complete opposite corner," Andrew muses.

I smile while pulling sheer tights above my knees. "I'm an all-or-nothing kinda girl."

"Yes, you are. Well, I get a ton of vacation days each year. I never end up using all of them. I can take a week off at the end of January and do the cross-country drive with you."

"Really? That's a long time to be cooped up in a car together, Andrew."

"There's nobody I'd rather drive three thousand miles with," he assures me. "We can stop in fun cities along the way. When's your last San Francisco work trip?"

Picking up my phone, I open the SkyLine employee app. "Looks like I finish a three-day trip January twenty-second. Then I'm off until February."

"Perfect. Okay, I will put in the request for vacation days right now. I'll get approved within an hour. They're not very strict around here."

"So we are driving cross-country together, huh?" I reflect. "I don't even officially have an apartment lined up. A flight attendant who lives in Jupiter offered me her spare room, but she's married, which might be awkward."

"You can stay with me," Andrew offers, clearing his throat. "My lease is up in April; I'll buy a house sometime before then. In the meantime, crash at my place. It's not exactly huge, but it can fit both of us. And then we can settle into the house, once I buy one."

I slide my arms into my uniform sweater, mulling over his proposal. "Andrew, that's a little intense. How could I move in with you? We aren't even dating."

"We're not?"

"Oh, I don't know…" I bite my lip. "Are we? And, anyway, there are bigger issues here. What if you hate living with me? I'm not exactly a neat freak, I have a bizarre sleep schedule, and I plan to adopt a cat. Possibly two cats. I might make a terrible roommate."

"First of all, I don't mind cats," he says. "I'd rather get a dog, but cats are cool, too. Second, I thought we were seeing each other. Casually. We don't have to be exclusive or official, until you're ready. In the meantime, I enjoy being with you. You mean a lot to me. Third, you can move into my apartment and then search for housing of your own, if you want. It'll buy you time to decide where you want to live. Think of it as a temporary situation. A trial period."

"That's a really nice offer," I tell him. "I have to head to the airport now, but I'll consider it."

"Okay," he says. "Safe flying today. Where do you end up for the night?"

"Atlanta. It's a short layover. What are you doing for New Year's?"

"Daryl invited people over to his apartment. Last year we went out in Las Olas and got shitfaced. My hangover lasted a week. I hope this year is more low-key."

"As someone who can't enjoy a proper champagne toast, please throw back one or two for me," I request. "No need to get buck wild like last year. A couple drinks will suffice."

"Deal. You're in Miami tomorrow, right?"

"Yes," I say, lifting the handle on my suitcase. "Land around five p.m."

"Looking forward to seeing you," he tells me.

"You, too," I respond, a little surprised by the sincerity in my voice.

****

Mackie texts me as I'm parking my car in the SFO crew lot. —*Have fun tonight, Cal. And Happy New Year*—

I send a quick response while unbuckling my seatbelt. —*You, too. It'll be a transformative year for both of us, Mack*—

When I open the driver's side door, a gust of wind sends chills down my spine. I glance up, briefly, to find a clear blue sky, a rare commodity in NorCal.

Dear small human, I think, mentally composing my next letter to the creature preventing me from drinking myself to oblivion tonight. *I'm not sure if or when you'll visit the West Coast, but I hope you find comfort here. I certainly have.*

The airport shuttle screeches to a halt. I continue writing while hoisting my suitcase onto the luggage rack. *Florida has a lot to offer; you will love the Sunshine State. You can play outside year-round. And visit the beach whenever you want. It'll be the perfect backdrop for a happy childhood.*

Someday, when you're older, maybe Dad will take you on a trip to San Francisco. And perhaps while you're there, you can sit on the park benches at the Ferry Building. They all face the Bay Bridge. The view is magical. It was the first place I visited when I moved here. It has become one of my favorite spots in the entire world, and I've trekked all over.

Maybe you'll inherit my gypsy heart. If you do, please remember your life is entirely up to you. There is excitement and delight to be found wherever you travel, and wherever you settle down. Essentially, you get to choose your own adventure. And there are so many to pick from.

Perhaps you'll be more stable and consistent, like your daddy. Whatever you are, just be perfectly—and unapologetically—you.

The airport shuttle cruises to a stop. I sigh, wondering when I became so sentimental about a child I don't plan to meet.

The airport is busy today. An enormous Christmas tree still glows brightly in the center of the terminal, even though Christmas ended a week ago. I check in on my phone because I'm running a little late and it would take too long to visit the crew room. Plus, I don't feel like talking to other flight attendants right now. Or anyone, really.

I find an empty section near my gate and flip open my laptop. Then I finish the letter to the unnamed human I'll never know.

****

"You're based in Orlando? Why'd you pick up a San Francisco trip?" I ask my coworker as we dump half-empty soda cans in the recycle bin. He's a muscular black guy with a deep, soothing voice and a chiseled body which seems to be protruding from his black-and-white uniform.

"Sounds like a hell of a commute," I continue. "Coast to coast, just to work a New Year's trip…"

He nods. "Yeah. I never would've done it, except I was visiting my cousins in Menlo Park. One of them has this crazy mansion. It's ridiculous. He worked for a startup in San Jose and became a millionaire, overnight, when they went public."

"Must be nice," I reflect. "How long were you visiting?"

"I flew into town the day after Christmas," he tells me. He meets my gaze, and I notice his eyes are a striking shade, amber with a hint of green. "I try to visit them once a year. We were really close as kids. Actually, they were like brothers to me."

The sun is setting; scattered orange and red beams filter in through the galley windows. A thin ray of light catches his silver wings. *Jordan.* I'd already forgotten his name.

"I'm glad you got to spend a week with your cousins, Jordan," I say. "Do you like living in Orlando? I moved there for a split second after college."

He shrugs. "Orlando never really grew on me. I was in Winter Park for a year, then I moved to Cocoa in April with my girlfriend. Well, *ex*-girlfriend."

"Girlfriend?" I repeat slowly, as though the word is foreign to me.

He looks at me and smiles. "Yeah. Some of us are straight, you know."

I shake my head and push the drink cart back into its spot in the galley, below the metal workstation. "Sorry. It's been a long time since I've flown with a straight male flight attendant."

"Me, too," he admits with a laugh.

"What's Cocoa Beach like? I visited once, during my college days, but I don't remember much."

"Cocoa is quiet," he informs me, leaning against the galley counter and crossing his arms. "It's really peaceful. Laid back. Which is nice in the beginning, but it gets old after a couple months."

"Makes sense. I love the constant, delirious buzz of

SF. There's always something happening, you know? It's the perfect city for an adrenaline junkie. Sometimes it can be overwhelming, but for the most part, it's energizing."

"Sure. After college, I moved to Los Angeles for a couple years. Everyone complained about the traffic and the crowds. Those aspects never bothered me," Jordan says.

"Why'd you leave?"

"I got sick of living paycheck to paycheck. I lined up work here and there: commercials, Indie films, voice-overs. But I needed financial stability in the end. I couldn't find it in L.A."

"You're an actor?" I reflect.

"Failed actor," he corrects me.

"Well, then, you're in good company; I'm a failed writer," I confess. "The industry is cutthroat."

"Tell me about it…"

The plane hits a bump, so I sit down beside Jordan on our jumpseat and buckle in. A few passengers glance up at us, visibly annoyed, as though the turbulence is something we can control. They lose interest after a few seconds and look away.

"Wait, you said you're living with your ex-girlfriend? How's that working out?"

He sighs. "It's as awkward as it sounds. She and I split up last month, but we should've ended a long time ago. I'm currently in the middle of moving to Delray Beach."

"Where is Delray?"

"Halfway between Fort Lauderdale and West Palm."

I emit a small shriek. A middle-aged woman in the

third row glares at me. I shrug and flash an embarrassed smile. With a dramatic sigh, the lady returns her attention to her iPad.

"Sorry I screamed," I whisper to Jordan. "It's just a big coincidence. I'm literally moving to the same area. I was awarded the FLL base starting in February."

He lifts an eyebrow. "You're moving? I thought you loved California."

"I do, but I need a change of pace. For a decade, I've been writing books, short stories, song lyrics and basically anything else you can think of. I moved from one big city to the next, never pausing to take time for myself. I guess I want a year to press the reset button. I plan to write with purpose. See how it feels to have actual *downtime*. I never rest or recover in SF. I rush to work, rush home, rush to open mic nights, rush to concerts at Dolores Park and happy hours in Nob Hill. Then I do it all over again."

"You want a fresh start," Jordan notes. "You'd like to create art without distractions. And finally clear your head."

I smile at him. "Exactly."

****

Our hotel in Atlanta is located beside the airport, in an area that doesn't have much to offer besides short-term lodging. The shuttle drops us off in front of the lobby, which twinkles with Christmas lights. While waiting for the driver to unload our suitcases, I glance through the parking lot in search of a restaurant within walking distance. Past the rows of cars and trucks, all I see is another hotel and an enormous gas station.

"Anyone hungry?" I ask my crew. "I might eat at the hotel restaurant. Doesn't look like there are many options nearby."

The pilots tell me they'll come downstairs to grab a bite, and Jordan also agrees to join us. Tess, the short redhead who's been flying in the back of the plane, informs the group she's too tired.

We check in and ride the elevator up to our rooms. Mine is simple, with white walls and light gray furniture. I slide out of my uniform at record speed, eager to get some grub. It's almost eleven o'clock; I never eat dinner this late. My stomach rumbles loudly as I hang my flight attendant dress in the closet. After changing into a hoodie and leggings, I check my reflection in the full-length mirror. The person staring back at me looks tired, but otherwise content.

I text Andrew while waiting for the elevator. — *Have fun with the guys tonight—*

His response arrives instantly. *—You, too. I hope your New Year's Eve is awesome. Can't wait to see you tomorrow, Callie—*

I smile.

The elevator doors fly open. Shoving my phone in the pocket of my sweatshirt, I make my way through the lobby. The hotel restaurant is dim and quiet, with lots of empty tables. Frost coats each window, adding a festive touch. Jazz music plays softly in the background while customers in business attire sip their drinks.

One waitress appears to be covering the entire restaurant. She sashays from table to table, dropping off cocktails with elaborate garnishes on top.

Nobody from my crew has arrived yet, so I select a corner booth and slide into the middle seat. The waitress appears within seconds, offering me a menu. When I say I'm expecting a few more people, she returns with three additional menus.

I'm browsing the appetizers, all of which sound delicious, when Jordan arrives.

"Hi, Cal," he says. He sits beside me, close enough for me to smell his cologne. He's wearing a gray V-neck sweater with vintage jeans. As he reaches for a menu, his arm brushes mine.

"You clean up nice," I tell him, nodding at his attire.

He smiles. "You, too."

"Liar," I say, glancing down at my faded sweatshirt and leggings. "I only had one cold-weather outfit in my suitcase. It was this or a strapless sundress."

Jordan lifts an eyebrow. "I'd like to see that, please. It's not too late to go change…"

I'm taken aback by the comment. Before I have time to respond, both pilots join us. They slide in to my right, filling up the rest of the booth.

"Does anything on the menu look good?" the captain, an older guy with a '70s-style porn star mustache, asks.

"There's a decent drink selection," Jordan tells him. "Haven't looked at the food yet."

"I could use a beer," the first officer notes. He grabs the drink menu from the center of the table.

The waitress returns to take our orders. I'm the only person at the table who asks for a nonalcoholic beverage. When I glance around to see if anyone noticed, my coworkers all appear unconcerned. They're busy discussing New Year's resolutions.

"Do you have one?" Jordan asks me.

I shrug. "Not exactly. Resolutions aren't really my thing; I set goals all the time, not just on January first."

"What are your current goals?" the first officer inquires.

"Hmm. Within the next few months, I would like to rescue a cat. I also wouldn't mind if I got something published. Not necessarily one of my novels, but a poem or short story would be fine. I'd love to see something in print."

Jordan nods. "Those are realistic aspirations. I hope you get published, Callie."

"Wait, you write books?" the captain asks, glancing up from his menu. "For fun?"

I nod. "Yeah. I'm a nerd. I wrote my first book several years ago. It's addicting. It's like getting a tattoo; once you have one, you want a million."

"Where are your tattoos?" Jordan asks.

I bite my lip. "Oh, I don't have any. It was just an analogy."

"So you're making comparisons to things you don't even have…" he notes with a goofy grin.

"I have a tattoo," the captain announces, catching everyone off guard. He lifts his shirt sleeve to reveal a faded anchor with a chain wrapped around it.

"Nice. I see you were in the Air Force," Jordan jokes, and we all burst out laughing.

The waitress arrives with our food and drinks. Eagerly, Jordan reaches for his overflowing pint glass. The pilots raise a toast, so we all lift our drinks into the air. I clink my water glass against their beer mugs; nobody seems to care that I have the most boring beverage at the table.

"Can I have some?" Jordan asks, eyeing my spinach-and-artichoke dip.

"Sure," I tell him. "If I can try your IPA."

He scoops a heaping pile of dip onto a tortilla chip and pops the whole thing in his mouth. "That's a fair trade."

I grab his mug and take a sip. It's hoppy, with a fruity aftertaste. "Kinda bitter, but not terrible," I note aloud.

"You can have more," Jordan tells me, reaching for another chip. "If you want."

I swallow another mouthful and hand the glass back to him. Then I lean back, sinking into the cushions. The pilots are talking about home improvement projects, but I'm only half-listening as I polish off my spinach-and-artichoke dip.

Dear small human, I think. *Happy New Year. This is a big year for you; you'll make your debut in a few months. I hope you like this strange, unpredictable world of ours. It can be jarring at times, but there are really sweet moments, too.*

"Cal," Jordan whispers, wrapping an arm around me.

I look down at his fingers around my waist, caught off guard by the tingling soaring through my body.

"Where'd you go?" Jordan asks, the corners of his hazel eyes scrunching up as his mouth forms a partial grin. "You were off in space. I ordered you an IPA. My treat, since I ate most of your food."

I swallow. "Thanks, Jordan. I'm trying to cut back, but maybe I can drink half of it."

"No problem. I'll finish what you don't," he assures me. "I also got a flatbread for the table to share. Seems we're all hungrier than we thought."

My phone buzzes from inside my pocket, but I don't dare to check it. Jordan's arm feels alarmingly nice, wrapped around my side. Mesmerized by the restaurant's tranquil atmosphere, I remain completely still as I attempt to figure out what, exactly, I'm thinking. Everything has been spiraling out of control lately. But in this exact second, the world seems perfect.

"You are beautiful," Jordan tells me, his eyes locked on mine.

"Huh?" I ask, tilting my head to the side. "I feel gross from flying all day. And I'm wearing workout clothes."

"Doesn't matter," he says. "You stand out, Callie. You're different."

The waitress sets our food and drinks on the table, pulling me from my thoughts. A flatbread rests in front of me, beckoning me to take a bite. I reach for a knife and carve myself a slice. Jordan releases his grip on my waist. He slides one beer mug toward me and raises the other one to his lips.

"We're calling it a night," the captain announces, placing a few bills in the middle of the table. "Early show for us tomorrow."

"Leaving already? You're not going to wait for the ball to drop?" I ask the pilots. "Just ten more minutes 'til midnight."

The first officer shakes his head. "Nah. We are old."

"Older than dirt," the captain tells us, chuckling as he rises from his seat. "Good night, guys."

"Night," I say as the pilots walk toward the elevators.

Jordan scoots closer to me. "Smile, Callie."

Suddenly there's a phone in my face. I grin as the

forward-facing flash goes off.

"Instagram story?" I ask. "Do I look dumb?"

Jordan shakes his head. "No, and most definitely no."

He shows me the image. Thanks to the lighting in here and our complementary complexions, the picture turned out great. Jordan's got a movie star smile, which helps.

"I don't post much on IG," he reflects. "But I do add photos to my website every now and then, even though I've been out of the acting biz for a couple years. Not sure why I still update it. Some dreams die hard."

"I'd like to see your website," I tell him. I reach for one last slice of flatbread. "Is it a blog? A portfolio?"

"Not a blog. It has my bio, union affiliations, and resume. I used to post career updates every time I landed a job, but I haven't done much lately. Aside from local theater in Cocoa."

"Theater? Do you sing, or just act?"

"Both," he says. "I'm better at acting, though."

"I suck at acting, but my singing voice is okay," I reflect. "Or so I've been told."

"I'd love to hear it."

I smile. "Maybe someday. If you're lucky."

"Hey, I can send you the photo. Type in your number." He hands me his phone.

"Really? Oldest trick in the book."

"Who cares if it's old, as long as it still works," he replies with a sheepish grin.

I type my number in his phone and hand it back to him. He looks at me for a second. The corners of his mouth move, as though he's considering saying something. I lean in just a tiny bit.

"Ten, nine, eight, seven—"

We both turn toward the television screen near the bar, where a countdown flashes in big, bright letters.

"Six...five..." I recite along with all the other patrons in the restaurant.

"Callie?" Jordan asks, scratching his chin as the countdown continues. "Is it, um, is it okay if I kiss you?"

"One! Happy New Year!"

I nod, fully aware I might regret this decision later. Guilt stirs in my core, but it's no match for the magnetic pull of excitement and intrigue.

Reaching for my face, Jordan guides me toward him. I close my eyes as his tongue slips inside my mouth. His lips are impossibly soft. Instinctively, my body melts into his.

When the kiss ends, I teeter forward, anticipating more. It's as though the world has stopped spinning and now what matters most is the tingling sensation where skin meets skin and tongue meets tongue. I sigh happily, then open my eyes.

"Thank you, Callie," Jordan murmurs. "Happy New Year."

Across the room, someone pops the cork on a bottle of champagne. I jump at the noise; it sounds like a firecracker. Or the sharp, painful crack of a whip.

Reality sinks in, hard and fast. The world resumes its circular orbit, except now it's spinning way too quickly, as though making up for lost time. Remorse spreads through my veins like poisonous venom.

"I...I have to go," I stammer, pulling my gaze from his. "I'm sorry, Jordan. Just super tired. It's been a long day."

"Let me walk you to your room," he offers.

"That's okay." I place some money on top of the stack left by the pilots. "Get some sleep. See you tomorrow."

I hurry toward the elevator, never looking back. The lock screen on my phone displays a series of notifications, including the photo from Jordan. I quickly scan the texts I received earlier tonight. Mackie sent me a sweet New Year's message and my roommates forwarded a couple photos from the house party they attended in the Mission District. Of course, there's a message from Andrew.

—*You deserve everything good in the year ahead. Happy New Year, California*—

I sigh and wait for the elevator to bring me to my floor. Then I hurry inside my hotel room, eager to scrub this night off my skin.

A message from Jordan lights up my phone screen while I'm washing my face. —*Didn't mean to scare you off. Sleep well, Callie*—

Without responding to anyone's texts, I turn off the light and crawl into bed.

Part Three: Go-Around

Chapter Twelve

January 1, 2020

I wake up with a headache and a bad taste in my mouth. Rolling over to my back, I stare at the ceiling, waiting for the pain to diminish. It does not.

I sigh heavily. Then I reach for the bottle of water on the nightstand and chug it. A rancid film lingers on my tongue. When I stand up and walk to the bathroom, I'm struck by a wave of dizziness.

I steady myself against the sink. Even with my eyes closed, the room feels like a carousel.

"I didn't drink enough for this kind of hangover," I mutter aloud. I hadn't come close to finishing my beer; two-thirds of it remained in the glass when I awkwardly fled the restaurant.

I grab my phone and search the internet for symptoms of morning sickness.

Guess you are saying hi, I silently tell the child who's most likely causing this discomfort. *Happy New Year to you, too.*

One article lists remedies for typical pregnancy ailments. Apparently, eating a small meal, complete with plenty of fluids, usually helps.

Battling the fatigue and vertigo, I pull last night's sweatshirt over my head and walk toward the elevators. I'm devouring a plate of scrambled eggs when my phone rings. Setting my fork down, I check to see who's calling.

"Good morning," Andrew announces when I answer the call.

"Hey," I say. "How was your night?"

"It was good. I left right after midnight. The guys were heading to some club, but I didn't feel like it. I only drank two beers, the whole night."

"One-and-a-half beers more than me," I reflect.

"Did you hang out with your crew?"

"Yes," I say, sipping water through a straw. "Since there's nothing near this hotel, we came down to the lobby bar. It was a good group. One of the flight attendants bailed, so it was just one other flight attendant and both pilots. And me."

"Did you stay up 'til midnight?"

I stab my fork into a mound of eggs. "I did. I went to bed right after, though. I was tired."

"Hopefully you slept well."

"I got a decent amount of sleep. But I had morning sickness today, which was weird. I woke up feeling off-balance. I'm at the hotel restaurant now, eating breakfast. I read an article about how food typically helps ease the symptoms."

"Damn. Sorry you felt crappy this morning," Andrew says, genuine concern in his voice. "Are you better now, or still uncomfortable?"

"I'm getting there. Breakfast helped a little. Still have a slight headache, but it's tolerable. The fatigue and dizziness are gone. Thankfully."

"Were you nauseous?"

"Not really," I muse. "It was mostly a headache. And intense pressure."

"I'm glad you're feeling better," he tells me. "We can take it easy tonight. I wanted to show you Coral Gables, but we can just eat someplace closer to your hotel instead."

"No," I protest, stuffing another bite of fluffy eggs in my mouth. "I'm pregnant, but not *dead*. Let's go to Coral Gables. It's such a fun area."

"You've been there before?"

"Yes. During college, I took a road trip to the Keys with some girlfriends. We were too poor to fly home for Thanksgiving break, so we drove to Key Largo and stopped in Miami along the way. I don't remember too much, except Coral Gables seemed upbeat and exciting. I'd love to see it again."

"Okay then, you got it," Andrew assures me.

I glance down at my watch. "Shit, I have to get ready to fly. Our airport van leaves in one hour."

"Be safe today, Cal. I can't wait to see you tonight."

"Same," I tell him, closing out the call. I swallow and flag down a server, asking for my check. Guilt washes over me, briefly, this time in the form of tightness within my chest. I grit my teeth and bear through it.

Dear small human, I hope you become a much better person than me.

****

Immediately after completing the drink service, I grab Jordan's arm and pull him into the galley. I've been scripting this dialogue in my head for hours.

My first instinct, when we both stepped onto this airplane, was to hide in the lavatory for the entire two-hour flight to Nashville. However, that felt like a cop-out. Plus, it would've solved absolutely nothing.

"Listen, Jordan, I need to apologize for last night," I tell him, avoiding his gaze. "I'm sort of dating someone. When you leaned in, with the mood lighting and the music and your fucking delicious cologne…well, I lost my head. I should've told you the truth from the beginning."

He nods and leans against the galley door. "Know what? I was afraid I had been too forward or aggressive or something. Don't beat yourself up, Cal. It was just a kiss."

"Yes. A really good one." I sigh.

"Don't remind me," he groans. He cracks a smile, his teeth bright enough to illuminate the entire galley. "It was *too* good. And for the record, I wasn't trying to hook up when I asked to walk you to your room. I really did want to make sure you got back safely."

"I appreciate it. My goal was to be as awkward as humanly possible and hurry out of the restaurant like a scared little kid."

Jordan laughs. "You succeeded."

"Thanks. I know," I say triumphantly.

"Callie…you're still searching for housing, right? For when you switch to the Fort Lauderdale base?"

I nod. "Felicity Daniels offered me a room in her house, but she's married, so it might be weird."

"I know Felicity," he says. "She was in initial training with me. Actually, come to think of it, you two have a lot in common. Felicity's a writer. She has a travel blog, and she writes company emails for SkyLine every month."

"She didn't tell me about the company emails," I note. "I've seen her blog, though. It's fantastic."

"Yeah, Felicity writes articles for the company newsletter. She wrote the one about the updated employee assistance program, and the one about our community outreach efforts. She's done a couple pieces in the airplane magazine, too."

"How awesome. Damn, I'm kind of jealous! I'll start looking for her name on SkyLine publications. How'd she get involved in that?"

"It happened by chance. Felicity worked a flight where the SkyLine CEO was sitting in business class, and they struck up a conversation. When he found out she was a writer, he appointed her to the Central Publications team on the spot."

"Seriously? That's lucky as hell." I gawk.

"She's talented, for sure, but she was also in the right place at the right time," Jordan notes.

"Hmm. Isn't that what all artistic pursuits boil down to, really?"

"Amen. Acting is the same. It's all about being in the presence of the right folks at the exact moment when it matters. Or, in Felicity's case, working the right flight." Jordan pauses. "You know, as cool as she is, I can see why you'd be hesitant to move into her house. I wouldn't feel comfortable living with a married couple, either."

"And you've lived with an ex-girlfriend," I tease. "So if anyone knows about uncomfortable living situations, it's definitely you."

Jordan chuckles. "Thanks. Come to think of it, my friend Karina has a spare room in Delray Beach. We went to high school together. She's a dental hygienist. I think you two would mesh really well. Maybe you could check out her apartment, see if it's a good fit."

"I'd be happy to meet with her. Where's the apartment complex? Close to 95?"

"Yep. Five minutes from the highway," he tells me. "It's near a ton of restaurants and a bike trail. There's a grocery store around the corner."

"Nice. Are the apartments new?" I ask.

"New-ish. Built within the last ten years. Look up *Atlantic Veranda Apartments* when we land. The two-bedroom units are about 1,600 square feet," he says. "With a balcony. Covered parking spots. And the beach is two miles away. Karina wanted me to move in with her, but I'm getting a one-bedroom in an apartment complex down the street. After the terrible living situation in Cocoa Beach, I kinda want my own place."

"This girl asked you to rent her spare room?" I muse, raising an eyebrow. "She's into you. Duh."

Jordan smiles. "I guarantee she isn't, Callie. She dated my sister for two years. Back in college."

"Maybe she goes both ways."

"Even if she does, there's some kind of code. You can't just switch from sibling to sibling. Plus, she knows my whole family. In fact, Karina still comes over for holidays sometimes."

"She's like a sister to you," I surmise.

He nods. "Exactly. I'll send you her number, if you want. I think you'll like her."

"Okay, sure," I say. "It would be nice to get my housing set up. Check another item off the list."

"You got it," he tells me. "Hey, my uncle lives in Biscayne Bay and he's taking me to dinner tonight, if you want to join us."

"Thanks for the offer, but I'll let you two catch up," I reply, sticking my hands in the pocket of my dress.

"Well, shit. That sounded bad, huh? I'm not trying to coerce you into meeting my family," he explains, shaking his head. "A couple of my buddies from college might meet up with us, too. I have history in Miami; I went to UM."

I laugh. "So you want me to meet your family *and* your close friends."

Jordan exhales slowly. "Okay, I'm going to stop talking now."

"Aw, don't worry about it. I'm just being a jackass."

"No, you're right. Some things sound better in my head than in real life. Guess I just figured if you were hungry, and you wanted to see a new part of Miami…hmm. Honestly, I don't know what I figured."

"Thanks for thinking of me. I'm actually hanging out with Andrew tonight," I inform him. "Otherwise I'd join you and your friends. We're gonna check out Coral Gables."

"You are? My old stomping grounds," he notes with a nostalgic smile. "I'm glad you have plans with your man. Coral Gables is beautiful. Have fun, Callie."

****

"I'm so sorry. I gave myself extra time, but traffic is insane," Andrew tells me with a sigh. "There's a huge wreck on 95 and the side streets are just as bad. Why don't you check into your hotel room and I'll come get you there? I'm about thirty minutes away."

"Not a problem. Seriously. I appreciate you driving to see me," I murmur, shifting my phone from one ear to the other.

"I wish I'd been on time," he reflects.

"It's fine, Andrew. Actually, this gives me a few minutes to change and relax after a long workday," I explain. "I'll see you in half an hour. Drive safely."

I close out the call and step onto the hotel shuttle. Jordan was picked up by his uncle at the airport and both of the pilots live in South Florida, so the only person besides me is Tess, the third flight attendant on our trip.

"Big plans tonight?" she asks me, grabbing a seat in the back of the van. She twists her long red hair into a bun on top of her head. "Sorry. Didn't mean to eavesdrop."

"It's okay," I say as I slide into the middle row of seats. This hotel van is larger than most, with four rows total. It's far too much space for the two of us. "I'm kind of dating this guy named Andrew. He's picking me up and we're going to Coral Gables."

"Sounds fun," she notes, her green eyes sparkling.

I pause. The whole crew has abandoned this poor girl, on the first day of the new year. And in a really exciting city. "Do you want to come with us?"

She waves her hand as the van starts moving. We both lurch forward slightly. "Oh, you're too sweet. I don't want to be your third wheel or anything. I'll just order some food at the hotel bar and call it a night."

"How painfully boring," I say with a sympathetic smile. "Look, Andrew is really nice. He'd love for me to bring a coworker along. I promise."

"Really?" she asks. "Are you sure?"

I nod. "'I'll text him now."

—*One of the flight attendants, a girl named Tess, is all by herself tonight. Is it cool if she comes along with us?*—

He responds quickly. *—Absolutely—*
—Thanks Andrew. Don't text and drive ;)—

We arrive at the hotel in minutes. It's at least eighty-five degrees outside, with a perfectly clear nighttime sky. While the van driver unloads our suitcases, I unzip my uniform sweater and stuff it in my backpack.

"Whatcha want to eat?" I ask Tess. "There are tons of choices in Coral Gables, if I remember correctly. Row after row of restaurants and shops."

She smiles. "I'll eat anything, really. I'm not picky. I appreciate you guys letting me tag along."

"Of course," I say. "Andrew is a decent tour guide, and I'm sure he will love having another person in his audience. He's lived in Florida his whole life."

"I've never lived anywhere but California," Tess explains. We wheel our suitcases into the lobby, a cozy room with a sprawling receptionist desk on one side. "So I appreciate the chance to see a new part of Florida."

"Lifelong Cali girl?" I muse. "I rarely meet a California native. Nearly all of my friends in SF moved there from someplace else."

"Oh, I don't live in San Francisco. I drive in from Sacramento," she tells me. She reaches for the airline sign-in sheet and places both our names on the list. "Left Sac to go to college in Santa Barbara, and then moved back to Sacramento after I graduated. Lame, huh?"

"Not at all," I reply, shaking my head. She hands me a hotel key and I briefly glance at the writing on the key packet. Room 328. "Just means you have more to enjoy on these overnights. Everything is new to you, interesting and inspiring and very different from what you grew up seeing."

She nods. "I've only been at SkyLine for three months."

"Seriously? You're a newbie?" I marvel. "I had no idea, girl."

We walk toward the elevators, passing a group of middle-aged folks on our way. The women are wearing stylish dresses and the men have button-up shirts and khakis. Everyone is talking excitedly, smiling a little too big and laughing a bit too loudly. *This city can bring out the best in you*, I reflect. In my experience, Miami's tropical vibe tends to make everyone more cheerful than usual.

I take the elevator to the third floor, typing Tess's number into my phone along the way.

"Calling you now," I say, steering my suitcase into the hallway. The hall is carpeted, a simple black-and-white pattern which complements the gray walls. "Save my number. I'll text once Andrew is here, and we can all meet in the lobby. Good plan?"

"Perfect," she says with a wave as the elevator door are closing. "Looking forward to it. Thanks again, Cal."

In my hotel room, I change into a black sundress. It's the only warm-weather attire I packed. The dress is cute and comfortable, a soft material that doesn't cling to my skin. I slide into black flats, thankful to be done with my work heels for the day.

Grabbing a seat in front of the vanity, I toss my makeup bag on the counter. The mirror is rimmed with lights, giving me a clear view of myself. My hair's a mess, thanks to the humidity, but otherwise I look decent. Surprisingly, there are no dark circles under my eyes. In fact, my skin appears luminous. I re-apply mascara and eyeliner. Then I put on a thin sweater, in case the temperature drops later.

My phone buzzes from the nightstand.

—Here—

—Room 328. Come on up— I smooth down my hair and inhale sharply. Leaning against the countertop, I contemplate my options: tell him now, tell him later, don't say a word.

"All bad choices," I mutter to nobody.

Andrew knocks, two quick raps on the door. I hurry to open it. He stands there, at the edge of the doorframe, a smile tugging at his lips. His gray polo hugs his body, reminding me how safe and peaceful it feels to curl up against his well-defined chest.

I blink, attempting to ignore the thought. Yet it persists. His clothing fits too well and, furthermore, I've seen what lies below the fabric. It's a satisfying, unforgettable image.

"Wow. Look at you," Andrew says appreciatively, his eyes fixed on mine. "You are gorgeous, Callie Schneider. Happy New Year."

I tilt my head to the side, basking in the glow of his compliments.

"Thanks, Andrew. We have a great year ahead," I predict, ushering him into my hotel room. "By the way, it was nice of you to let Tess join us tonight. Turns out she's brand-new to SkyLine. She's still bright-eyed and bushy-tailed."

"I'm glad we can show her around town. I reached out to a couple of buddies who live here, hoping they could meet up with us. This way, Tess won't feel like a third wheel."

"Smart thinking," I say, sitting on the edge of the bed. "Guess I can text her now and tell her to meet us in the lobby."

Andrew makes his way toward me. "Maybe wait just a couple minutes?"

I look up at him. "Sure."

He takes a seat, his hip grazing mine as he sinks into the bed. Smiling, he tucks a strand of hair behind my ear. "It's only been a few days since I saw you, huh? Feels like longer. Hopefully you haven't had much pain. I was sorry to hear you got sick this morning."

"I felt better after eating something. The dizzy, uncomfortable part didn't last long."

"Still, I hate seeing you in any kind of pain. I also hate knowing there will probably be more morning sickness to come. At least once you move to Florida, I can take care of you each time you feel shitty."

"Cook me bacon?" I request, cracking a smile.

"Obviously," he scoffs. "And scrambled eggs, and breakfast crepes."

I scoot an inch closer, nestling into his neck. He wraps an arm around me. *Say it now?* I debate. Andrew tilts my chin up, so I'm facing him. His eyes are bigger than ever, two spheres of sincerity and warmth.

"Sometimes I wonder when you're going to get sick of my bullshit," I reflect, sighing. "I'm not exactly the easiest person in the world to deal with."

He chuckles. "Fine by me. I don't mind your bullshit."

But you don't know everything I've done, I note internally. I pause for a moment, unsure of myself and my motives.

Then I press my lips to his, enjoying the familiarity of this kiss. Andrew is cautious and thoughtful, adjusting his arm around my back so I can lean into him. He kisses my mouth first, then my ear, then my neck. His lips are warm and gentle on my skin.

I tilt my head back. His hands migrate down to my waist, in no rush to arrive at their destination. I sense both desire and caution in his touch; his eagerness is equally matched by restraint.

Briefly, I open my eyes. This hotel room is just dim enough, just quiet enough that if I don't speak up, we could both get lost in this moment.

I clear my throat.

"Hmm. Maybe we should go," Andrew murmurs, reading my mind. "Otherwise, we might stay here all night. I'd love to—"

"We are on the same page," I interrupt, well aware of all the things he would like to do in this hotel room because I want to do them, too. "Tess would think we stood her up, and I'd go to bed hungry."

Andrew rises to his feet and pulls me onto mine. "Which would be an atrocity. Let's get some food."

We walk down the hallway, hands clasped together. As we ride the elevator to the first floor, I text Tess to meet us downstairs. Andrew and I meander through the lobby. We are relatively quiet, exchanging wordless glances every now and then.

Surprisingly, the silence isn't awkward. With Andrew, the quiet moments feel as natural as the loud ones.

Within seconds, Tess steps off the elevator. She hurries toward us, waving a braceleted arm cheerfully.

Aside from the receptionist, there's nobody else on the first floor. The only background noise is the whirring of the air conditioning high above our heads.

"Hi guys. Nice to meet you, Andrew," Tess says. "Thanks for letting me tag along."

"Nice to meet you, too," Andrew responds. "I'm glad we can show you around South Florida. This is your first time in Miami, right?"

We walk outside together, a blast of tepid air swirling around our faces. I glance at the sky as we advance toward Andrew's Mazda. Hundreds of stars shimmer overhead.

"I was here once before, but on a super short layover. I didn't leave the hotel," Tess explains.

We pile into the car and buckle up. Tess is in the back seat. I'm riding up front with Andrew, his hand resting on my knee. We cruise down streets glittered with fluorescent lights and quirky storefronts.

"This city is beautiful," Tess reflects, her voice filled with wonder.

"Miami is the busiest, flashiest city in Florida," I tell her. "I love the glamour of it. It's totally different from Orlando or Tampa, which feel more residential."

"Hmm. I haven't been to Tampa yet, aside from a quick layover where the only thing I saw was the inside of my hotel room," Tess clarifies. "What are the big Florida cities like? I visited Daytona before, when I was younger. Don't remember much."

"Daytona gets busy during Bike Week and spring break; the rest of the year, it's just a quiet beach town," Andrew explains. "It's a quick drive from Jacksonville, which feels like the Deep South more than Florida."

I nod in agreement as we cruise to a stop in front of

a red light. A luxury car pulls up to our left and a shiny stretch limo sits on our right.

"Let's see, I went to school in Gainesville, which is a fun college town," I tell Tess. "SkyLine doesn't fly into Gainesville; the airport is tiny."

"Gotcha. How's Fort Myers?" Tess asks. "I have a long overnight there in a couple weeks. I'm hoping to visit the beach."

"We were just in Fort Myers," Andrew recalls, pulling into a massive parking garage. We wind around, level after level, searching for an open spot. "It's a sleepy little retirement community, but the beaches are a lot less crowded than in other cities."

"The crew hotel is literally on the water," I say. "You walk out the back door, and the ocean's right there."

Tess releases a contented sigh as Andrew parks the car. We're probably a dozen floors up; the garage is completely packed. There are motorcycles, rusted sedans, expensive cars, and everything in between.

"Sounds awesome. I can't wait," Tess notes. "I've been in California my whole life, where the beaches are too cold to go swimming. I'm excited to *finally* enjoy the water."

We exit the car and walk toward the elevators, stopping briefly to check out the view. There are large square cutouts in the garage walls, essentially windows without any glass. Tonight, the sky is clear enough for us to see all the way to the water's edge. Andrew's fingers find mine as we marvel at the bright lights of this South Florida metropolis. His hands are cool but not clammy, and soft to the touch. I've never been a fan of romantic displays of affection before. But with

Andrew, this feels normal. It feels right.

After soaking up the spectacular view for a few moments, we ride an elevator down to the street level and meander toward a large roundabout, passing bars and boutiques along the way.

"How does everyone feel about Mexican food?" Andrew asks.

"Sounds good to me," Tess says.

"I'm in," I declare.

Andrew leads the way to a restaurant with a vintage golden awning. The interior strikes me as both trendy and rustic, exposed beams stretching across a low ceiling. The walls have been stained various neutral colors, with the grain of the wood visible. There's a taco bar on one side and a liquor bar on the other. A hostess seats us at a big booth; it's more than enough space for the three of us.

Andrew checks his phone while Tess and I glance over the menu.

"My buddy Connor might join us," Andrew announces. "He lives in Coconut Grove, which isn't far from here."

"Someone else is coming?" Tess asks, looking up from her menu.

Andrew nods. "I have a couple friends in Miami. Guys I know from college. I invited Connor and Luis to meet us. Haven't heard back from Luis yet."

We order guacamole and queso to start. I hadn't noticed my rumbling stomach until we set foot in the restaurant, but now I'm keenly aware of my hunger. Today was hectic and stressful, between my guilt and morning sickness. In the midst of the chaos, I hadn't eaten much.

Our queso arrives right away. I let Tess take the first scoop before reaching for the bowl. Andrew and I share a small, round plate, intermittently munching on tortilla chips. As we eat, I lean into him. He slips an arm behind my back and we sit like this, casual and carefree, while Tess talks about the cities she'll be visiting this month.

****

Connor slides into the booth just as our entrees arrive. He greets Andrew with a quick side hug, slapping him lightly on the back.

"Hey. I'm Connor," he says, extending a hand to Tess. She shakes it hesitantly, then smiles.

"I'm Tess. I'm a flight attendant on Callie's trip."

"And I'm Callie," I add, even though I get the distinct feeling Connor already knows this. "Nice to meet you."

"You, too. You both work for SkyLine, right?" Connor asks. "Man, I flew on them for Thanksgiving and I had a rough experience. Two screaming babies and a grown man who wouldn't stop projectile vom—"

"Yep, it happens. Sorry 'bout your luck," I interject with a laugh. "Tess has only been at the airline a couple months, so it's definitely not her fault. As for me, well, I was off Thanksgiving. Intentionally. The end of November is amateur hour."

Tess pokes a fork in her carnitas and looks up at me. "But you don't mind working New Year's, Callie?"

I shake my head. "Nah. New Year's is a lot calmer than the rest of the winter holidays, in my opinion. And I only worked on Christmas because someone paid me $500 to pick up her trip."

Andrew grabs a taco and raises it toward his

mouth. "I'm definitely glad you worked Christmas."

"I bet you are," I say, shaking my head. I dig into my taco salad hungrily. "That was the night we reconnected after a few weeks of silence."

"Weeks, or years? Andrew's been talking about you forever, Callie," Connor says.

"Dude, shut up," Andrew instructs, grabbing another taco. "We met in the middle of November and then she ghosted me."

"Ghosted?" Tess repeats.

"Well, no," I say with a sly smile. "I didn't exactly *ghost* Andrew. I was certain he wasn't interested, and I thought we were just, you know, going separate ways. I had no idea he wanted to see me again."

Tess raises an eyebrow. "But what is ghosting?"

"Oh, it's basically ditching someone," Connor says. "If a person stops responding to all calls and texts, just vanishes without a trace…then you got ghosted."

Tess makes a face. "Sounds like an awful thing to do."

"It was," Andrew says, nudging me. The corners of his mouth turn upward. "But I forgave her."

I roll my eyes and stuff a forkful of salad in my mouth. Tess and Connor are chatting about the vast differences between California and Florida. I glance at Andrew, polishing off his second taco, and realize there's really nowhere I would rather be.

Chapter Thirteen

January 2, 2020

Andrew's eyes are shut. I yawn and reach for him, running two fingers through his dark hair. He smiles, opens his eyes for a split second, then closes them again. I sit up, my back against the headboard, mentally composing the first few lines of a letter to the unnamed person in my belly.

Dear small human,

Some topics are worth broaching. Even if they are painful or jarring. For me, the toughest conversations involve apologies. I don't like admitting I screwed up. Maybe you'll be less prideful than me; maybe apologies won't be as difficult for you.

I glance down at Andrew. His rhythmic breathing assures me he's fast sleep. Tossing the sheet off my legs, I slide out of bed. This hotel suite is large, with a separate sitting area connected to the bedroom. I walk toward a small table positioned a few feet in front of the door. Then I flip my laptop open and begin to type, occasionally looking up to see if Andrew has moved. He remains on his side, dreaming away.

I don't want to tell your father what really happened two nights ago, I type. *But he deserves better than my worst...so I'm going to be honest with him.*

I've avoided some important conversations in the

Lisa Wilkes

past. When I got hired at SkyLine, I didn't tell my parents I was going to become a flight attendant until after completing the two-month initial training. I was certain they wouldn't approve. My older brother, your uncle, is so straight-edge and successful. He's a perfect human, while I'm a category 5 hurricane. I thought my parents would be disappointed by my career choice.

In addition, I was worried I might fail the training. I had a lot on my mind back then; while trying to get my first book published, I kept running into brick walls. As a result, my self-esteem plummeted. Along with my ability to concentrate.

By some miracle, I completed training. I passed all my exams, donned a uniform, and finally informed my parents I was a flight attendant. Long after the fact.

They weren't disappointed or embarrassed. In fact, they were just plain hurt. And for good reason.

Mom and Dad couldn't understand why I'd intentionally left them in the dark for months. It would've been easier to explain the situation in the very beginning. But my fears got in the way of healthy communication.

I hope you take control of your fears, little one. When the world seems scary, please remember you are a product of love and determination. Although your arrival was a shock to me, it was the biggest gift your father has ever asked for. Make no mistake, you have been on his mind for a long time.

Anyone who enters the world under those terms, surrounded by affection and anticipation and gratitude, is surely strong enough to master even the scariest of circumstances. You are bigger than whatever issue happens to be plaguing you in the moment. You're brave and honest and adored by a father who embodies sincerity.

You are made of stronger stuff than I am, child. You're going to do great things.

Sincerely,

Your mama

I hear rustling in the bedroom, so I quickly shut my laptop.

"Good morning," I say while approaching the bed. Andrew smiles, motioning for me to come lie down with him.

"Morning, Cal," he murmurs in my ear once I'm snuggled up beside him. "What time is it?"

I grab my phone off the nightstand. "Almost eight."

"Have you been up a long time?"

"Nah. Maybe half an hour," I tell Andrew, rolling over to face him. He gently wraps an arm around my waist, pulling me a few centimeters closer. Our legs are tangled up together, with our toes touching.

"Did Tess have fun last night in Coral Gables?" he asks.

I nod aggressively. "Absolutely. Everything is still so new to her; I'm sure she was glad to get out of the hotel and visit a new part of town. Plus, your friend seems great."

"Connor can be a mess sometimes, but he's cool," Andrew notes. "Too bad we didn't make it to Coconut Grove. Next time, for sure."

I groan. "My fault, sorry. I was wiped out by ten o'clock. Guess I didn't get enough sleep the night before. It was painful trying to keep my eyes open."

Andrew shakes his head. "Don't worry about it,

Callie. It was New Year's Day, so we were all exhausted."

"Even coming back to the hotel early, I think Tess had fun. She loved Coral Gables. I'm glad we got to walk around and grab drinks after dinner," I note. Then I catch myself. "Well…all the *non-pregnant* people got to drink. Must be nice."

"I bet that part is awful," Andrew says quietly. "Sorry, Callie. I wish you could drink with everyone."

"It's okay. Liquor has lost its appeal. A byproduct of the changing hormones, I guess." I place my hand on Andrew's chest, near his shoulder. I'm mesmerized by the perfect angles of his body.

"When do I get to see you next, Cal?" he asks, closing his eyes and resting his chin on my head.

I pause.

There are a million responses I could give him. I could easily whip out my phone and check for my next Florida layover. Or I could figure out which weekend I want to fly to West Palm and look at apartments.

But there's a different topic I need to address first.

I take a deep breath. "Andrew, I have to tell you something."

His eyes fly open. He readjusts himself so he can face me directly. "Hmm. This doesn't sound good. What's up?"

"Well," I begin. "I wasn't sure I should tell you this, but I think it's worse to pretend it never happened. I know we're sort of dating. Or at least figuring some things out. I really enjoy spending time with you. But…"

Andrew blinks.

"*But*," he repeats. He glances at me, his eyes wide

with kindness and worry.

I look away.

"I got wrapped up in the moment on New Year's Eve and, uh, I ended up kissing someone in the hotel bar," I say, staring at the artwork on the wall. It's an aerial shot of downtown Miami, probably a few decades old. The skyline has changed drastically since then. "I screwed up, Andrew. Big time. You were celebrating with your friends in West Palm while I was making out with a complete stranger. You deserve better. It wasn't my finest moment. I'm sorry."

He tilts my chin up so I am facing him once again. We are still lying on our sides, the generic white bedsheets halfway covering us.

"Thank you for telling me," he says. "It was just a kiss?"

I nod. "I don't know what happened, Andrew. The clock struck midnight and then I was kissing someone. I'm a shitty person sometimes. I don't have any excuses."

He rolls over onto his back and scratches his head. "Look, I will never force you into an exclusive relationship. I appreciate you explaining what happened on New Year's, but you don't owe me anything. If you want to kiss someone else, or sleep with him or date him, that's your call."

"The thing is, I *don't* want to kiss someone else...at least, I don't think so. Look, Andrew, I haven't had a boyfriend since college. I got used to making my own decisions and navigating this world alone. But everything has changed recently. I like being with you, and only you."

"You know I feel the same way, right?'

I swallow. "I do. Life has been an ongoing nightmare lately. I'm pregnant, and I'm keeping this massive secret from my friends and family. It sucks. It's lonely as hell. Sometimes I feel like a fucking liar with no soul."

"I'm so sorry, Callie."

"It's not your fault," I point out. "It's just tough. There are a million crazy thoughts floating through my mind. I'm a disaster, Andrew. I want to be with you, but I need to get my head straight. You know?"

"You're dealing with a lot at once, Callie. I don't want to add pressure during this chaotic time. No need to plan our whole lives right now. We can go slowly. No rules. If you're ready to be exclusive someday, then we can take that route. Please don't agonize over it."

"But what about everything *you* want?" I ask, realizing I haven't considered Andrew's goals this entire conversation. It's been about me: my guilt, my indecisiveness, my confusion, my anguish. "Is this what Andrew David Goldberg desires, deep down? To do our own thing for an indefinite period of time, without commitment or exclusivity?"

He pauses. "Well, I want you to know all your decisions are supported and respected."

I curl up against his chest, fully aware he didn't answer my question.

****

"Did you guys have fun last night?" Jordan asks, sitting down beside me on the jumpseat. He's holding his company-issued iPad in one hand and a can of soda in the other.

I quickly close my laptop. I'd been writing another letter to the unnamed child growing inside me. "We did. Tess came with us, actually. We went to a Mexican restaurant in Coral Gables. How about you?"

"Grabbed dinner with my uncle. Afterward, I met up with a couple college buddies for drinks. I stayed with one of my best friends, who lives downtown."

"Sounds great," I say. "Are you going to catch a flight home tonight, or do you have to wait 'til tomorrow?"

Jordan checks his watch. "We should be twenty minutes early into SFO, which means I'll have about an hour before the Orlando flight. Plenty of time."

"Long day for you," I note.

"Nah, not really," he insists, leaning back against the paper-thin jumpseat cushion. "I saw my cousins, hung out with my buddies in Miami, and met you. Overall, well worth the five-hour transcontinental commute tonight…"

I shake my head. "Meeting me has been a highlight of your trip?"

"Obviously. You inspire me to get back into acting, Cal. I've been out of the loop for a while, but I love seeing your creative ambition. I'll be first in line to buy a copy of your book when it's published."

"You might be waiting a long time," I warn with a dry laugh. "But thanks. I hope you have an easy transition back into the world of theater."

Jordan pauses. "Hey, did I ever text you Karina's number? You should reach out to her. I think you'd love the apartment complex. The location is unbeatable."

I scroll through my phone. "Nope, I don't have it. Send me her contact info when we land."

"Will do," he says just as the captain announces

we're on our final descent into SFO. We stand up and walk through the cabin with the trash cart, making sure everything is secured for landing.

Chapter Fourteen

January 3, 2020

I type furiously, editing the "Description" section for the thousandth time.

A series of open letters to a child I'll never meet.

Sighing, I stab the backspace button. Then I watch the cursor erase every character with a vengeance. "Technically, I'll meet the kid," I murmur to my empty apartment. "While pushing it out of my body."

Letters not meant to be read by their recipient, I type. Then I delete that sentence, too, because it sounds cold and institutional. Like a formal statement to a professor as a thesis proposal.

I drum my fingers on the metal part of my laptop. Uploading the individual letters had been relatively easy, except for a few small formatting issues. But writing the informational sections was a whole different ballgame.

Written with love, addressed to nobody/everybody, I type, clicking the "update" icon. I attach a photo of myself in the galley of an Airbus, my back to the camera. A glowing sunset serves as the backdrop, outlining my dim silhouette.

The photo is artistic and nostalgic. Best of all, it has zero identifying markers, upholding the anonymity of my blog.

"Description section complete," I declare triumphantly. There's a knock on the door.

"Hi, Callie," Mack practically sings from the sidewalk. Her voice floats in through the open windows.

I hop up from my bed and rush to the door. Mackenzie tackles me in a hug, nearly knocking me into the wall.

"Good to see you, too." I laugh into her hair.

She pulls away, still gripping my shoulders, and smiles. A cloth bag, full of clunky items which are most likely crafting materials, dangles from her arm. "Happy New Year, best friend. How was your trip? How are you feeling these days? I want details."

"New Year's was good," I tell her as we walk toward the living room. It's the middle of the afternoon, so we have a couple hours to ourselves before Tammy and Linda get home. "How about you?"

"Dave and I ended up at his coworker's house for a small party. It was okay," Mackie notes. She sits down next to me on the couch. "New Year's Eve is far less exciting when you can't get shitfaced."

"Tell me about it." I chuckle. "Oh God, Mack, something happened on my trip. Don't judge me."

"I'd never do such a thing," she promises. "I love your stories, Cal."

"Not this one," I say, shaking my head. "This is a bad story. I kissed the flight attendant on my trip. A guy named Jordan. He's Orlando-based and I had never seen him before last week. The Atlanta hotel bar was dark and loud. He's so charismatic and so damn hot. I just lost my head."

"And this is a bad story because...?" Mackie trails

off, raising an eyebrow.

"Because I'm kind of dating someone. Andrew is the nicest person ever, and I kissed a complete stranger behind his back."

"Listen, Cal, there's no such thing as 'sort of' being in a relationship," Mack points out. "I'm on Team Andrew all the way, trust me. He sounds like a legitimately good dude. But you're either a couple or you're not, right? And, to my knowledge, you two are not a couple. Not yet. I can understand why you feel guilty, but don't beat yourself up over it. Did you tell Andrew what happened?"

I nod, staring out the window. The sky is full of fast-moving black thunderclouds. They cast ominous shadows over the city.

"Was it a rough conversation?" Mackie asks.

"Yes," I groan. "It was so uncomfortable."

"How'd he respond?"

I sigh. "He was really sweet. He said he isn't going to force me into a relationship, and I'm free to do what I want until I'm ready to possibly consider a future with him. But that's part of the reason I feel bad, ya know?"

Mackie furrows her brow. "Not really."

"I feel guilty because it's obvious that Andrew *does* want a relationship. Even if he's too polite to admit it," I explain, looking Mack in the eye. "He's a fantastic person, but our situation is messed up. There's no perfect ending in a world where I'm giving birth to Andrew's child and then signing away all my rights. How could this possibly turn into something real?"

"You're the only person who can answer that question," Mackenzie says gently. "Maybe it wouldn't work. Or maybe you'd figure it out somehow. When I met Dave, he was dating someone. Remember? A few weeks later, he was unexpectedly single. From then on, we were inseparable. Life is freaking weird and unpredictable. It's messy as hell."

She reaches for my hand. We sit like this for some time, a tangle of worries and sympathies and enduring love.

"Hey, what's in the bag?" I finally ask, nodding toward her cloth satchel.

"Crafting supplies. My friend Cora is sending a huge batch of cards to a retirement home in Alameda. They're already collecting for Valentine's Day. What do you think? Want to share some love with lonely old people?"

"Sure, why not," I say with a smile. "I could use the karma points."

****

I tuck the last letter into Mack's bag, which is overflowing with sealed red-and-white envelopes. Altogether, we wrote twenty cards, filling blank pages with inspirational quotes and warm wishes.

"A few months ago, we would've celebrated the completion of this altruistic task with a glass of wine," Mackie notes.

I snort. "More like a whole bottle."

"It's weird I don't even want alcohol these days," she says. "I just miss the social aspect of it. How 'bout you?"

I rise from the couch, stepping into the kitchen to pour myself a glass of seltzer. Without even asking, I pour an extra one for Mackie. She will accept it. She always does. "Same here. The lure has gone *way* down."

"Have you been sick at all? I bet flying gets tough in the second and third trimester," Mackenzie predicts.

"I had morning sickness yesterday, but it only lasted a few minutes. Woke up with a raging headache, stomachache, and general discomfort."

"Ugh. The worst," Mack sympathizes.

"As for flying, it depends on the person," I surmise, handing her a cup of seltzer. "Some women leave work during the second trimester. But I've flown with pregnant ladies who are ready to pop, and they seem to be doing fine. Apparently, their doctors clear them to fly until they're just about ready to deliver the baby."

Mackie cradles her glass of bubbly water and tilts her head to the side. "I'm impressed. Judging by my terrible symptoms a few weeks ago, I predict I'll be completely useless at work by the third trimester."

"Lots of time to stay in bed and write cards to old people you've never met," I reflect with a half-smile.

"Definitely," Mack chuckles. "Speaking of writing, are you still working on letters to the baby?"

I gasp. "Oh, shoot, I forgot to show you. I spent all morning tweaking this. Hang on a second."

I dart into my bedroom and grab my laptop. When I flip open the screen, my blog stares back at me, shades of blue and silver with bold black writing.

"All right, here's the preliminary version," I announce, returning to the living room. Mackenzie finishes her seltzer and sets the empty cup on the coffee table. "Sorry if it sucks. I compiled all the entries into an anonymous blog. Figured they'd be more accessible this way, in case the general public cares to read them."

Mackie places the lightweight computer on her lap.

Her face is illuminated by the glow of the screen. She remains silent for a few moments, scrolling through posts while I hold my breath.

"Callie," she murmurs. "Damn, girl."

"What? How is it?" I inch closer to her, peeking over her shoulder. She's scrolled down to my sixth blog post, a letter I'd written several days ago.

"*In the aftermath of absurdity, a shred of hope remains. You, tiny human, are the source of wide-eyed anticipation; you lit a spark inside your father,*" Mackenzie reads. "It's emotional and addicting. I've never seen a blog like this before."

"Thank you," I say, my voice cracking just a little. "Sometimes I suspect my writings are boring as hell. Look, I know you have to say these nice things; as my best friend on the planet, it's your job. But it still feels great to think maybe, just maybe, I'm not the worst writer ever born."

Mackenzie shakes her head vehemently. "Callie, I love you enough to give you honest feedback. I'd tell you if the blog was lame. I mean, I'd say it nicely. But I wouldn't go on and on about how unique, fascinating, and well-written it is. I would make suggestions on how to improve it."

I pause, weighing the logic of her assertion. "Okay, then. I love you, Mackenzie."

"Good thing. You're my maid of honor, after all. You'd better love me."

I shriek. "Oh God, I just realized when I fly back for your wedding, I'll definitely be showing. In front of all those people, Mack. I'll have a huge belly and everyone will ask a thousand questions."

Mackie bites her lip. "Shit, I didn't think of that.

We will be, what, seven months pregnant by then? Visible bump, for sure. Can you tell everyone you're a surrogate?"

"Will they believe me?" I ask, certain that nobody would trust such an obvious lie. I've spent the last decade adamantly declaring my love for alcohol and coffee. "I'll just tell them the truth. Surprise baby, after what I thought was a one-night stand. God, I don't know. It's your special day and hopefully everyone will focus on you. You'll have a bump, too..."

Mackie places a hand on my arm reassuringly. "True. I'll be massive and hideous. In fact, I'll need to buy a new wedding dress. Shit. Give me a day to think. We will figure something out, Cal. I promise."

Lisa Wilkes

Part Four: Clearance

Chapter Fifteen

January 4, 2020

—How's your day off?— Andrew texts around noon.

I reply while dodging the crowd already gathered in front of The Fillmore. *—Good. How's work coming along?—*

—It's fine. Are you free tonight? I can call you once I get home. Would love to hear your voice—

I stare at the intersection of Geary and Webster, trying to judge whether traffic is light enough for me to jaywalk. After a moment's deliberation, I make a run for it. *—Meeting an old friend for lunch, but I'll be home after that. Feel free to call later today—*

—Thanks, Cal. Will do—

I duck inside the world's smallest Japanese restaurant, the first place I dined at when I moved to SF four years ago. There are only a few tables in the restaurant. Luckily for me, one happens to be empty. I weave around customers to reach the vacant table.

My friend Trevor walks in as I'm glancing over the menu. He strolls toward me with a grin on his face.

"Hey, Callie," he greets me with a hug. "Man, it's been a long time. We missed you at Hotel Utah last week. Frankie played one of her new songs, which was great. And this guy I've never seen before did slam poetry. I was skeptical, to be honest. He wasn't bad, though."

I tilt my head to the side. "Sorry I missed it. God, I haven't been to SoMa in forever."

"Too long, girl. Have you written any songs lately? Any new material for me to learn?" Trevor asks.

"You're such a good sport, memorizing all those chords and standing in as my guitarist," I reflect. "I have no problem singing in public, but I sure as hell won't play guitar in front of a crowd. I suck so much."

"Somehow, I doubt that," Trevor says skeptically. The waitress comes by for our drink order, and we both get green tea. I order brussels sprouts for an appetizer, my stomach rumbling loudly enough for people across the street to hear it.

"I actually have some news," I tell him. "Most of my girlfriends already know, but I haven't had a chance to tell any of my musician buddies yet. I'm moving to Florida at the end of the month."

Trevor's jaw drops. "Really? Back to Gainesville?"

I shake my head. "Actually, this time I'm going to Fort Lauderdale. It was a sudden decision. I plan to be in Florida for less than a year. I just needed a change."

"Why?"

"It's hard to explain. I keep inching closer to thirty," I say with a shrug. "Not that thirty is old, but I'd hoped to be published by now. I want to pursue my writing without distractions. Stop doing everything half-heartedly and really *focus*. For once."

"Can't you do all those things in SF?"

I pause. Outside, the sun is beginning to peek through the thick clouds. Tiny golden fingers reach down from the sky. This might be the only time all day the yellow orb makes an appearance. Through the restaurant's oversized windows, I spot pedestrians unzipping their jackets and taking off their scarves, hats, gloves.

"There's more to the story," I confess before my brain can register what my mouth is saying. "Yes, I do want to work on my writing. As always. But, umm, I'm pregnant. It was a total surprise. Anyway, I decided to carry the baby to term. But I don't want to raise a child."

Trevor's eyes grow wider than I've ever seen them. "You're giving it up for adoption?"

"Sort of. Turns out the father actually wants a kid, so I'll sign over my rights once the baby is born."

"Holy shit," Trevor says. "I had no idea you were going through all this."

"Most people don't know," I admit. "That's part of the reason I'm moving to Florida for a while. I don't want my friends asking questions once I start showing. It's a bizarre situation; I just want to be anonymous for the next few months."

"Makes sense," Trevor notes as the brussels sprouts arrive. The vegetables remain in the center of the table, steam rising from the plate, while both of us just stare.

"I can't believe I blurted everything out," I say. "Damn, it feels good to tell the truth. I've been lying so much these past few weeks. My parents think I'm moving to Florida to save money."

"Your secret's safe with me," Trevor promises. "Shit, when my brother got locked up last year, you were the only person in San Francisco I told. We know all of each other's skeletons in the closet."

"We really do, don't we?" I grab a brussels sprout with my chopsticks and take a bite. "I've been writing letters to the baby, notes that he or she will never read. Not sure why I started. Guess I needed to release all of my confusion and worries."

"How many letters have you written?"

"Dozens. I have at least twenty blog posts already…"

"You started a blog? Can I see it?" Trevor inquires.

I quickly navigate to the site on my phone, then hand the device over to him. "Here you go. I kept it anonymous. Haven't figured out how to publicize the thing yet, since I don't want anyone knowing I wrote it."

Trevor scrolls through the blog while I finish my appetizer. The waitress returns and we both order cucumber rolls.

"Thoughts?" I ask, Trevor's eyes still glued to the phone screen.

"It's great. I've never read a collection of letters like this…and certainly not ones addressed to a child who will never see them," he muses. "It's really creative. These letters are about more than an unexpected pregnancy; they're about hopes and losses and self-acceptance."

"Wow. Thanks," I say. "Means a lot to me."

"You should create a dummy Instagram profile. Link it to your blog, make it untraceable. Edit all photos so your face isn't discernible. You could be like the Banksy of the literary world."

I mull over his suggestion. "You might be a genius, Trevor. I couldn't figure out how to get exposure since I don't want the blog linked to me in any way. This is a brilliant solution."

"Let's create your new Instagram account after lunch," he says, smiling. "I'm good at this stuff. I can blur certain parts of a picture with an editing app on my phone. We'll keep your identity hidden, Cal."

Our cucumber rolls arrive and we both dig in. When I glance out the window, I notice the sun has retreated. Pedestrians are, once again, bundled up in multiple layers of clothing, shivering as they trek across the city.

****

"Any plans for the night?" Andrew asks, his voice bouncing off the kitchen walls.

I adjust the speakerphone volume. Then I lean back in my chair, sipping chamomile tea. "A few of my friends are going to the Urban Art Museum. It stays open late on Thursdays, and everyone usually gets drinks after. I'm debating going. If I can motivate myself to head back outside, into the cold."

"Send photos if you go," Andrew requests.

"Sure. Whatcha up to?"

"I'll head to my sister's house for an hour, before my nephew Cameron goes to sleep," Andrew tells me. "Last week, my sister told me he's been asking to see me."

"Where do they live?" I ask.

"Boca. Not a far drive, and traffic should be light by now," he says.

I glance at the clock above the microwave. 3:50, which means it's almost 7 p.m. in Florida. "I bet your nephew loves when you visit. How old is he?"

"Five," Andrew informs me. "Cameron's energetic and funny as hell. He's been through a lot, but you'd never know it. He adjusted so well to everything."

"Since he's adopted," I murmur. "Sorry. I didn't mean to sound creepy. Just saw some photos on your Facebook profile, so I put two and two together."

"My sister, Julia, has wanted kids her whole life. The process wasn't easy, Cal. Especially since she's single. She waited years to be matched with Cameron. She was a nervous wreck the entire time. It was definitely worth the wait, though; Cameron's the best."

"I'm glad he's got a great family now," I reflect. "Have fun tonight."

"Thanks, Callie. Where are your layovers tomorrow?"

I thumb through my schedule on my phone. "Hmm...Memphis and Santa Fe."

"No Florida layovers this month, huh?"

"I tried to get one, but there was nothing to trade into," I tell him. "Which is fine, because I'll visit after this trip. Crap, I almost forgot to tell you: I plan to fly into West Palm on my days off, to figure out my housing situation."

"Where are you hoping to live?"

"Well, my coworker gave me the contact info of a friend in Delray Beach, this girl named Karina. She's a dental hygienist. She has an open room in her apartment and rent is really cheap. It's furnished, too. Have you heard of Atlantic Veranda Apartments?" I ask.

"Yes. One of my buddies lived there for a year. It's a good location. The apartments are big and modern," Andrew says.

"Good. I texted this girl about the room and she said she's got some free time next week. I'm thinking I'll fly to West Palm on Monday, rent a car, and drive to her place."

"Don't forget, my offer still stands," Andrew says. "You're more than welcome to move in with me, even just temporarily. Completely up to you."

I smile. "I haven't forgotten, Andrew. I think it would be best to find my own place for now, but if I change my mind, you'll be the first to know."

"At least let me come get you when you land on Monday," Andrew insists. "You can use my car during the week, to check out apartments. My office building is only a couple blocks from my apartment; I'll walk to work."

"You're too much," I tell him, chuckling at his absurd generosity. "Why are you so nice all the time?"

"Dumbest question ever. Because I like you, duh."

I laugh. "Fair enough. Have a good night, Andrew."

****

"What's going on, Mack?" I ask, curious about the cryptic text she sent me earlier today: —*Something to tell you ASAP. Meet me in front of the museum, before we go inside—*

"I have news."

"But it's cold out here," I say, my voice both whiny and pleading. "Can we have this conversation inside the building, maybe? Everyone's in there. Tammy, Linda, Maria, and Candice."

Mackenzie's brown eyes are radiant, shining through the otherwise dark night. Cars fly past us, a blur of headlights and roaring engines.

"Callie, I figured it out," she says breathlessly.

"Huh? Figured what out?"

"Everything," she murmurs, grabbing my hand.

Her fingers are much warmer than mine. "I don't want a big wedding. Not now. The situation changed when I discovered I was pregnant. I don't care about planning my 'special day' anymore. Dave and I just want to go to City Hall, preferably next week. Ten people total. I still want you to be my maid of honor, obviously. What do you say, Cal?"

I blink. "Seriously, Mack? Have you lost your marbles?"

She laughs. "No. Maybe I'm finally regaining my sanity."

"Is this really what you want?" I ask her. "Why would you change your mind so suddenly? This better not be to save my reputation, Mackenzie. You can't let my mistake dictate the terms of your wedding. I refuse to allow it."

Mackenzie shakes her head. Loose waves of shiny brown hair tumble from her beanie. "No, Cal. I started brainstorming because of our conversation two days ago. It occurred to me that I don't want to get married seven months pregnant. I don't want the stress and chaos. Dave and I can have a big ceremony next year, if we choose. After life calms down. But I don't care about a huge, complicated reception anymore. As long as my parents are there, and Dave's siblings, and you...you guys are all we need."

"What about the expense? Haven't you guys already paid for everything?"

"We crunched the numbers," Mackenzie tells me. "At this point, all we'd lose is the deposit on the venue and the caterers. Everything else is refundable because we are still so far from the wedding date."

"And you really, truly want this?" I ask, trying to

gauge her body language and facial expressions. There's no sign of insincerity.

"I want this," she assures me. "I've already called my parents. They love the idea. My wedding dress fits me, since I'm not showing yet. Now we just need to select a day and write our vows. Will you still be my maid of honor, Callie Schneider?"

I wrap her in a hug, mystified by her change of heart.

"Of course. Duh," I tell her. "I wouldn't miss it for anything."

****

Forks clink against plates as we walk into Rory's Diner. The sound is almost rhythmic, a symphony of silverware colliding with dishes. Tammy and Linda went home after the museum, leaving the four of us to grab a bite.

We sit at a booth near the kitchen. I'm on the edge, next to Mackie; Maria and Candice are across from us. When the kitchen door swings open, the scent of fried eggs wafts toward our table. Without any warning, I gag. Muttering something unintelligible to the girls, I sprint toward the bathroom.

I make it to the stall just in time.

The taste of bile lingers in my mouth long after the violent retching has ended. I'm exhausted beyond belief, which is baffling because I felt fine ten minutes ago. I wipe my mouth with toilet paper, flush, and contemplate what to tell my friends.

Food poisoning, I think, staring at myself in the mirror as I scrub my hands. Thankfully, there are no chunks of vomit on my clothes.

"Hate to say this, but I have to go home. I'm

sorry," I tell the girls once I'm back at the table. "I must've eaten something bad; I got really sick just now. You guys enjoy your food."

Mackie grabs her jacket. "Nope. You're not walking home alone, Cal."

I hold up a hand. "Thanks, Mack, but I'm only a few blocks from here. Less than ten minutes. I just need to rest. I'm sure I will wake up tomorrow feeling normal again."

"We'll get you an Uber," Maria offers.

I shake my head. "No, thanks. I can walk home in the time it would take for an Uber to arrive. Hey, I had a great time at the museum. Sorry to cut the night short. I'll see you ladies soon."

I zip up my coat and dart into the cold night.

Andrew texts me as I reach the corner of Ellis and Van Ness. —*Goodnight, beautiful*—

—*Hey, Andrew. Late night for you, huh?*—

—*Yeah, I stayed and talked to my sister for a while after Cameron fell asleep. Just got back to my apartment*—

The light changes, so I jog across Van Ness. —*Gotcha. I'm on my way home. I threw up at a restaurant with some girlfriends. Who knew morning sickness also happens at night?*—

Seconds later, my phone buzzes with an incoming call. I accept it just as my feet touch the curb on the west side of Van Ness.

"Hey, Andrew."

"Callie, I'm so sorry you're sick."

"I feel okay now," I tell him, sidestepping a small puddle that might or might not be human piss. "Out of nowhere, I got super nauseous. Then I was in the bathroom, vomiting uncontrollably. So gross."

"Are you still nauseous?" he asks.

I turn onto Gough Street. "Not really. It was fast. The smell of eggs hit me, and it was *foul*. Completely overpowering."

"I wish I were there with you."

I pass a strip of restaurants and corner stores. "There's not much you could do, Andrew. But thanks for wanting to help."

"Hopefully you feel fine the rest of the night."

A man walks out of a restaurant carrying a big brown bag. As he passes me, I catch the distinctive scent of Italian food. It smells cheesy and garlicky.

"Well I just walked past someone with takeout and it smelled amazing, not repulsive," I inform Andrew. "So that's a good sign."

"Hopefully," he says. "Hey, Callie, I've been thinking…you should probably have a prenatal doctor's appointment, right? Your first one. Why don't we schedule it for when you're in town, so I can come with you. I'll find a good obstetrician and book your appointment. I can pay whatever insurance doesn't cover."

"That's actually a great idea," I say. "To be honest, I hadn't even thought about a doctor's appointment yet. I'm probably overdue."

"I read online that the first appointment is typically just before the two-month mark," Andrew reflects. "Which means you are right on track. Okay, I'll set something up. When are you flying to town? Monday?"

"Yes," I respond as I arrive at my apartment building. "I'll fly to West Palm on Monday and stay until Wednesday or Thursday, at the latest. Hey, guess what? My best friend decided to get married at City Hall instead of doing a big wedding like she originally planned. I'll be her maid of honor sometime next weekend."

"Wow. Is it just going to be a few people?"

"Yes," I tell him. I slide my key into the lock and step inside. It's warm in my apartment and I can hear the television playing in the living room. "Ten people total. I already have my dress for the wedding. Thankfully, it still fits. I'll just show up, make sure Mackenzie is calm and happy, and watch my best friend marry *her* best friend."

"Isn't SF's City Hall iconic? I remember reading it's an architectural masterpiece or something…"

I step into my bedroom, eager to change into pajamas and crawl into bed. The nausea has passed, leaving me dead tired. "Yes, it's stunning. I'll send lots of photos after Mackenzie's wedding."

"Thanks, Callie," Andrew says. "Are you home now? The background noise sounds a lot quieter."

"I'm in my bedroom, safe and sound," I inform him. "I already feel a hundred times better than I did before. Gonna brush my teeth and then hopefully sleep for ten hours."

"Okay. Goodnight, Callie."

"Night, Andrew."

Chapter Sixteen

January 5, 2020

"Do you mind? Just for a second. If not, it's okay," the nervous mother tells me, eyeing the bathroom door. A tiny infant squirms in her arms. "I can hold him on my lap while I pee…"

"No, no," I say. I reach forward, accepting the wriggly baby. "I'll take care of him. Don't worry about it."

The passenger ducks into the bathroom, shooting me a grateful smile as she closes the door.

I glance down the aisle. The other two flight attendants, Brittany and Jonah, are assisting various passengers toward the back of the cabin. Outside, the sun's beginning to set; bright orange rays peek through partially opened window panes. From the looks of it, half the passengers are sleeping and the other half are watching television on their phones.

"Well, hello there," I tell the baby in my arms, scanning his face for any signs of discontent. He blinks up at me, two big blue eyes full of curiosity. "Don't cry, okay? You can pee or poop. You can even grab my hair. But please don't make a scene. Got it?"

He yawns, showing off his toothless mouth.

I pull the child closer to my chest and step toward the jumpseat cautiously. Once I'm sure I have solid footing, I unfold the bench and sit down.

"This is called a jumpseat," I inform him. "It's where flight attendants go when our heels are killing us. I've written many short stories in this spot."

The kid reaches for my sweater and hoists himself closer to my face.

I smile. "You're strong, for a teeny tiny little guy."

He tilts his head to the side, studying my shirt. His eyes land on the shiny gold wings with my name engraved on them. After a few seconds of deliberation, he leans forward and starts suckling my wings.

"Nothing tasty there," I assure him, gently pulling his mouth from my shirt. "I promise there's no milk buffet hiding under these metal wings. Your mom will be back soon. She has the good stuff."

The child touches my wings with his finger, then places his head near my shoulder. I can feel his heartbeat against mine. A faintly sweet scent emanates from his head, some combination of soap and milk and happiness. I inhale deeply, savoring the smell.

The mother emerges from the bathroom, wiping her hands on her jeans. Thanking me profusely, she reaches for the baby. As she carries her child down the aisle, back to their seats, I can't help but smile.

Nice try, kiddo, I think. *You probably thought you could win me over with your adorable face. You are a cute baby, sure. But I still don't want one. At least, not right now.*

I pull my laptop from the storage bin and flip it open.

Dear small human, I type. *I'm seriously considering getting a cat...*

****

Mackenzie calls me while I'm getting ready for bed.

"Hey, lady," I say, mouth full of foamy toothpaste.

"Hi, Cal. Sorry it's late. I remembered you're in a different time zone *after* dialing your number," she says. "Are you brushing your teeth or something?"

I spit into the hotel sink. "Yes. I'm in a hotel in Memphis, getting ready for bed. It's only ten o'clock here, but I figured I should catch up on sleep now. Next week is going to be pretty insane."

"Tell me about it. That's actually why I'm calling you. Dave and I were able to schedule our wedding at City Hall next Friday, at 11:30 a.m. Does that work for you?"

"Absolutely," I tell her. I set my toothbrush on a hand towel lying flat on the bathroom sink, then head toward the king-sized bed. "Holy crap, Mackie. You'll be married in less than a week. Wow. It's really happening, girl."

"Shit just got real," she agrees. "Actually, shit got real when my pregnancy test turned up positive."

"No kidding. That's the *realest* shit can ever get," I note. "All right, so Friday at 11:30 you get married, and then I assume we eat lunch after? Are you hiring a photographer, or do you want me to take photos? I don't mind."

"Dave's cousin in Marin is a professional photographer, so he'll snap pics for us. But I appreciate your offer," Mack says. "And yes, lunch after. My only regret is that we can't get blackout drunk in the middle of the day with everyone else."

"At least you'll have me there to commiserate with you." I laugh. "We can drink club soda with lime. Like complete losers."

"It's a plan," Mackie responds enthusiastically. "Dave's in San Jose tonight, at his brother's place. He's got an early meeting in Palo Alto tomorrow. I promised him I'd have the details of our wedding worked out by tomorrow night, Cal."

"What else do you have to do?" I ask.

She sighs. "Pick a hair stylist. And write the vows…"

"I can help with the vows," I volunteer. "I mean, if you come up with the ideas, I'll weave the words together. If you want."

"Yes, please," Mack murmurs. "Thanks, Callie. I know what I want to say, but I keep getting tripped up. Okay, I'll compile some thoughts and you turn them into something coherent. Good plan?"

"Great plan. Just make sure Dave realizes I'm still your number one. Forever. I've known you longer," I declare, sitting up against the headboard.

Mackie laughs. "Dave is fully aware. He knows his soon-to-be-wife already has a wife."

"Excellent."

"Hey, Callie, what's Memphis like? Nashville's the only city in Tennessee I've been to before."

I walk toward the window, marveling at Beale Street's twinkling lights. People spill out of the bars, filling both sides of the street. This hotel is fairly soundproof. But even without auditory assistance, I can imagine the excited hum of street performers and small bands, playing jaunty renditions on the curb.

"Don't tell anyone, but I actually like Memphis a tiny bit more than Nashville."

"What?" Mackie asks. "Really? I've heard

Memphis is rough…"

"It can be. Most flight attendants think it's grimy. But there's something authentic about Memphis. It's the birthplace of blues, and a hotbed of political activity back in the '60s. Don't get me wrong, Nashville has its own charm. But Memphis is a little smaller, a little more historical, and also more *real*."

"You make it sound cool," Mack notes.

"It is. This place is very different from Nashville, where everyone looks perfect. They're all trying to be the next big star. Here, people are motivated by something else. Memphis music reflects a genuine love of the game."

Mackie sighs. "Tell me again why you're *not* going out with your crew tonight…"

"This baby is zapping my energy," I admit. "I go through phases of pure exhaustion. Tonight seemed like a great opportunity to sleep as much as humanly possible."

"Well, maybe you can meet your crew for an hour? Give yourself a curfew, let's say midnight. Back in the hotel and tucked into bed by twelve."

"It does look fun down there," I reflect, gazing out the window once more.

"Where are your coworkers?"

"They were planning to meet at Sully's, because there's barbecue and live music there. I wouldn't say no to some pulled pork right about now. Or maybe some brisket."

"Do it," Mackie instructs. "It sounds delicious. Go enjoy your night and tell me all about it."

"Really? I don't know. I'm already in my jammies."

"It'll take you five minutes to get dressed."

I snort. "Oh my God, Mackenzie. This is why I fell in love with you. You've always been that little voice encouraging me to live it up. My co-conspirator since day one."

"Aww, thanks," she gushes. "Listen, when you're pushing out a baby and in the worst pain of your life, you'll be like, 'Wow, I'm so glad I enjoyed Memphis that one night, instead of going to bed early like a grandma.' "

"Doubt it," I smirk, changing into a sweater and jeans. I tug at the waistband, realizing these pants won't fit me in a month or two. "When you're in labor and screaming in agony, you'll think to yourself, 'Holy hell, I hope my kid makes better decisions than my irresponsible BFF.' "

"Oh, whatever." Mackie chuckles. "Now go destroy the town, you sexy pregnant lady."

"One hour, max," I declare. "Back in my hotel room by midnight. Fast asleep by 12:01."

"Be safe, Callie. Send photos if you can. I'll be up for a while. Might find a movie to watch."

"Okay, Mack. Have a good one."

"You, too," she says before ending the call.

I reach for my purse. Then I glance in the mirror one last time, to make sure I don't look like I just rolled out of bed. Which I basically did.

A text from Andrew illuminates my phone. —*Sleep well, Cal. I can't wait to see you in a few days*—

—*Thanks, Andrew. You, too*—

My hair looks decent tonight, wavy with lots of volume. The dark circles under my eyes have vanished, mercifully, and my cheeks are a healthy shade of red. I apply a thin layer of lipstick, then I'm out the door.

Even though it's January, the air isn't terribly cold. On the van to the hotel, our pilots had mentioned something about Memphis being unseasonably warm right now. As I dart across the street, I'm grateful for this heat wave.

BlueStreet Cafe is loud, with dramatic melodies pouring onto the street. There's a souvenir shop next door with tons of vintage guitars and faded old concert T-shirts. Although the store is closed, the display case illuminates the dark night, casting oddly shaped shadows onto a large stretch of sidewalk. I pause for a second, musing at the miscellaneous items with intricate backstories.

Across the street, a man plays guitar, harmonica, and drums. He's rigged his instruments together so he can use them simultaneously. I glance at the guy, impressed by his musical abilities but even more amazed at his creativity. Fumbling in my purse, I grab my phone to send a photo to Mackenzie. The nighttime backdrop is too dark, though; the picture doesn't turn out. With a shrug, I continue toward Sully's Pub.

Once inside the bar, I spot my crew at a table toward the back. College flags dangle from the ceiling, representing at least a dozen state schools. A Florida Gator grins down at me, outlined in bright orange.

I snap a photo of the Gator flag and send it to Mackie. Her response arrives before I reach my coworkers' table. —*Eww. What a dumb restaurant*—

I smile at the text. Mack's a Georgia alum. I don't bother showing her the Bulldog flag hanging in front of the stage.

"Oh, hey, guys," I say to my crew members,

grabbing the last open seat at the table.

"Hi, Callie. What a nice surprise," Jonah tells me. "Glad you made it."

"Me, too. I was exhausted, but I decided to venture out of the hotel room anyway. I can't stay too long," I reflect, glancing around the table. "Where's Brittany?"

"She went to meet up with some friends who live here," the captain tells me. She's a pretty brunette with reading glasses resting on her head. I vaguely remember flying with her before, but I can't recall when or where. I also have no idea what her name is.

"Gotcha. What did you order, Captain?" I ask, nodding toward her mostly empty dish. The edge of the plate is lined with potato chips.

"Cajun chicken sandwich," she tells me. "It was good."

"Let's get you a menu," the first officer suggests, flagging down a waiter.

"I know what I want; same thing as last time. Brisket salad, please," I tell the waiter.

A band ascends the stage, hauling instruments and bulky equipment. The lead singer has shaggy hair down to his shoulders. He looks like he's in his mid-thirties. The other two guys are younger and more clean-cut.

As the band maneuvers across the stage, pressing foot pedals and testing the microphones, I am reminded of the first time I sang at open mic night in SF. I was a complete mess, riddled with anxiety. I wasn't worried my voice would shake or I'd sing off key; instead, I was afraid people might find my lyrics boring.

"The last band was really good," the first officer says, leaning toward me.

Startled, I gasp. Then I shake my head

apologetically. "Shit, sorry. I was in my own little world."

He stares at me for a moment. His eyes squint as his mouth forms a tiny smile. "Did you pre-game in your room?"

"Definitely not. I'm cutting back on booze. It's my New Year's resolution," I lie. "Just getting food tonight."

"Well, damn," Jonah says from across the table. "I was hoping to go bar-hopping later."

"Early night for me," I say, flicking my wrist. "But you guys have fun. Memphis is a cool city."

The band begins to play, chords slicing through the air with determination. This song has a driving beat. Suddenly, I find myself tapping my foot. Whatever type of music this is, some mix of rock and pop and blues, I like it.

My salad arrives as the band wraps up its first song. I hungrily stab a forkful of brisket. Across the table, Jonah's laughing about something with the captain.

"Where are you based?" the first officer asks me.

"San Francisco," I respond between bites. "But I'm moving to Florida by the end of the month. Switching to the Fort Lauderdale base. How about you?"

"Chicago," he says. "Tanya commutes from Indianapolis. I live just north of the city."

"Tanya. That's it. I'd forgotten her name. I've worked with her before, maybe a couple years ago," I muse. "She's nice, huh?"

He nods. "She's great. I've only been at SkyLine for six months, but she's by far the best captain I've flown with."

"Just six months? You're a newbie. Welcome to the circus, man. Do you like it here?"

The band begins a fast song, lights swirling around the stage in sync with the bass. People stagger onto the dance floor. They hold their beers high, occasionally bumping into each other.

"I love working for SkyLine," the first officer says. "Worked at a commuter airline for six years, based out of Phoenix. It was okay, but the trips were long and difficult. We used to do six legs a day, then end in some random town in the Pacific Northwest, like Walla Walla."

"Walla Walla? SkyLine tends to fly to bigger airports," I say, cracking a smile. "Although I got stuck in Toledo one time. After we diverted."

"Sounds riveting."

"Actually, it was really fun. I had a good crew. We Ubered to a small downtown area. Two streets packed with clubs and restaurants. It was cooler than any of us expected. Ended up playing darts at a funky dive bar."

The first officer smiles. "You know, I'm not surprised. Sometimes the least exciting layovers create the best memories."

"True. But the big cities are really fun, too," I muse. "One of my first trips here, I had double New York layovers. I stayed out in Manhattan until sunrise and barely slept. Totally worth it."

"Yep," the first officer says with a nod.

The band shifts to a slow song. Folks slowly return to their bar stools, ordering another round of drinks. I glance at their cocktails and pint glasses, envious of everyone who gets to drink freely.

"What's your name?" I ask, returning my focus to

the pilot beside me. "Sorry. We all introduced ourselves on the plane, but I already forgot."

"Shawn," he tells me. "I didn't forget your name, Callie."

I swallow the last few bites of salad, cleaning my plate. "It's easier to just call you guys 'Captain' and 'First Officer.' We switch pilots so often, I can't keep track of names."

"That's one thing I miss about the commuter airline," Shawn notes. "We kept the same crew all three days."

In some ways, that could be dangerous, I muse, recalling the times I'd ended up in a pilot's hotel room without necessarily meaning to. It had only happened once or twice, but I'd ducked out of there as soon as possible. Having to engage in small talk the next day would've been painful; instead, we'd flown to opposite corners of the country. Mercifully.

"I like switching it up," I inform Shawn. "Keeps things interesting."

He shrugs. "Guess so."

Across the table, Jonah jumps to his feet. "Who wants to dance?"

The band finishes the setlist and starts packing up their equipment. Hip-hop music blares through speakers. People return to the dance floor, swaying and laughing.

I shake my head. "I don't know…"

Jonah frowns. "C'mon, Callie. You're going to make me go out there all alone?"

"Tanya will go with you," I say, volunteering the captain. She frowns at my suggestion. "Okay then, Shawn will dance."

"The hell I will," Shawn scoffs, taking another swig of beer. "I'm not drunk enough."

"Then let's get you another IPA." I laugh, flagging down our waiter.

****

I pull Jonah toward me, shouting that I want to send a selfie to my best friend. Jonah grins and wraps his arm around my shoulder like we've known each other for decades.

"Get my good angle," he demands, tilting his chin downward.

We stop dancing long enough to smile for three photos. The forward flash blinds us, a burst of light in this shadowy bar. Around us, people continue dancing, unaware they're in the background of our shot.

"I like the second one," Jonah says as he thumbs through the pictures. "Add me on Snapchat. JonahTwink229."

I raise an eyebrow. "Twink?"

"Are you surprised?" He snorts. "You work for an airline, Callie. I doubt I'm the first twink you've met…"

"Fair enough," I admit with a chuckle. I send him the photo and then text it to Mackie, too. "Hey, I should head back to the hotel. It's past my bedtime."

"Be safe, Callie. I'm gonna go make friends," Jonah tells me. Before I can respond, he disappears into the crowd. The music speeds up, bringing more and more people onto the dance floor.

I look around for Tanya and Shawn. Our table is completely deserted; the waiter is collecting empty plates and pint glasses.

Maybe they left already, I think. Checking my

phone, I realize I've missed my midnight curfew by half an hour. I grab my jacket, eager to return to the hotel.

"Callie," someone says behind me.

I turn to find Shawn in front of the bar, polishing off his beer. He sets the empty glass on the counter and nods at me. "How was dancing?"

I shrug. "I was voted Best Dancer."

He smiles. "I bet you were."

"I assumed you and Tanya had left," I tell him.

"Tanya called it a night when you and Jonah got up to dance. She said she was tired. You heading back to the hotel now?" he asks.

"Yes."

"I'll come with you. It's too late for you to walk back alone."

I frown. "Shawn, it's barely midnight. In San Francisco, I've trekked home later than this a billion times. In the freezing cold. While shitfaced."

"Really? Sounds exciting, but also dangerous."

"Excitement and danger fuel me. What can I say? I live on the edge."

"I can tell," Shawn says, chuckling as we march up Beale Street. There are lots of food stands and local musicians; it doesn't feel like midnight, with all these vendors filling the street. We pass a juggler, then a mime, and then a contortionist.

"Where are you guys heading tomorrow?" Shawn asks me.

"Three flights to Santa Fe. You?"

"Two flights home to Chicago. Thankfully," Shawn says as we reach the hotel. "I'm still recovering from the holidays. Pretty sure if I had to work an extra day, I'd fall asleep in the cockpit."

"Like you've never done that before." I chuckle. The lobby is quiet and calm, the polar opposite of what we just saw on Beale Street. To our right, there's a water cooler infused with lemons and strawberries. We each fill a plastic cup before heading toward the elevator.

"This month's been brutal," Shawn assures me as we sip our fruity water. "Holidays are a shitstorm when you're battling your ex over visitation."

"Divorced?" I guess. "Couple of kids?"

Shawn presses the button and we wait for an elevator car. "Yes and yes. My girl's three, my boy is seven."

"Is it hard to be gone so much?"

He nods. "Thankfully, I don't have to commute to Phoenix anymore. I missed weeks at a time, back then. I would come home and my kids had grown four inches taller, it seemed."

"I can imagine," I empathize as the elevator doors swing open, even though I can't imagine it at all. "You live in Chicago, right?"

"Yeah. North side. In a city called Wilmette," Shawn says. "Go Cubs."

I laugh. "I'm a Giants fan. It's a requirement, if you live in SF. I grew up in Boston, though. Back in the day, I went to every Red Sox game. My parents still live there. They're obsessed."

Shawn sighs. "Nobody's perfect…"

I elbow him in the ribs, pressing the button for the seventh floor. Shawn hits a different button, illuminating the oversized 9.

"Come watch a movie with me," he says as the

elevator shoots upward. "I'll find something on my iPad."

I pause. "Shawn, I need to sleep."

He reaches for my arm, turning me until I face him. "Just an hour. I won't keep you up late."

"Can everyone *please* stop hitting on me?" I murmur, shifting my gaze down to my feet. "Seriously. I've been single the last six years and now, when I'm in literally the worst spot of my entire life, everyone decides to chase me."

Shawn lifts an eyebrow. "Look, I don't have any expectations. I'm not an asshole, Callie. I just want to hang out; it's still early."

The elevator stops abruptly. Doors fling open.

"This is my floor," I tell Shawn. I sigh, then wrap my arms around his neck. My head rests comfortably on his shoulder. The doors close while we are standing like this. "Well, fuck…"

"Now you have to come up," he says with a smile. The elevator begins its trek to the ninth floor.

I pry myself from Shawn's shoulder. "The thing is, I'm kinda dating someone. And it would be nice to wake up in the morning *not* feeling like the worst human on earth."

Shawn nods. "Okay. I'm not trying to interfere, Callie."

We reach his floor, and he tentatively steps into the hall.

"Goodnight, First Officer," I say with a weak smile.

He tilts his head to the side, standing two feet in front of the elevator doors. "Goodnight, Flight Attendant."

The doors close and I return to the seventh floor. Inside my hotel room, I lean against the counter for a minute before washing my face. I stare at myself, at the image of someone approaching thirty and still struggling to make choices that aren't self-destructive.

Then I change clothes and slide into bed.

Chapter Seventeen

January 6, 2020

"Callie," Jonah says breathlessly as he steps into the galley. "Check your board. We've been rerouted."

"Huh?" I ask, looking up from my laptop. I'm halfway through another letter to the creature in my belly. "Where are we going?"

Jonah shows me his phone, which has our trip pulled up in oversized print. Instead of spending the night in Santa Fe, we now have an eighteen-hour layover in Sacramento. And we are scheduled to arrive home mid-afternoon tomorrow, as opposed to the original return time of 10 p.m.

"Looks like we actually benefited from this reassignment," I note happily. "We are done for the day once we get to SMF, huh?"

Jonah nods. "Pretty sweet. Tomorrow we work one flight to Portland, then deadhead home."

I smile. "You must be good luck, Jonah. I can't remember the last time I got a half-decent reroute."

"You're welcome," he says. "Hey, I'm going to do a quick water service because main cabin's starting to get needy."

I glance at my watch. "One hour left. Here, let me help you."

We set up the cart with water and coffee, then

make our way down the aisle.

****

"You ended up someplace else, not Santa Fe?" Andrew asks me as I walk past the Capitol Building.

"Yep. Sacramento. Last-minute reroute. Hang on a second." I snap a photo of the state capitol and text it to him.

"Wow. Really cool building. I'm guessing your crew hotel is downtown…"

"It is," I respond. "That's the state capitol building. I got in early enough to walk around a little before sunset. There's a lot to do here. It's no SF, but Midtown and East Sac are really fun. There's even a bar with mermaids swimming in a giant fish tank."

I continue walking up 12th Street, evaluating the restaurant options. My stomach has been rumbling for the last half hour.

"Nice. Fort Lauderdale has one of those, too," Andrew says. "Have fun, Callie. Stay warm."

"I will. Heading back to the hotel soon," I inform him. "Just needed a little fresh air."

"Be safe," he replies. "How many days?"

I smile, because I know exactly what he's referring to, even though his question is somewhat vague. "I'll be in West Palm in three days."

"Three days. Can't wait."

"Me, neither," I say, pausing in front of a hole-in-the-wall Mediterranean restaurant. "Talk soon, Andrew."

I tuck my phone in my pocket and glance inside the restaurant, which has a bistro feel. Daily selections are listed on a giant chalkboard. I scan the list of available meals, my eyes sweeping from side to side while the delicious scent of gyros floods my nostrils.

I walk up to the counter and order chicken shawarma to go. Then I grab a seat on a bar stool. I scroll through my texts, searching for the long note Mackie sent me earlier today.

"Here we go," I murmur aloud, eyes fixed on my phone screen. Theirs is a sweet, intricate love story, the kind that almost never happens in San Francisco. Or anywhere on earth, for that matter.

—*Themes for vows: met Dave during my third year in SF, at a party I crashed on my way home from Nob Hill. He was in a relationship back then. I knew right away he was different from anyone I had met before, but we were just friends because he wasn't single. Loved his mathematical brain, completely different from my creative and quirky side. He played ultimate frisbee on a local league; a few months later, I went to the game because my coworker was on the opposing team. David was there, was now single. It was a nice surprise.*

He asked me to get a beer with him after the game, just us, and we went to this little bar in Outer Richmond. I can't remember exactly how it happened but we started talking and we just kept talking. And talking. And talking...ended up watching the sunrise over Ocean Beach. We both had to work the next morning, but neither of us cared. Inseparable from then on, calling and texting all the time. Moved in together five months later. Best roommate of my life: goofy, funny, sweet, and patient. It was a true partnership. My friend, sidekick, and teammate.

I never wanted to get married, but my perspective changed when I met Dave. Everything made sense with him.

A year after moving in together, I proposed during a Giants game, drunk off my ass. He said yes but also said he'd give me a proper proposal someday. A month later, up in Napa, he got down on one knee. I screamed "YES!" before he even popped the question. Found out I was pregnant a few months later, can't wait to welcome a baby with my life partner by my side—

I tap my fingers on the bar, contemplating how to tell Mackie's story with the humor, energy, and optimism she exudes. A waiter hands me a big bag of food, all wrapped up for the two-block trek back to my hotel.

Once I'm in my hotel room, eating my shawarma cross-legged on my bed, the words come to me. I grab my laptop, typing furiously.

David, we met at an impractical time. Lots of people claim the odds were stacked against them but, in our case, the odds didn't even exist. You were off limits. I was determined never to fall in love.

Within a few months, everything changed. Your frisbee skills needed some help, but your conversation skills were expert-level. I remember walking through the streets of our city with you. Familiar places suddenly felt brand-new. I realized the lifestyle I'd never previously considered was the one I was meant for. Life made sense with you; it still does, and it will forever.

I proposed to you because I was certain. You proposed to me because you shared my confidence. Thank you for building a home, a future, and a family with me. Thank you for embracing the unexpected and finding beauty in the unknown.

I promise to celebrate your strengths as well as your weaknesses. I vow to continue learning and growing with my best friend, during the summits as well as the valleys. You are all the best parts of me and everything I'm working toward. I am grateful for your unwavering support. Also, thanks for understanding I'm already partly married to Callie.

I smile at the last line, knowing full well Mackie will strike it from the record but also find it comical. Finishing up my dinner, I e-mail the vows to Mackenzie with the comment, "Extremely rough draft, feel free to change anything/everything."

Chapter Eighteen

January 7, 2020

In Portland, the customer service agent announces our airplane will be terminating for the night.

"Your SFO flight is three gates down," she says. "I can radio Phil so he prints your boarding passes in advance."

We wheel our suitcases to Gate 14, approaching the desk in unison. The flight's already boarding; people are lined up single file in a neat little row. It doesn't appear the plane will be full.

"Hi, there," I tell the SkyLine customer service agent, a skinny guy who looks like he's fresh out of high school. "Are you Phil? We're the crew from Flight 842, deadheading to SFO."

He hands me three boarding passes resting beside his keyboard. They're still warm from the printer. "Here you go. Fifty-four open seats, so I gave you each your own row toward the back."

"Thank you," I say, dispersing the tickets to Jonah and Brittany.

We board the empty airplane and find our seats. Freezing air blows down from the vent above my head. I zip my sweater all the way up, curling into a ball by the window to conserve some heat.

The last few passengers are trickling onto the

aircraft when I spot a familiar face.

"Hello, Callie," Zack Friedman says with a mischievous smile. "Is this seat taken? Of course not. What a coincidence; you must be deadheading home."

He tosses his backpack on the floor and settles into the middle seat, right beside me.

"Hi, Zack. I forgot you commute from here," I reflect, offering him a hug. "Heading to work, I assume?"

"Yep, I have a flight tonight checking in at eight p.m. One leg to Seattle, twenty-four hours there, and then Vegas tomorrow."

"Nice. How have you been?"

"Same old, same old," he notes. We buckle up as the flight attendants march into the aisle and begin their safety demo. "I've been talking to a few buddies in LA. We're looking for a three-bedroom apartment. Ideally, something in Echo Park or Silver Lake...but let's be honest, we'll take anything affordable."

I nod. "I hear you. SF's the same way; everything is overpriced, so you end up living wherever you'll be slightly *less* broke."

The plane takes off, jutting through big, black clouds. The higher we ascend, the darker the cabin becomes. Zack turns on a reading light so we can see each other.

"Yeah. I've been saving up, but I'll still be poor for the first few months after the move." Zack sighs. "Hopefully we'll find something by March. I'm done with Portland."

"Good luck, Zack. I'll miss seeing you around campus," I tell him, referring to the crew room at SFO.

He lifts an eyebrow. "You'll still see me, Callie.

Practically every LA trip has an Oakland or SF layover built into it. I'll text you whenever I'm in town."

I gasp. "Oh, shit. I forgot to tell you I'm moving to Florida at the end of January."

Zack tilts his head to the side, and I can see the wheels in his brain turning. "Which part of Florida, Callie? West Palm Beach, by any chance?"

Blood rushes to my cheeks. "Uhhh, maybe."

Zack's eyes widen. "Oh my God. Are you moving in with Andrew? What the hell? A few weeks ago, you were asking me for his number, and now you're moving to Florida?"

I bite my lip. "Here's the deal: I got in touch with him the day I saw you, right before Christmas. We met up in Orlando during my trip, and we have been hanging out ever since then. We're basically dating. But it's not official yet. Or maybe it is? Shoot. I don't know, to be honest."

Zack smiles. "Just admit it already. You're madly in love with the guy."

"Not exactly. You have a vivid imagination." I laugh. "Andrew is great, and I really enjoy spending time with him. But we're not moving in together."

"No? Is the sex terrible?"

"You lunatic. We haven't done it since November," I say, rolling my eyes.

"I thought you just watched Netflix the night you met…"

I smile. "Touché. If you must know, the sex was amazing. It was mind-blowing and passionate and different than other guys I've been with. When I'm beside Andrew, I crave it. I think about it all the time. However, I've been trying to keep my hands off him until we figure out our relationship. Things are still…complicated."

"Wow. A magnetic pull and an undeniable attraction," Zack says, grabbing my hands. "So what's the problem? Why aren't you two shacking up?"

"He offered, but it's too soon. Look, I really do like Andrew. He is fantastic."

"And sexy," Zack adds.

I nod in agreement. "And sexy, yes. But Andrew isn't the reason I'm moving to Florida. At least, not the main reason. This is something I'm doing for *me*; I need a change of pace."

Zack stares at me skeptically.

"Hey, do you know a flight attendant named Jordan?" I ask. "He's around your seniority. Was Orlando-based for the longest time, but now he's switching to FLL. He sent me the info of his friend who lives in Delray; I'm going to check out her apartment next week. She has a spare room, so I'll probably live there."

"Jordan Crossley? I definitely know him. He was a month behind me in initial flight attendant training," Zack informs me. "Solid guy. He's really chill and fun. Did you fly with him recently?"

"Yeah, we had a New Year's trip together," I say, intentionally omitting the rest of the details. "Jordan seems great."

"He is," Zack agrees. "Callie, I'm trying to piece all this together. I'm confused why you'd leave SF, especially if you're *not* moving in with Andrew. I was under the impression you love the Bay Area."

"I do. But I need a fresh start."

"You're pregnant," he gasps.

I blink. "What?"

"Holy shit, Cal. I'm just kidding. That would be a fucking disaster. You love your freedom. I cannot picture you stuck at home with a screaming baby."

"Me, neither," I say. "I'm in no hurry to have kids. You're right, I'm gonna miss SF like crazy. But Florida is calling my name. Not because of Andrew, not even because of money."

"Then what's your motivation, Cal? What's pushing you to leave San Francisco?"

I sigh. "I'm disheartened about my writing. I thought I'd be published by this age. I'm getting older and I feel so scattered. I can't fully immerse myself in my passion when I'm lost in the crazy chaos of San Francisco. There's too much background noise, too much pressure. My writing always gets placed on the backburner. In Florida, I'd be able to focus on my dream. As for Andrew...I'd rather go slowly. For the first time, I actually like a guy enough to *not* want to screw things up."

"How sweet. You really care about this handsome hunk. And you want the world to see your art," Zack murmurs. "Nothing wrong with either of those things."

The flight attendant reaches our row, asking if we want anything to drink. We shake our heads politely, and she pushes the cart down the aisle.

"Well, Cal, I sincerely hope you get published," Zack continues. "Hey, if you ever need an extra pair of eyes, I'll gladly help. I'm always looking for a good book. Do you have a blog or something?"

"I do, but it's not up and running yet," I lie. "I've written a couple books, but I'm better at short stories. I can tweak the diction and syntax until they're perfect...or damn near perfect, anyway."

Zack smiles. "Sounds complicated."

I wave my hand. "It's not. Writing is my favorite form of self-expression. I think Florida will provide me with endless inspiration. While San Francisco is awesome, it's time for something new."

"I feel the same way," Zack notes. "Portland has become stale."

"Then it's smart to switch up the scenery. You'll gain a whole new perspective when you move to Los Angeles," I assure him.

"Thanks, Callie. Florida will revive you," he predicts. "Plus, this works out really well for *me* because now I have a great excuse to visit you in PBI. And accidentally wind up in Daryl's bed."

"True," I say with a laugh. "You're welcome, buddy."

Chapter Nineteen

January 8, 2020

Mackie is sitting on an oversized blanket, rainbow-themed and far too big for the two of us. I vaguely remember buying that blanket with her years ago, when we watched the Pride Parade from Civic Center, cheering as loudly as possible. We'd painted our faces and given each other fake tattoos. Mackie had worn a neon miniskirt. She'd convinced me to put on a pink tutu, typically the last thing I'd be caught dead wearing.

I smile at the memory. Back then, we were both fairly new to SF. We were thrilled to be part of something bigger than ourselves. That was my first Pride Parade, and I haven't missed one since.

Mackie waves at me, hands flailing above her head. Dolores Park is calm today. Vendors meander around the park selling edibles. Several food trucks are parked on 20th Street, with lines of people waiting to order lunch. But here, in the center of the park, there are unoccupied patches of green grass.

"You picked the perfect day for a picnic," I tell her, grabbing a seat on the blanket. Birds soar overhead, occasionally chirping at each other. A few small clouds linger in the distance, puffs of white amid a bright blue sky. Mackie's sweatshirt, useless on a warm day like today, rests in a pile beside her shoes.

"This weather is beautiful, right? Hopefully my wedding day is like this," she reflects. "How was your trip?"

"Really good," I tell her. "Almost slept with a pilot, but I decided against it."

Mackenzie's eyes widen. "Damn. What happened?"

"The night I texted you from Memphis, I ended up walking back to my hotel with the first officer. A guy named Shawn. We're riding the elevator up to our rooms and he asks me to 'watch a movie' with him," I say, using air quotes. "Which is code for naked Olympics."

"No kidding," Mackie snorts. "You turned him down?"

"Yes. I don't know what is going on between me and Andrew. But I'm tired of waking up in the morning feeling like the scum of the earth. Until we figure out this incredibly strange *thing* we're doing together, I don't need any distractions. And I'd like to have a clear conscience."

"You know how I feel," Mackie says warmly. "I don't think there's anything wrong with exploring your options. Since you're not officially a couple. But if you'd prefer to stay focused on Andrew, then good for you for sticking to your convictions. I wish you the best, whether you end up with Andrew or the sexy flight attendant from New Year's or nobody, for that matter. You're fucking fierce, Callie. You're about to move to Florida and write like crazy and grab life by the balls."

I laugh. "Shit, I still can't believe I made out with Jordan. I'm about to meet his childhood friend in

Delray Beach, did I tell you? I'm flying to West Palm tomorrow to look at apartments and this girl has a spare room in a nice part of town."

"I bet it works out perfectly..." Mackie trails off, her gaze shifting toward the street.

"Everything okay?" I ask, trying to see what she could be looking at. There's no unusual activity on Dolores Street. Cars and bikes speed by, their metal parts reflecting the bright sunshine.

Mackie doesn't answer me. Instead, she lifts a container of veggie tabouli from her bag and places it between us. Then she reaches for two plates and silverware. "Dive in, Callie. I also have hummus and pitas, and some baklava."

"Yum," I say, piling tabouli onto my plate.

"Listen, I'm proud of you," she tells me as I take my first bite of food. "You are making smart decisions and following your gut."

"Well, it's easier to think clearly when I'm not wasted," I admit with a chuckle. "This fetus is a buzzkill but also a good influence."

"You have such a unique, weird little way of phrasing things. I love you, Callie Schneider."

"Back at ya, Mackenzie."

She pauses. "Okay, I need to tell you something. Here's the deal: I lured you here today, under the guise of a picnic lunch, because my hormones are out of control and I am really starting to miss you. Even though you haven't left yet."

I swallow. "Mack, I'm gonna miss you like hell. Try to remember it's just for a few months; it's not forever."

She smiles weakly, tears welling up in her eyes.

"You're the best thing that's happened to me. I'm marrying David in less than a week, but you were my first real friend in this city. You were there when I met him, and then re-met him, and then realized I was falling in love. You wrote my vows, for Chrissake. You're literally the closest friend I've ever had. You're my other half."

Under brilliant rays of sunshine, on the most cheerful day San Francisco has seen in ages, everything suddenly feels broken.

I choke back tears. Pushing my plate to the side, I lean toward Mackenzie and place a hand on her knee. She looks up at me, eyes glistening.

"What am I supposed to do without you?" she whispers, dabbing her eyes with a napkin. "God, how selfish of me. You're off to start a new chapter of your life in Florida, to find inspiration and get published. You're about to give Andrew the best gift anyone can ever give another person. You are such a beautiful soul. I'm fucking greedy, Callie, because I want you here during my pregnancy. I want us to go through this together. Step by step. I pictured us doing this in unison, equally bloated and nauseous and scared and excited."

I stare at my hands, certain if I look up at Mackenzie, I'll burst into ugly sobs.

"Getting pregnant was the biggest mistake of my life," I say quietly. "I'm not ready to raise a kid. Sometimes I'm so lost, Mack...like I'm still figuring out how to be the person I always imagined I was. That pregnancy test in December scared the shit outta me. I'll tell you what, as harrowing as this experience has been, I couldn't have survived it without you. You are strong when I'm a crybaby. You're caring and thoughtful. Who writes cards to senior citizens she's never met? My best friend, that's who."

Mackie sniffs. "Because I'm a dork."

"Because you are incredible," I correct her. "I moved to the Bay Area knowing zero people. If you were the only friend I made this entire time, that would be perfectly fine by me. You're my sister. You always will be. We're still in this together, every single day. I'll just live a little farther away."

She nods, tears streaming down her face. "Will you come visit?"

"Duh," I tell her. "Do you think I love my job because of the crazy-ass passengers? Not a chance. It's the flight benefits, Mack. I fly free. I'll come visit SF often…just maybe not around any of our other girlfriends. I don't want to answer too many personal questions."

"I'll pick you up at SFO every time," she promises. "We can drive to Alameda. Somewhere nobody recognizes us. Drink tea together and swap stories about how terrible our pregnancies are progressing."

"Deal," I tell her. "We will hold each other's hair back while we puke."

Mackie sighs, collapsing against me in a defeated hug. "Remember the good ol' days? When we threw up because we were shitfaced, not because of morning sickness?"

"Best moments of my life," I assure her. "Two train wrecks taking excellent care of each other."

"I love you," she murmurs into my shoulder.

"You bet your ass I do, too," I say, my arm wrapped tightly around my best friend.

Part Five: The Stopover

Chapter Twenty

January 9, 2020

I text Andrew the moment we touch down in West Palm. —*Just landed. No rush. I'm in the second-to-last row so it'll take forever to deplane—*

—*Already here, in remote parking. I'll head to Arrivals soon. Can't wait to see you—*

West Palm Beach Airport is calm today, much slower than the last time I was here. The holiday rush has ended, replaced by half-empty airport restaurants and quiet terminals.

I hurry toward the exit. Andrew's Mazda cruises to a stop just as I wheel my suitcase through the double doors. He hops out of the driver's side and scoops me up in a big hug.

"Welcome back, Callie," he says.

"Thanks," I respond. Instinctively, I lean forward and kiss him.

"I'm glad you're here," he murmurs after our kiss. Then he hoists my bags into the trunk and opens the passenger side door for me. "How was your flight?"

"Not bad," I say, buckling my seatbelt. "Standby flights stress me out, but this one was wide open. I got a whole row to myself."

"Did you take a nap?"

I shake my head. "Nope, I did some writing."

"What are you working on?" Andrew asks as we merge onto Belvedere Road and then 95.

"Damn. I thought I told you already…I created a blog."

"A travel blog?" he guesses.

I inhale sharply. "Nope. I've been writing letters to the baby. Not letters I actually want the kid to read someday. More like, um, notes that help me sort through my emotions, curiosities, and fears."

I hold my breath while waiting for a response. Until now, it hadn't occurred to me how strange it would feel to tell Andrew about dozens of letters which indirectly, and sometimes directly, involve him.

Keeping his eyes on the road, he reaches across the console and grabs my hand. "I'd love to read your blog, Cal. If you're okay with that."

"Sure. Feel free to tell me if my letters are cheesy or boring or too personal. Honest feedback helps a lot, even if it's negative."

"You got it. Although I'm sure I will love them."

We park in front of Andrew's complex and he carries my bags to his apartment. The unit looks different than I remember. To be fair, I was three sheets to the wind last time I set foot in this place. It's incredibly clean and cozy. It has an open floor plan, no doors except for the ones leading to the bedroom and bathroom. There's a wraparound couch in the living room, flanked by cherry wood end tables. They match the coffee table and media console.

I grab a seat on the couch, sinking into the cushions. With a contented sigh, I lean back until my head is resting comfortably against a tall pillow. Andrew places my bags in the bedroom, then sits down beside me.

"Are you hungry?" he asks.

I tilt my head. "Not starving or anything, but I can always eat."

He looks at his watch. "Traffic might be bad right now. What if we grab dinner in an hour?"

I smile. "Sounds great to me."

"Maybe I can check out your blog in the meantime," he suggests.

I sit up and type the web address into my phone. "Sure. Here you go. Sorry in advance if it sucks."

"Oh, stop. I know you well enough to know it's not going to suck," he insists.

"Don't say that 'til you see it," I warn with a half-smile.

While Andrew reads my blog, I lean on his shoulder. A big window next to the television reveals the last traces of daylight. The sun flickers on the horizon, briefly, as though waving goodbye.

Palm trees shimmer beneath the emerging moon. Their leaves cast shadows on the wall, dancing around me as Andrew immerses himself in letters to our unborn child.

I close my eyes, sinking deeper into the space between his cheek and his collarbone. He smells good, a cologne I've grown to love over the past few weeks. Without pulling his gaze from my phone, Andrew slides an arm around me. His touch is tender and reassuring.

"Callie."

"Mmm?"

"You have a gift, Cal. This is incredible."

I open my eyes. "You don't have to say such nice

things, Andrew."

"I do," he insists. "Because it's true. You're carrying my baby, so I have an emotional attachment that other people might not have. But your writing doesn't rely on a personal connection. Your letters are honest and compelling. No backstory required. Actually, the anonymity adds to your blog. Makes it more relatable, in a way."

"Really?" I ask, placing my hands on his chest so I can face him directly.

He tucks a strand of hair behind my ear. "I'm a thirty-year-old man who knows nothing about being pregnant, living in San Francisco, or flying around the country every week. Yet I had a tough time putting the phone down. I just wanted to read another post, then another, then another. You grabbed my attention and kept it the whole time. This is good stuff."

I smile. "Thank you, Andrew."

"Somebody's going to discover your talent," he tells me, his brown eyes fixed on mine. "You are something special, Callie Schneider."

"Nah, I'm just a free-spirited stewardess who got knocked up," I say. "By a really good guy, it turns out…"

"Yeah? I guess he's *okay*." Andrew laughs.

He leans in to kiss me, small kisses at first and then bigger, more dramatic ones. After a moment, Andrew pauses. He pulls away, carefully inspecting my face. I detect genuine wonder in his gaze, as though he's discovered a priceless work of art. The admiration in those brown irises is foreign yet compelling.

Why do you like me? I muse, a half-smile spreading across my lips.

We've slept in the same bed numerous times, cuddling and talking and falling asleep to the sound of each other's heartbeat. I fought my cravings. I played it safe, because I was terrified Andrew would change his mind. Or, worse, he'd decide he really, truly cared about me. After all, how could I ask him to love someone so broken? Would he be signing his own death certificate? I've always been a ticking time bomb, two seconds away from some irrational decision.

Yet Andrew views my eccentricity as a gift. To him, it's a treasure.

And, now, we are tangled up together on a couch in his living room, our silhouettes drenched in moonlight. I'm straddling Andrew, his face resting squarely in my hands. In my entire lifetime, I've never felt so desired.

The handsome stranger on Clematis Street was supposed to be a one-night stand, yet he's become my lifeline.

And I am unable to deny my attraction longer.

I pull Andrew's shirt over his head, tossing it behind the couch. One glimpse of his chiseled chest sends shivers down my spine. He slides a hand under my sweater, his palm cool against my stomach.

"Are you sure this is what you want?" he asks, eyes brimming with concern and hope and curiosity.

"Absolutely. I've wanted it for a long time," I say, clearing my throat. "I've wanted *you* for a long time, Andrew."

I wrestle out of my sweater and jeans as quickly as possible. In my bra and panties, I lead him toward the bedroom. Once inside, he hoists me onto the bed effortlessly. With Andrew standing directly before me, our knees meet at a ninety-degree angle. I seize the opportunity to wrap my legs around his waist. Then I turn my face upward. As I kiss him, he unfastens my bra.

His fingers glide across my chest, sending tiny tremors of excitement through my core. He places my breasts in his mouth, one at a time, and licks them gingerly. Each flick of his tongue is slow and deliberate.

Then he moves down my stomach. He kisses my side, my waist, my hipbones. It's as though he is determined to graze every inch of skin.

I writhe in pleasure, aware that an orgasm lingers just on the horizon. I have been touched before, but never with this much attention to detail. Ecstasy spreads through my body, radiating from the exact spot Andrew's tongue is massaging.

He pauses, interrupting my steady climb toward euphoria. I glance down with curiosity as Andrew removes my panties. He sighs appreciatively. As his face disappears between my thighs, I lean forward, reaching for the top of his head with one hand. His thick brown hair slides through my fingers like blades of grass swaying in the breeze. Andrew's face sweeps from left to right, slowly. Then he licks up and down. Electricity flows from his tongue to my body's most intimate parts. I gasp for air as I approach climax.

The long-awaited orgasm spreads from my core to my arms, legs, fingertips. A moan, almost animalistic in nature, escapes my lips. It echoes off the walls, testifying to my state of bliss.

Amazed at the sensation lingering in my extremities, I pull Andrew toward me. His chest glistens with sweat, a product of his hard work and determination. He places an arm behind my back, cradling my neck with his hand. I close my eyes as he glides inside of me in one swift motion.

As the thrusting continues, steady and smooth, I grasp the pillow behind my head. "Why did we wait so long?" I murmur, my voice barely audible.

"Worth it," he tells me, his breath warm and comforting in my ear.

Chapter Twenty-One

January 10, 2020

"How's your morning been?" Andrew asks.

I shift my phone to my left ear. "Really good. I forgot how much I missed the Florida sunshine; SF is foggy year-round. I do need to buy some sunglasses, though…"

"There's an extra pair on the counter, black-rimmed with oval lenses," he tells me. "They're yours."

"Thanks, Andrew," I say. "How's work?"

"As exciting as you'd expect." He laughs. "I'm getting a burger for lunch, which is the highlight of my day. Besides coming home to you tonight, obviously."

"Aw. Well, I hope your food is delicious," I tell him.

"Thanks. Have you eaten yet?"

"Nope," I say. "I'm heading out in a second. Meeting Karina for lunch, then checking out her apartment after. She's off work today."

"Nice. I have a good feeling about the apartment, Callie," Andrew says. "Let me know how everything goes."

"I will," I assure him. "Oh, and I'll pick you up from work tonight. It's the least I can do since I'm stealing your car for the day."

"Don't worry about it. My office building is really

close; I can walk home."

"It's not up for debate," I insist. "I will come get you, Andrew."

"So stubborn. There is no convincing you otherwise." He laughs.

"Honestly, my motives are selfish. I need you to conserve your energy for later tonight, mister."

"Oh, really?" he asks. "In that case, yes, please."

"You're welcome," I say with a smile. "And, also, thank you."

"I can't wait to see you. Last night was fucking spectacular," he reminds me, as though I could have forgotten the magic of our lovemaking. "Shoot, I gotta go. My burger's ready."

"All right, Andrew. See you in a few hours," I say, closing out the call.

I check my reflection in the hallway mirror, smoothing down my hair with my hand. I reach for sunglasses and keys, sitting in a bowl on the kitchen counter. Andrew's keychain is a Florida State Seminole. Shaking my head, I make a mental note to surprise Andrew with a UF Gator keychain. Which he will most definitely hate.

Chuckling to myself, I head out the door.

Traffic on 95 is light; I make it to Delray Beach in about fifteen minutes. My GPS steers me to a cute, beachy building with a thatched roof.

When I tell the hostess I'm looking for a friend, she leads me to a table beside the kitchen. Karina waves at me, a smile illuminating her face. High cheekbones and flawless skin accentuate mocha eyes, which happen to be framed by long, perfect eyelashes.

She could easily be a model, I think, taking a seat

at the table.

"Hey, Callie. Nice to meet you. Jordan has told me so much about you; I already feel like we are friends," she says.

"Really?" I ask, hoping the surprise in my voice isn't too noticeable. "Wow. Hopefully he said good things. It's great to meet you, Karina. Thanks for making time for me on your day off work."

She nods. "Absolutely. I hope you like the apartment."

"I have a feeling I will," I predict, certain I will love the place even though I haven't seen it yet.

"Do you like flying for SkyLine? Jordan's told me some stories about the crazy shit he's seen on the plane," she says. "Sounds like an interesting gig."

"It's pretty exciting," I agree. "After flying for a year or two, I thought I'd seen it all. Seriously, I was convinced I'd witnessed every insane thing on the planet. Yet passengers are always coming up with ways to outdo each other. Last month, a lady boarded the plane with a parakeet tucked into her purse. We only found out because the bird kept singing throughout the flight. I have no idea how she smuggled it through security."

Karina shakes her head. "Wow. My job is far more boring than yours. I look at teeth all day."

"But you're helping people," I point out. "You're making a difference. I'm just pouring mixed drinks and flying around the country."

"Which sounds fantastic," Karina muses dreamily. "Hey, on an unrelated note, have you been here before? It's a South Florida chain. Not exactly fine dining, but it's really fun. They designed it to feel like a tiki bar.

You gotta try the popcorn shrimp; it's delicious. I also like their mixed seafood platter."

"It all sounds good," I say.

Our waitress arrives, informing us of the daily specials. Karina and I both order the shrimp. Then we lean back in our chairs and continue chatting like old friends.

****

"This is the place," Karina says, welcoming me into a spotless living room. A glass coffee table sparkles in the ample sunlight. Behind it, there's a gray couch and a patterned rug. An island separates the kitchen from the main room, with bar stools propped against it.

Just beyond the kitchen, a long hallway leads to both bedrooms. The tiled floors look like they've been cleaned recently.

"It's so darn cute," I murmur, admiring the apartment. Karina has decorated it tastefully, with a few black-and-white photos adorning the walls. It's not empty, nor is it cluttered. I love the minimalist aura of this space.

Karina leads me down the hall. She stops in front of the first bedroom, opening the door so I can look inside.

"This is my bedroom," she explains. "Sorry for the mess."

"It's definitely not messy," I assure her. The bed's made, the nightstand and dresser are immaculate. A loveseat sits in one corner, to the left of a bay window.

"They're both master bedrooms," Karina tells me, closing the door.

I follow her to the second bedroom. It's twice the

size of my room in SF. There's a queen bed in the center of the room, two dressers, and a desk.

"This is amazing," I reflect, walking toward the desk. "Oh my God, I could do so much writing here. My room in San Francisco barely fits my twin bed and nightstand, let alone a desk."

"Jordan told me you're a writer," Karina says with a smile. "What are you working on?"

"I have a couple of unpublished books," I tell her. "Right now, I'm starting a blog."

"Wow. What a cool talent to have. I'd love to write a book, but I don't have the attention span."

"You'd be surprised. It seems daunting at first, because of the length. But once you get into the rhythm of writing each day, it becomes addictive," I tell her. "It's my favorite hobby, for sure."

"Well, mine is beach volleyball," Karina informs me. "There's a volleyball net in the courtyard, next to the pool. Sometimes the neighbors will start a game."

"Sounds amazing."

"My old roommate, Ben, used to play every chance he got. He was really good."

"Where does he live now?" I ask, glancing inside the bathroom. It has a double sink and a frosted-glass shower.

"He got engaged and moved in with his girlfriend," she tells me. "Fiancée, I guess? They're getting married in May. They bought a place in Miami. I thought about keeping the extra room open, instead of adding someone else to the lease, but Jordan told me you're cool. And I wouldn't mind the help with rent each month."

"Thanks," I say. "Karina, I seriously love this

apartment. I just have a couple questions. How long is the lease? I'm coming to Florida to work on my writing, and for a change of pace...but I might move back to SF in about a year."

"I renewed my lease in December, so it'll be up in 11 months. I talked to the leasing office and they told me it would be easy to add your name."

"The timing is perfect," I reflect. "Okay, secondly, is the furniture staying? I'm leaving my stuff in San Francisco and subletting my room."

"Yes. Some of it is my old furniture, and some was Ben's. He and his fiancée got all new stuff, so he left this."

"Sounds good. All right, last and final question: do you like cats? I've been wanting one for about a decade," I hold my breath while waiting for her response.

"I adore cats," she says. "I actually got a kitty when I first moved to Delray, right after college. She was such a sweet girl. I rescued her from the pound when she was already a senior citizen, almost eleven years old. She lived to be seventeen. I had to put her down last year, because she got so sick. But I'd love to have another cat in the apartment."

"Well, then, it's settled," I say, unable to contain my excitement. "I can't wait to move in. This is half the price I'm paying for my apartment in SF and twice the size. I think we will be great roommates, Karina. The complex looks like it has so much to offer."

"It really does," she says. "We're close to everything. Plus, there's a pool, clubhouse, gym, and volleyball court."

"I'm sold," I murmur.

She smiles at me. "Welcome to Florida, Callie."

****

"You're getting dessert," Andrew tells me. He signals our waiter, then asks for a dessert menu. "You have to. Please. Since we can't do a champagne toast."

I snort. "Well, technically we *can* toast with some bubbly. But I'd be cut off after one glass."

Andrew sighs. "I'm sorry you can't drink, Callie."

"Don't worry about it," I say, glancing at the dessert menu our waiter left on the table. There's a red velvet cheesecake, which sounds divine. "Liquor doesn't even appeal to me lately."

"After the baby's born, we should go out drinking," Andrew suggests. "My parents can watch the kid for a night, and I'll take you downtown. Introduce you to the best artisanal cocktails you've ever tasted."

"Hmm. Sounds pretentious," I note, smiling against my will.

"It's not," Andrew says, his eyes widening. "I mean, whatever, maybe it's a little pretentious. But there's this bar in CityPlace you would love. Their mixed drinks will blow your mind."

I tilt my head to the side. "You're going to hang out with me after I pop out this kid?"

"Obviously," Andrew responds without hesitation. He flips the dessert menu around so he can look at the selections. "Which one do you want?"

"Cheesecake," I inform him. "I won't eat the entire slice, though. Will you have some?"

"Yes."

He reaches under the table and clasps my hand. I've grown used to the feeling of his fingers woven through mine; it's a warm, comforting sensation.

"Thanks for letting me stay with you this week," I say. "And steal your car. And take up all your time."

"Of course. Thanks for giving me something to look forward to every day after work," he tells me with a smile. "You know, Cal, I'm really happy you found a place you love. Delray is great. I can't wait to help you move into your new apartment."

"Why are you so nice to me?"

He shrugs nonchalantly, attempting to stifle a smile. "We've already discussed this. Because I like you."

Chapter Twenty-Two

January 11, 2020

The waiting room is fairly empty; there's only one other couple here, sitting on the opposite side. I flip through a pregnancy magazine, briefly skimming the articles without absorbing any of the information in them. Andrew's hand has been on my knee since we arrived. He's reading work emails on his phone. Behind us, an air conditioner hums steadily.

A nurse calls my name, breaking the silence.

I place the magazine back on the end table. Then I rise from my chair and grab my purse.

"Can I head back there with you?" Andrew asks, looking up at me.

"Well, I think the first part is a physical exam, urine sample, bloodwork...all the boring stuff," I tell him. "Why don't you stay out here for now, and then I'll call you back for the ultrasound?"

He nods. "Sure. Come get me if you need anything, Cal."

"I will," I promise.

I follow the nurse through a small white door. We walk down a long corridor, making small talk. I respond politely without actually knowing what the hell I'm saying; my heartbeat feels loud and frantic, pounding in my ears. Being here, in a medical facility with white walls and high-tech equipment designed to monitor growing babies…well, suddenly it's starting to feel a lot more *real*.

The nurse measures my height, weight, blood pressure. She requests a urine sample, so I chug a bottle of water, then fill the small plastic cup to the brim. The nurse sticks a needle in my arm, gathering some blood.

Overall, the scene feels much more dramatic than it really is. *Calm your shit*, I instruct myself. *There will be more doctor's visits like this one. Pull yourself together.*

My heart rate slows when the nurse leaves the room. I lean back against the white exam table. It feels stiff and cold below me, an unwelcoming bench with very little padding.

The doctor arrives after a couple minutes. She's a pretty Indian woman in her late thirties.

"Hello, Callie," she says, smiling warmly. "Nice to meet you. I'm Doctor Pritika."

"Hi," I say quietly.

"How have you been feeling? When did you discover you were pregnant? Do you have a family history of heart disease, hypertension, mental health issues?"

She proceeds to ask a flurry of questions, which I answer to the best of my knowledge.

After a physical exam and pap smear, she assures me the fetus and I are in good shape.

"Umm, I don't know if this matters, but it feels important," I say, staring at my hands. "I'm not planning to keep the baby. I mean, I'll give birth. But the father is going to raise the child. I'm signing away all rights."

Doctor Pritika doesn't bat an eye. "For now, we are

focused on your health as well as the baby's. Your decisions are yours to make, Callie, and what you've chosen is perfectly fine."

"Thank you," I say, impressed by her level of acceptance.

She smiles at me. "I have seen many women who are giving the baby up for adoption, women who are still considering abortion...all of those choices are personal ones. As your doctor, I simply want to ensure you are in the best physical state possible. My job is to support you throughout your pregnancy."

"Thank you," I murmur.

"Are you ready for the ultrasound?" she asks gently.

I nod, then ask if Andrew can join us for the next part. A nurse escorts him into the room. He strolls in, beaming, and clasps my hand.

"This might feel a bit cold," Doctor Pritika warns as she applies cool gel.

I inhale sharply while waiting to view the activity inside my uterus.

Andrew's eyes are glued to the screen. He emits a small gasp when a shape begins to appear.

"Is that the heartbeat?" he asks, a faint rhythm filling the room.

"Yes," Doctor Pritika tells us.

Oh my God, I think. *You're really in there, little one? I can see your outline, but I still don't feel like you are living and growing inside my body.*

"Can you tell what gender it is?" Andrew asks.

Doctor Pritika shakes her head. "Not yet. We'll be able to determine the sex at your mid-pregnancy ultrasound, in another eight weeks."

"I see," Andrew says. He squeezes my hand gently and looks at me.

I smile up at him. Then I return my attention to the screen, to the child I never anticipated and still don't feel connected to. I silently beg the fetus to be kind to its father. He is, after all, a genuinely good guy.

Chapter Twenty-Three

January 12, 2020

"Thanks so much," I say, wrapping him in a hug. "You take great care of me every time I visit."

"I can't wait 'til you're back," he tells me. "And I'm so glad you found an apartment, Cal."

"Me, too."

An officer strolls past, gruffly demanding we move our vehicle.

"Guess that's my cue." Andrew smiles. He pulls my luggage from the trunk of his car. "When will I see you next?"

I tilt my head to the side. "This weekend is going to be insane. Damn. Mackenzie gets married tomorrow. Wild, huh? Then I'm back to work on Saturday, at like 4 p.m., but I think it's West Coast layovers."

"Gotcha," he says. He slides his arms around my waist. "Maybe I can come to SF next weekend. You shouldn't have to travel to me all the time; I can put in the effort, too."

"Oh, did you think I was coming to Florida to visit *you*?" I tease, trying not to smile too big. "I was here on some important business and you just happened to be in the area."

"Lucky me." He laughs.

I place my hand behind his head, kissing him

fervently.

"Have a good day at work," I say, grabbing the handle of my suitcase.

"Thanks, Cal. Fly safely."

I plant another kiss on his lips, then head toward the double doors. The airport is as empty as it had been the day I arrived; I breeze through security and linger near the gate, waiting for my plane to land. An hour before the flight, I walk up to the desk. The gate agent gives me a business-class seat.

"Thank you," I tell him, staring at the paper ticket in my hand. "It's been a long time since I flew in business class."

"Enjoy it," he says cheerfully. "We're so empty today, you'll have the whole row to yourself."

Before taking my seat in the third row, I greet the lead flight attendant. I thank him profusely, explaining I was in Florida preparing for my move to Fort Lauderdale. He congratulates me on my new base.

"Fort Lauderdale is great," he says. "I moved up to Providence because my fiancée got a job there. But I was based in FLL for two years. Honestly, it's the best base in the system."

"I'm excited to try it out," I note with a smile. "Thanks again for the upgraded seat."

Since the gate agent said I'd have the whole row to myself, I toss my backpack onto the open seat next to mine. Each side in business class has two giant seats instead of three cramped ones, like in main cabin.

With a contented sigh, I settle into the big, comfy cushions. Then I open my laptop.

Dear small human, in a couple weeks, I'll have a new residence on the East Coast. My life will be flipped around, a complete 180. For the first time in a long time, I'm excited about all the upcoming adjustments. Thank you for inspiring such drastic changes.

"Excuse me," someone says, stirring me from my thoughts.

I look up to find a pretty woman dressed in a pencil skirt and matching blazer. Her hair's pinned back in an intricate up-do.

"I'm sorry; this row was probably empty before, but I had to rebook my flight just now," she explains apologetically. "I missed the Miami flight earlier this morning, unfortunately. Our meetings ran late."

"Oh gosh, it's no problem. Here, let me move my stuff," I say, reaching for my backpack. I pull my laptop cover from the seatback pocket and check the area once more, to ensure I cleaned everything.

"I think I got everything. It's all yours," I inform her with a smile.

"Thanks again," she says. She sits down, buckles up, and slides her black briefcase under the seat in front of her. "Sorry if I stink. My Uber was hot as hell; I asked the driver to turn up the A/C, but it must've been broken."

"You smell perfectly fine," I assure her with a laugh. All I can detect is a floral perfume; there's no hint of sweat.

She shakes her head. "You're sweet, but I promise I do not."

The crew begins its safety demo. I glance at the female flight attendant, a petite brunette, showing passengers how to put on life preservers. She looks slightly familiar, but I can't recall where I've seen her.

"You definitely don't need to apologize. It's been a

whirlwind week for me. I feel like a complete mess," I tell my seatmate. "Scattered and disheveled and a little out of it. I haven't slept much."

She turns toward me, close enough for me to see every detail of her face. The lady's complexion is absolutely flawless. She seems a few years older, most likely in her mid-thirties, but her skin is insanely smooth. Not a wrinkle in sight. She doesn't have the leathery look of people who have spent years worshipping the Florida sun.

"Are you flying home, or going on vacation?" she asks, adjusting her dark-rimmed designer glasses with two fingers.

The plane speeds up, preparing for takeoff. Engines roar behind us.

"Guess I'm going home. Well, kind of," I respond, tilting my head to the side. "I live in SF but I'm moving to Florida by the end of the month. Yesterday, I signed a lease for my new apartment. It's in Delray Beach."

"Fantastic. I'm in Miami, in the Design District. South Florida is amazing. I mean, it's totally different from the West Coast," my seatmate clarifies. "It has its own appeal, though."

I nod. "At first, I was hesitant about moving. I went to college in Florida, and I do love the endless summer here. But I've gotten used to the excitement of San Francisco. It's got this crazy, appealing chaos. Wild and busy and energetic. I wasn't thrilled about switching coasts, but I'm really warming up to the idea. Things are falling into place. I'd forgotten how peaceful and soothing Florida is. In college, I sat outside on the quad when I was studying for finals each semester. It's hard to be stressed when you're lying on a beach towel in the middle of February."

"Agreed. Where'd you go to school?" she inquires as we ascend through fluffy white clouds. I lower my window shade, concealing the blinding sunlight.

"UF."

"Really? Me, too. I'm a bit older than you, though."

"What was your major?" I ask. "I studied History. God knows I never used it, but I minored in English and I took a ton of really fun creative writing classes."

"Same here. I was a double major, Journalism and Mass Communications. I'm Gina, by the way."

"Nice to meet you," I say, extending my hand. "I'm Callie. I'm actually a SkyLine flight attendant, just flying standby to get back to SF."

"I bet it's a really fun job," she notes, her eyes sparkling. "To be honest, it's always been my secret fantasy to be a stewardess. Seems so glamorous."

I chuckle. "Sometimes it is. Other times, it's exhausting. But I love it, despite the hectic schedules, delays, and unhinged passengers."

She snorts. "I can imagine. You must see some real winners."

"Every day." I nod emphatically. "Most travelers are great, but every now and then we have to deal with someone insane. My patience has been tested a few times. On the plus side, it makes for some good stories."

"Well, I'm always looking for good stories," Gina tells me. "Discovering new talent is the best part of my job. I love writers who can weave together a unique tale, one I've never heard before."

I pause, unsure if I heard her correctly.

227

"Um, what do you do for work?" I ask slowly.

She pulls a mirror from her purse and reapplies her fiery red lipstick. "Oh, I thought I mentioned that already. I'm the VP of Publishing for Wondrous Words, the anthology division of Clarity Books."

"Clarity Books, as in the publishing house in Miami Beach?" I murmur, even though I already know for a fact this is the *exact* company she's referring to. I sent a couple manuscripts to them years ago, right after completing my first two novels. I never got anything back, not even a rejection letter. Which is common for the big publishers; if they wanted my novel, they would've found a way to contact me. Silence meant they couldn't care less.

"That's the one," she says. "I was lucky enough to get my foot in the door right after college. Worked my way up to my current role, and now I'm in charge of finding authors who are a good fit for our publishing house."

"I'm insanely jealous," I confess. "It's ironic that you've always dreamed of being a flight attendant, because I'm completely in love with your job."

She raises a slim, perfectly tailored eyebrow. "I don't usually get such an enthusiastic response from people; to the outside world, my career seems mundane."

"Are you kidding? I'd love to work in the literary field. I'm obsessed with the written word. In fact, I was working on my blog during boarding."

Gina leans toward me. "Really? A travel blog, I assume?"

I clear my throat. "No, although I definitely have enough short stories saved on my laptop to start one of those someday."

"Interesting. What's your blog about, then? And can I see it?"

"Of course," I say. With shaky fingers, I unfold my tray table from the console between our seats. Then I set my laptop on top, angling the computer to give Gina a clear view of the screen.

"Dammit," I say. "I need Wi-Fi to access the site."

"No problem, I have a code. All the VPs at Clarity Books get one, since we fly on SkyLine so often." She types her password into my laptop.

"Wow, thanks," I say. I navigate to the website in two short clicks. "There's an Instagram account linked up to the blog. I wanted to keep it anonymous."

"Can I read the blog from the IG page?" she asks.

"Sure," I tell her. I log into my account, surprised to find I have nearly two thousand followers. Trevor's hashtags really worked, apparently.

"Mmm. I love this persona," Gina notes. Her eyes move from left to right at superspeed as she reads through my blog. She clicks the keyboard, scrolling through various posts.

I hold my breath the entire time. After a few minutes of silence, the lead flight attendant comes by for our drink orders. I smile politely at him and shake my head.

Gina asks for merlot, then turns her attention back to me.

"This is pure gold," she tells me. "It's raw and stirring. Your letters are filled with conflicting emotions, yet they always circle back to hope. It feels like the narrator sincerely wants this kid to turn out fine."

"You...you like it?" I stammer, still processing her critique.

"Like it? I love it," she declares. "Tell me, Callie, are these letters true? Or pure fiction?"

"I—"

Gina waves her hand. "Actually, never mind. I don't want to know. The writing is so captivating, it honestly doesn't matter. You have achieved something marvelous with this blog. I believe people would be very interested to read these letters. Looks like you already have a large audience. A couple thousand followers in less than a week...not bad."

Goosebumps spread across my arms and legs. "Thank you. Wow."

"You've got style, Callie," she continues. "I'd love to put you in one of our upcoming anthologies. There's a poetry book we'll release by the end of this year. We also plan to do a compilation of romance vignettes."

I nod, hanging on every word.

"Obviously, your blog doesn't directly align with either of those topics. It's not poetry and it's not a traditional love story," she notes aloud. "But luckily for you, we're also publishing an inspirational book this year. We're seeking short stories about grief, loss, and hope."

"My letters fit in that category?" I murmur.

"For sure," Gina says. "Your letters are tragic, but they're also undeniably hopeful. Callie, I believe you'd make an amazing addition to our inspirational series."

I gasp.

How can this possibly be real? I reflect internally. Flashbacks run through my mind, tiny snippets of heartache and rejection. Countless times in the past, I'd approached the idea of publication with fierce optimism. Every single time, I had watched my dreams dissolve. Slowly and painfully.

Is this time different? I wonder, tears welling up in my eyes.

Gina frowns. "Are you okay, Callie?"

"Yes, I'm great," I assure her. I swallow, blinking away the tears. "Just trying to wrap my head around everything. Gina, I'm honored that you would consider including my letters in a book."

She reaches into her wallet and hands me a business card:

Gina Theolonis ~ VP of Publishing
Wondrous Words, Miami Beach
Anthology Division of Clarity Books

"Can you fly back to Florida next week?" she asks me. "I'd like to introduce you to my colleagues."

"Yes," I say without hesitation. "I work Saturday through Monday, but I'll catch a flight to South Florida as soon as my trip ends. Is Tuesday good?"

"Perfect. I'm speaking at a symposium in Marin County tomorrow, then catching the redeye back to Miami. If you don't mind, shoot me an email tonight. Send me all your contact info, including the Instagram handle. I'll set up an official appointment for you."

"No problem. What time should we meet?"

She thumbs through a calendar on her phone.

"How about three p.m. on Tuesday?" she suggests.

"Sounds great. I'll be there," I promise. "I can't wait, Gina."

****

I lean against my car, staring up at the night sky. The highway is probably a mess; it's Thursday night, during the tail end of rush hour, which means 101 is undoubtedly a shitshow. I predict I'll be stuck in bumper-to-bumper traffic for an hour or longer...but I'm unfazed by this prospect.

The world is shades of pink and purple tonight, brighter than it's been in ages.

"Callie, I am thrilled for you," Andrew says, his voice full of emotion.

I smile. All around me, airline employees walk to their cars. I'm perched against my driver's side door, staring dreamily into space.

"Is this real?" I ask Andrew. I shift the phone against my ear. "I've heard about other flight attendants having fortuitous encounters on the plane, but I never imagined I'd be one of the lucky ones."

"It's one hundred percent real," he tells me. "You have so much talent, Callie. The world is finally going to see it."

I inhale deeply. "Things could still fall through, Andrew. I've gotten my hopes up before, only to have them ripped to shreds. The literary industry is fucking brutal."

"True. But this is the most promising opportunity you've ever had," he points out. "You didn't tell the exec from Clarity Books to read your blog, she asked to do it. And you didn't have to fish around for compliments; without any prompting, she told you she enjoyed your writing. Repeatedly."

"She did. I still can't believe it," I muse.

"You really impressed her," he says. "I'm so proud of you, Cal."

"Thanks, Andrew."

"On a more selfish note, I'm happy you're

returning to Florida next week for the appointment at Clarity Books," he reflects. "I would've flown to SF to see you, but this works out well, too. You can borrow my car again. Obviously."

"You're the best," I tell him. "Thank you."

"Don't mention it. Hey, I just thought of something. I've been in touch with a lawyer about the adoption paperwork we'll need to sign in a few months. Maybe I can ask her for a referral, someone who specializes in contracts? When Clarity Books offers you a publishing deal, you should have a lawyer read it over to make sure it's fair."

"Wow. That hadn't even crossed my mind."

"I just think it would really help to have a lawyer," he reflects. "One who will get you the best book deal."

I sigh happily. "This is wild."

"It was bound to happen," Andrew assures me. "Honestly, I'm surprised it's taken this long for someone to recognize your talent. But I'm glad you're finally getting the attention you deserve."

I'm silent for a moment. The employee parking lot is emptying out; a few cars remain, scattered throughout the massive lot. Probably the redeye crews or late-night flyers.

The air feels crisp and cold against my skin. Its silence is unusual for the Bay Area. There's no wind at all, not even a slight breeze. The calm air balances out the thoughts swirling through my mind.

"I miss you already," I admit when I finally find my voice.

"Me, too."

"Andrew, what are we?" I ask.

"We are two people who accidentally broke a

condom in November," he says with a laugh. "Seriously, though, we are two adults trying to figure things out."

"What are we figuring out..." I trail off.

"Where to go from here," he says. "There's no rush. We can take our time and let things progress naturally. I know you're overwhelmed; I will never pressure you into anything."

"Maybe I want us to be more," I tell him, my confidence surging. "Maybe I'm ready to be your girlfriend, in spite of the absurd circumstances and all the unknowns these next few months hold."

"Are you sure, Callie?"

"Yes."

"Good. It's official, then. For the record, I've wanted to be with you since the day we met," he says. "Thank you for taking a chance on me. I have no idea what the future holds, but I know exactly how I feel about you."

"Same here. I didn't want to like you, Andrew. I fought like hell, trying to ignore my feelings. I found a billion reasons why we would never, ever work. But, in spite of everything, I'm falling for you. You're literally the nicest person I've ever met."

"And you're the most interesting person *I've* ever met."

"Well, thank you," I say. I unlock my car door, nearly half an hour after arriving at the employee lot, and toss my suitcases into the backseat. "Shit, speaking of making things official, Mackenzie gets married tomorrow. I have so much to do tonight."

"Are you excited to be her maid of honor?"

"Absolutely. But it's surreal."

"I wish I could be there with you, Callie. If City Hall is half as nice as I've heard it is, it'll be a beautiful ceremony," Andrew comments.

"City Hall is every bit as stunning as you've been told," I assure him. "I'll send lots of photos."

Chapter Twenty-Four

January 13, 2020

City Hall stretches before us, glistening white stairs leading to three identical arched doorways. The building's creamy façade, with a dome positioned on top, looks like something straight out of a fairytale. Majestic figures protrude from the gable, ancient heroes etched in stone.

Dave and Mackie pose for photos in front of the entrance. Mackenzie's hair is wrapped up in a braid that encircles her whole head, with tiny strands of tinsel woven into the braid.

I reach into my silver wristlet and retrieve my sunglasses, sliding the frames over my nose. It's hot today, much warmer than any of us expected. Fluffy clouds dot the sky. Birds soar overhead, tracing circles and figure-eights around the historic building.

Leaning against a pillar, I smile at the happy couple. Dave's cousin, Kevin, snaps the last few pictures. He assures the bride and groom that all the images look fantastic. Mackenzie breathes a contented sigh.

She shields her eyes from the sun and walks toward me. I hand her a water bottle, figuring she must be thirsty after standing in the hot sun.

Mackie chugs some water and leans in.

"We got our marriage license yesterday," she whispers. "Here goes nothing."

I look her squarely in the eye. "You got this, Mack."

She reaches for my hand, squeezing gently. "I love you."

"And I love you. As you already know," I tell her with a smile.

Mackenzie's parents are a few feet away from us and Dave's brothers are standing on the other side of the pillar. Everyone's dressed nicely, bowties and shiny shoes and pearl necklaces. We walk inside the building together, an eclectic group here to support Mackenzie and David as they tie the knot.

Exactly six guests are allowed on the rotunda for the ceremony. Mackie chooses me, her parents, David's brothers, and his cousin. Together, we ascend the grand staircase to reach our destination.

Ornate columns stretch high above our heads. People line the rotunda's second-floor balcony, waiting their turn to get married. In front of us, an elaborate door is flanked by huge sculptures of celestial beings. A chandelier dangles from the ceiling, its golden hue perfectly matching that of the sconces. No matter how many times I've seen this building, I'm still mesmerized by its sheer beauty.

I stand to Mackie's right, across from Dave's youngest brother. The officiant begins speaking, his voice echoing off the rustic walls. Mackenzie turns her head toward Dave. Although I can't see her face, I am certain she is tearing up.

The observers on the second floor remain silent as the officiant continues his opening monologue. I glance up, briefly, at an older man in a dark blue suit. He looks like he's around seventy years old. He's clasping the hand of his partner, a handsome Asian male who appears to be the same age.

Never too old to fall in love, I reflect internally. Without warning, my eyelids become damp, which is absurd because the ceremony has barely begun and I promised myself I'd hold it together. For Mackie's sake.

Dabbing my eyes, I turn my attention back to my best friend.

The officiant recites a few lines about the emotional union of two souls. He then gives the floor to Mackenzie, whose vows I practically know by heart because I heard them this morning. In Mackie's bedroom. Before anyone else was awake. Wearing a tank top and shorts, and choking back tears, Mack had recited the words to an audience of one: me.

"David, we met at an impossible time," she begins. Her voice is soft but steady. She inhales sharply before continuing.

"Many couples claim the odds were stacked against them. In our case, there were no odds at all. You were with someone else at the time and I was not interested in falling in love.

"A few months later, the world flipped upside down in the most amazing way. I saw you at a frisbee game, single and very social. The rest is history. I remember walking through the streets of our city with you. All these familiar places suddenly felt brand-new. With you, everything made sense. It still does, and it will for the rest of our lives.

"I proposed to you because I was certain. You

proposed to me because you shared my confidence. This summer, we will welcome our first child into the world. There's nobody I'd rather create a future with than you. Thank you for embracing the unexpected, finding beauty in the unknown, and loving me so well.

"I vow to continue learning and growing with you. Day after day. Year after year. I love you immensely, David, and I look forward to a life spent alongside my best friend."

I clear my throat loudly.

Mack cranes her neck toward me. "Oh, shoot. I mean my soulmate and life partner. I already have a BFF. She is very possessive."

Laughter slices through the air, lightening the mood.

"Noted," Dave says with a chuckle. He begins his vows with a description of why he fell in love with Mackenzie.

I glance at the older couple on the balcony once more. The two men are looking at each other, totally enamored, as though there's nobody else in the room...or the entire world. I smile up at them, and the beauty of this building, and the illogical yet poignant entity that is love.

****

The hostess leads us to a private room in the back of the restaurant. Windows stretch from floor to ceiling, giving us a clear view of Civic Center. The sun's still shining, periodically interrupted by passing clouds. Soon, SF's infamous fog will roll in. Possibly before we finish our lunch.

I take a seat next to Mackenzie's mother. She wraps an arm around me, pulling me in for a side hug.

"We heard you're moving to Florida," she says, eyes widening. "We are going to miss you, Callie. It's been great having you over for holidays. And thank you for being such a good friend to Mackenzie. She truly adores you."

"I'll miss you guys, too. Don't worry, I'll still come visit," I say. "And I'm not moving to West Palm forever. Just a year or so."

"To work on your books, right?" she asks.

"And my blog," I add. I consider telling her about the potential book contract with Clarity Books, but quickly decide against it. Mackenzie and David are seated at the center of this long, rectangular table. They're laughing and ordering appetizers for the whole group.

This is their day, I reflect. I'll share the good news with Mackenzie and her family some other time. Today, we celebrate the marriage of two amazing people. One of whom happens to be my best friend on the planet.

Chapter Twenty-Five

January 14, 2020

The view from my Portland hotel is unimpressive. Through the window, I spot a half-empty parking lot and, behind it, a small stretch of highway. I tug the curtains closed, then collapse on the bed.

My phone buzzes with a text from Andrew.

—Are you at your hotel now?—

—Yes, settling in— I respond. I pull an old-school, spiral-bound paper notebook from my backpack. Although my laptop is inside my suitcase, fully charged and ready to be used, tonight I need something more substantial. In this moment, I want to feel something solid in my hands.

I grab a pen from the nightstand. Its shiny gold barrel is inscribed with the hotel's logo, written in cursive. I press the pen to paper and let the words flow through me.

Dear small human, I begin.

My best friend got married yesterday. I've always been skeptical of marriage, especially big, showy weddings. This one was small, though. It was intimate and sincere. In my opinion, it was everything a wedding should be: namely, an exchange of promises between two people who are madly in love.

You might get married someday. It's perfectly fine

if you don't; love comes in many forms, and you can have a meaningful life without a spouse. If you do get married, however, please choose someone who makes you a better person daily, someone who inspires you to try things you're scared of and pursue things you excel at...or want to excel at. I believe a significant other should love you the way you are while acknowledging your potential for greater things.

Your dad is a good example of the qualities you should look for. His selflessness is admirable; he's always eager to take care of others. He's also loyal, reliable, and smart as hell.

I didn't want to love him, little one. There's a messy road ahead, and I'm incredibly confused. But I know this much: some people are genuinely good. Those people are worth being with, even if the circumstances don't make sense. Your father is a gem. You'll know exactly what to seek in a life partner, because you will see firsthand what genuine love looks and feels like. You'll learn from the best.

Sincerely,

Your mom

Just as I'm finishing the letter, my phone buzzes with an incoming call from Andrew.

"Well, hi," I say.

"Hey, Callie. It's not too late, is it?" he asks.

"Nah," I tell him. "It's only nine-thirty on the West Coast. I'll do a little more writing, and maybe watch some TV before bed."

"Okay, great. I was just calling to say goodnight," he tells me. "What are you writing tonight? Another blog post?"

"Yep."

"Can I hear it?"

I pause. When I'd written the letter, I hadn't considered how Andrew would feel about it. "Do you want to? Full disclosure: you're featured in it."

"Now I'm even more curious," he reflects. "Please."

"All right, here goes nothing," I say. I read the blog post aloud, start to finish, unsure whether it's cheesy or intrusive or downright creepy.

"Callie, I'm not really that amazing," he insists once I've finished reading the letter. "I only *wish* I were as perfect as the person you describe."

"I think you are," I argue. "You're different, Andrew. You're giving and patient. You put up with me, even when I'm rude or selfish."

"Maybe you don't give yourself enough credit," he says gently. "You've never been rude or selfish to me. I'm just thankful I get to see you in two days."

"Two more days, huh?" I muse. I return the notebook to my backpack, then lean against the headboard. This bed is super soft, with a thick comforter and half a dozen pillows.

"Yes, forty-eight hours until you're here in Florida," Andrew notes. "I appreciate you sharing your letter with me. Your writing is incredible."

"Thank you," I tell him. "It's easy to write when the topic is something—or, rather, *someone*—you really like."

Part Six: Touchdown

Chapter Twenty-Six

January 16, 2020

"You should run," Monica, the flight attendant up front with me, suggests. We strap into our jumpseats as the plane descends through 10,000 feet, approaching SFO. "Seriously. Your West Palm flight leaves twenty minutes after we land. Just open the door and sprint. I bet you'll make it. Patrick and I will handle the deplaning process, girl. We don't have commuting flights to catch."

"I appreciate it," I tell her, adjusting the straps on my seatbelt. "Really, this means a lot to me. If I miss my flight, the next nonstop isn't until tomorrow morning."

"Don't mention it. You'd do the same for us," Monica says, and it's true. We all do favors for each other, especially when there's a close connection to be made.

We glide onto the runway, an impressively smooth touchdown. As soon as we pull up to the gate, I disarm my door and grab my suitcase from the coat closet. I thank Monica one last time. Then I sprint up the jet bridge as fast as I can in my three-inch heels.

I'm slightly out of breath when I reach the gate. The customer service agent smiles at me.

"Don't worry, we're not closing out the flight for

another ten minutes. No rush," she assures me. "Nine open seats on the plane. I gave you a window seat in mid-cabin."

"Thank you so much," I tell her, accepting the boarding pass she hands me. "I was worried I wouldn't get to Florida tonight."

"You'll make it there. Enjoy the beach," she says with a smile.

—*On my way*— I text Andrew as I board the plane. —*Sorry it's so late. ETA 11:15*—

His response arrives before I even set foot on the aircraft.

—*Definitely not too late. Can't wait to see you. Fly safe, babe*—

I exhale slowly. Nobody has referred to me as their "babe" in years. Since moving to SF, I've been Callie, Cal, or California. Nothing else.

—*See you soon*— I reply. Biting my lip, I contemplate exactly how lame it would sound to use a pet name for him.

After a moment's deliberation, I type —*Looking forward to it, baby*— Then I send the message before I can second-guess my word choice.

I introduce myself to the flight attendants and grab a seat in the middle of the plane.

****

"I thought about saving the surprise for tomorrow but decided against it," Andrew says as he unlocks the door to his apartment. We step into the living room, moonlight pouring in through the windows. He flicks on a lamp.

"Surprise?" I echo, frowning.

He smiles. "Hopefully you don't hate it."

"Hate what?" I ask.

"You'll see," he assures me confidently.

I look up at my boyfriend, impressed that he got me something special and even more shocked he was able to keep it a secret this long. Andrew never struck me as the clandestine type; he's honest to a fault.

Something brushes against my ankle. Startled, I kick my leg.

"What the hell…" I mutter, glancing down. A full-grown cat stares up at me with golden eyes, cocking his head to the side. He marches forward, determined to rub my leg again, despite my spastic response.

"Andrew? Is this my surprise?" I ask, a smile working its way across my lips.

He nods slowly. "It's a weird gift, and a big commitment. I will gladly keep him if you have any concerns. It's just…I know you wanted to rescue a cat this year. Well, this little guy was on death row at the animal shelter. He was about to be euthanized. I swear to God, I went in just to see what cats were available. When I heard he was going to be put down, I couldn't say no. He's so affectionate."

I throw my arms around Andrew. "Thank you so much. He's perfect."

"You're welcome, Callie. I can keep him here until you're settled into your Delray apartment," Andrew tells me. "Then he's all yours, if you want."

I bend down, petting the kitty. His fur is sleek and soft, a beautiful shade of gray with one white patch on his chin. He nuzzles my hand, purring loudly.

"Your motor's running," I inform the cat with a laugh. "Nice to meet you, sweet boy. Sorry about your difficult past, but you're safe now. For all the rest of your days, you'll be happy and loved."

"Isn't he friendly?" Andrew muses.

"Yes. You found me the perfect fur baby," I gush. "What a beautiful cat. He's a Russian Blue, right?"

Andrew shrugs. "I have no idea, actually. His paperwork says he's six years old, neutered, and up-to-date on all his shots. He was the only all-gray cat at the shelter."

Gently, I scratch behind the kitty's ears. He leans his head back in pure bliss. "What's his name?" I inquire.

"The shelter called him Cloudy," Andrew says. "But you can change it, if you want."

"Hmm. I'll think of a special name for you," I tell my new pet. "Since you have a new home, you'll get a brand-new name, too."

I pick him up and rise to my feet. With the cat in my arms, purring happily, I kiss Andrew.

"I love my surprise," I say. "Thank you, babe."

"Glad you approve. This is a big week for you," he reflects, eyes shining brightly. "You're about to land a book deal tomorrow. I wanted to get you something meaningful, something you really loved."

"Well, you succeeded," I inform Andrew, leaning in for another kiss. "Okay, I think I know what his new name should be."

"Great. What should we call him?"

"Silver Fox," I say, lifting the kitty so he's closer to my neck. He presses his wet nose against my shoulder and kneads his paws into my shirt contentedly. "SF, for short."

Chapter Twenty-Seven

January 17, 2020

I wake up with Andrew's arms around me and his right leg tucked between mine. Silver Fox is curled up in a neat little ball to my left. His tail sweeps from side to side, brushing against my tank top.

"Morning, baby," I say softly. SF opens one eye and yawns dramatically.

"Mmmm," Andrew murmurs. "Good morning."

I roll over to face my boyfriend. "Oh, I was greeting my *other* baby. But good morning to you too, handsome."

He snorts. "SF has been here one day and already takes priority over me? Fine. I see how it is."

I kiss Andrew's forehead, then his lips. "Thanks for accepting the hierarchy."

He pins me to his chest, tickling me with one hand.

"Stop!" I shriek, wriggling from his grip. I hop to my feet, the hardwood floor cool against my toes. "You are ridiculous."

"Just making sure you're alert and excited for the day ahead," he tells me, sitting on the edge of the bed. "You're welcome."

I sink into his lap, enjoying another kiss before marching to the bathroom to get ready.

As I'm putting lotion on my face, an ache strikes

my back, toward the bottom of my spine. The discomfort migrates to my abdomen.

"Holy shit," I wince, leaning against the sink with both hands.

"What's wrong, Cal?" Andrew asks as he steps out of the shower.

With one hand still propped against the counter, I reach around to my back. "There was a really strong pain right here, then it moved to my stomach. God, it hurts."

"Morning sickness?"

I shake my head. "Not sure. Maybe? I'm not nauseous. Just uncomfortable."

Andrew holds my waist so I can stand upright. "Is this better, or worse?"

"It feels the same," I say, inhaling deeply. "Damn. It's like cramps, but a million times stronger."

"Do you want to lie down?"

"That's okay. I think it's easing up a little."

"You sure?"

"Yeah. Yes, it feels better," I say with a nod. "Is this some weird pregnancy symptom?"

"I have no idea," Andrew admits, concern radiating from his big brown eyes.

"Me neither. I'll research it," I assure him, reaching for my makeup bag. "Later."

"Maybe you ate something bad?" he guesses.

"Nah, it's probably stress," I reason. "I'm worried about the meeting today."

"You are? Why?"

"Because it's fucking terrifying," I confess, sighing heavily. "Did I tell you I sent two manuscripts to Clarity Books during college? I wrote my first novel at age eighteen. They didn't want my books. Didn't even care enough to send me a rejection letter. I wasn't worth one single piece of paper, or one three-sentence email."

"But things have changed," Andrew reminds me. "I'm sorry you had a negative experience in the past; you deserve better. It was an oversight on their part to dismiss your novels. Everything is different now, though. Their VP told you, in no uncertain terms, she wants to print your letters."

"True."

"You have nothing to lose and everything to gain, Callie. Keep your head up. You've already been told you'll be published. Today is just a formality, where you get to iron out the details."

"Thanks, Andrew," I say as I apply mascara. "I hope you're right."

****

The lobby is every bit as stunning as I'd imagined. White walls display life-sized characters from Clarity Books' most famous novels. Some of the books have been turned into movies over the years, while others have become popular series. I study the murals, recognizing every face except one. A couple of the books are saved on my iPad, and a few more rest on my bookshelf in SF.

In a small state of panic, I realize I'm currently sitting in the building where these novels transitioned from obscurity to international sensations.

I instruct myself to breathe. Slowly. The entire scenario is so surreal that, if I'm not careful, I might faint. Or have a heart attack.

Cold air filters down from vents in the ceiling. I

attempt to focus on the goosebumps covering my legs, because they're real and tangible and safer to think about than my invisible, overwhelming fears. I place a hand on my frigid legs to warm them. With its cool surface, the white leather couch below does me no favors. A tremor runs through my body.

If only I'd thought to bring a sweater, I lament.

Heels click down a hallway, their rhythm similar to that of my anxious heart.

Gina appears beside the receptionist's desk. Her breathtaking knee-length dress fits impeccably and probably cost ten times what mine did.

"Hello, Callie," she greets me, offering a firm handshake.

"Hi, Gina," I say as I follow her down the hallway. "How was the writer's symposium last weekend?"

"It was great, until I found out my redeye was canceled," she responds with a quick laugh. "Although, in hindsight, it was a fortunate twist of events. With an extra day in San Francisco, I finally got to be a tourist. No meetings or deadlines looming on the horizon."

"Did you visit the Wharf? Alcatraz?" I ask. "Golden Gate Park is awesome, too."

"I walked through Little Italy and ate one of the best meals of my entire life," she says. "What's that part of town called?"

"North Beach," I supply. "Such a cool area."

"Yes. Afterward, I saw the sea lions at Pier 39."

"Sounds like you made the most of your extra time in SF," I reflect with a smile. "It's easy to get lost in adventures there."

Gina gestures for me to step inside a conference room. A long table fills the room. It's flanked by ten black chairs with thick padding. Only two chairs are presently occupied.

"Hi, I'm Callie," I say, shaking hands with a middle-aged black woman and a slim man who looks a little older than me. The woman introduces herself as Donna and the male says his name is Justin.

"Callie lives in San Francisco, but she's in the process of moving to Delray," Gina announces to everyone. We take our seats.

"Welcome to South Florida," Donna says with a comforting grin.

I nod. "Thank you."

Gina folds her hands and looks directly at me. "Callie, Donna is responsible for the anthology I was telling you about, the one your letters align with. Her job is to select appropriate excerpts and compile them, so the book is a seamless blend of inspirational stories. Justin runs our in-house editorial team. All of Clarity Books' novels are edited for content and grammar."

I swallow, hanging on her every word.

"They've both read your blog in its entirety, via the Instagram page," Gina continues. "Everyone thinks your letters would be a wonderful addition to the anthology, which has a working title 'Heartlines.' "

Donna jumps in. "We're anticipating entries from about ten authors. So far, we have a short story about a man with a double life, another one about a teenage girl whose brother beats cancer, and a thirteen-thousand-word epic poem about a mythical warrior."

"Such an eclectic mix," I murmur.

"We're hoping to have the book printed by October, so it's available for the holidays," Justin chimes in. "October might sound far away, since it's only January, but the editing process can be really complex. We'd like to get the ball rolling as soon as possible."

"We want to include your letters," Gina informs me. "We'll need to start the process ASAP, so everything's ready to print by autumn. Can you read through this contract by next week?"

She slides a stack of papers toward me. With trembling fingers, I lift the stapled packet and skim the first page, which describes my compensation as well as my obligations to the publishing house. The document is full of legal jargon and bullet points.

"Do you have a lawyer?" Justin asks.

"Yes," I tell him.

"Good. Sit down with your lawyer and comb through the contract to make sure you agree to these terms."

I look up from the stack of paper. "I will."

"Your blog is a decent length; we plan to include all the letters you've posted," Gina says. "But feel free to write a few more, to give your readers a sense of closure. It's still somewhat open-ended, as of your most recent post."

"Sure. I'll add a couple letters, with a definite ending," I promise her.

"We printed a hard copy of the contract for you, but we're also forwarding one to your email address," Gina says. She stands up and shakes my hand once more. "Thank you for coming in today. We look forward to working with you, Callie. And think of a pen name, if you'd prefer to publish the letters under a name other than your own."

"A pen name," I repeat, dumbfounded. *Real*

authors use those; established novelists with a presence and a following.

Gina nods. "It's completely your choice. Thank you for taking the time to meet with us, Callie."

"It's an honor," I respond.

After saying goodbye to Donna and Justin, I walk down the hallway, the same way I came in. Everything feels different this time around. I step outside, where an endless stream of sunshine awaits me. The contract rests squarely in my hand, several sheets of white paper which rectify a decade of frustration.

All this time, I wasn't good enough, I think as I march through the parking lot. *I tried so hard. I lost sleep, lost weight, lost hope. I was never worth anyone's time or consideration.*

But now, on this warm January day, I've been offered a chance at something tangible.

I step inside Andrew's car and dial his number.

"How'd it go?" he asks breathlessly.

"They want my blog," I tell him, laughter swelling up inside me. Adrenaline flows freely through my veins, a rush of energy so powerful that I am tempted to scream. "I did it, Andrew. They offered me a contract. Oh my God. I'm going to be in a book."

"I am so proud of you," he says emphatically. "Congratulations. We have to celebrate tonight."

"Yes," I say. "Shit, I can't believe this. Wow."

"Did they email you the contract? I can forward it to the lawyer."

"Good idea," I comment, putting him on speaker so I can rifle through my inbox. "Okay, I sent it to you. Gina wants a response by next week."

"This is it, Callie. All your dreams are coming

true," Andrew notes.

"They really are," I agree.

****

We're finishing dinner when my back stiffens up, the same way it did this morning. I freeze, hoping the pain will dissipate. Pressure radiates from my spinal cord to my side. It grows stronger with each passing second, until it's dizzying and all-consuming and unbearable.

Across the table, Andrew describes his latest work project. I try to listen, but the throbbing is too intense. I can hardly breathe, let alone focus on Andrew's eagerness to design a high-speed rail to Tampa. I hunch my back in an attempt to lessen the pain. It doesn't help.

The waiter drops off our check. Grimacing, I grip the edge of the table.

"Callie, are you okay?" Andrew asks, noticing my discomfort.

"I don't know," I admit. "It feels like this morning, except worse. I've never had cramps like this. Holy shit."

He tosses several bills on the table and rushes to my side. "Here, let me help you stand."

I nod. "Thanks."

I cling to him as we walk toward the exit. The sharp pangs have migrated from my back to the pit of my stomach. By the time we reach the car, Andrew is practically carrying me.

It's a five-minute drive to Andrew's apartment. I keep waiting for the pressure to ease up, but it never does. Once we're in his living room, I lie down on the couch, perfectly flat and still. I stare up at the ceiling, blinking away tears. Silver Fox rubs my shoulder, purring loudly. It takes all the strength in my body to reach over and pet him.

"What can I do for you, Callie?" Andrew asks. He kneels beside the couch, holding a glass of water and a bottle of acetaminophen.

I swallow two pills, praying they kick in quickly. While I wait, SF licks my arm with his sandpaper tongue. I glance over at him, at his striking golden eyes and the tiny patch of white on his chin. I lift my hand to pet him, then decide against it. This pain is like nothing I've ever felt before. I set my hand on my stomach, gently, as though this can somehow reduce the torment.

"Will you help me to the bathroom?" I beg Andrew. He reaches under my back and lifts me. I hold his neck, burying my face into his chest.

"Should we go to the emergency room?" he asks when we reach the bathroom. "I'm worried about you, Callie."

"I don't know," I murmur. "I'm not sure what to do."

I sit on the toilet and clutch my stomach.

When I look down, there's no urine in the bowl. Only bright red blood, full of clots. Big, dark chunks of flesh. Blood continues pouring out of me. I watch in disbelief. For an instant, I almost forget my pain.

"Andrew," I say meekly, afraid he won't hear me. "Andrew?"

He rushes to my side. For a split second, he freezes.

"I don't understand what's happening. What is this?" I ask, half-crying and half-pleading.

He grabs me, grabs a towel, and then we're out the

door.

The next hour is a blur of streetlights and white walls, the sterile kind you'd only find in a hospital. Andrew holds my hand as I'm placed on a stretcher and rushed to an examination room. The doctor asks if I'm pregnant, if I've had any unusual symptoms lately. Can I pee in a cup, can they draw blood, have I ever had a miscarriage before?

I swallow at the word "miscarriage."

I look at Andrew, seated beside me, searching his face for disappointment or disgust or anger.

All I find is concern. He holds my hand. He blinks, telling me I am going to be okay and he will stay here the whole time. He says he won't go anywhere. He says I'm the strongest person he knows.

But the child you wanted, I think. *Is the baby okay? How could this happen?*

A nurse hands me a paper cup with medicine inside. I don't ask what it's for, I just swallow the pills and lean back, delirious from the pain.

As I'm falling asleep, Andrew uses his finger to wipe tears from my eyes. I hadn't even realized I was crying.

Chapter Twenty-Eight

January 18, 2020

Sleep comes in bursts, one short-lived nightmare after the next. As the sun begins to rise, I stare at the ceiling. Andrew's knocked out, one arm tucked under me. Silver Fox is snoozing, too, at the foot of the bed. I'm the only one who can't find peace.

I didn't want you, I silently tell the child who no longer exists, as of last night. *I was going to give you up, let your father raise you. He's more fit to be a parent.*

The clock on the dresser informs me it is 6:30 a.m., which means it's only 3:30 on the West Coast. I blink, wishing it were later and Mackenzie were awake. I'd give anything to hear her voice right now; she would comfort me, and tell me it's okay, and assure me this isn't my fault.

Andrew stirs. He opens his eyes, looking at me for a moment. Then he takes his free hand and runs it through my hair, sweeping a few unruly strands away from my face.

"I'll take the day off," he says softly. "You shouldn't be alone today, Callie."

I nod. "Thank you."

When I walk into the bathroom, I discover I'm still bleeding. The doctor had said this might happen for a few days. I stare at myself in the mirror, at a reflection which appears no different than it did yesterday. Despite the world being flipped on its head.

Blinking away tears, I peek into the bedroom. Andrew has fallen back asleep, with SF resting beside him. I smile at my boys, a hollow grin, then step into the living room.

My physical pain has decreased significantly. It's been replaced by a pervasive emptiness. I take a seat on the couch, laptop in hand, wondering how a body can feel so completely vacant. If the doctors had told me they'd removed every organ inside me, I would've believed them.

You weren't mine to keep, I reflect. *How can I miss something that was never mine?*

I open my laptop, staring at a blank screen. SF saunters from the bedroom, his eyes fixed on me. He hops onto my lap. Reaching over him, I begin to type.

Dear small human...

The cursor flashes at me aggressively. It reminds me of a heartbeat, perhaps my own. Or perhaps the one I heard on a sonogram last week.

"Goodbye," I murmur aloud. At the sound of my voice, Silver Fox looks up at me. I stroke his head, watching him close his eyes in delight.

Sighing, I return my attention to my laptop.

If there's a heaven, maybe I will meet you there one day. That would be wonderful.

I'm sorry you didn't get to see this world through your own eyes, little one. I'm sorry you didn't get to fall asleep in Daddy's arms, or take your first steps while gripping his hand, or taste solid food for the first time.

Part of me feels responsible for this; I probably

could have done things differently. I could've been more cautious from the moment I discovered you existed. Whatever I did wrong, I apologize. I wish I could go back and do it again. This time, I would protect you from start to finish.

You changed me, helped me become a better person. My entire adult life had been about myself. Until you came along, that is. Suddenly, I was willing to be selfless. That was your influence, small human. You inspired kindness and hope. You changed my perspective and, more importantly, my heart.

You also rekindled a joy within your father. He is so loving; he would have given you the world. You reminded him that the dissolution of his marriage, years ago, did not determine the outcome of his life story.

Andrew will probably have kids someday. He will share with those children all the love he has for you. That kind of affection doesn't fade, baby; it grows and multiplies. You are alive and well through the warmth your father exudes. You might have left us physically, but that's only one aspect of your being. Andrew and I are both affected by your spirit. We have changed drastically, thanks to you.

For years, I've been afraid to open my heart. It started the day I received my first rejection letter from a publishing house. Silly, right? But heartbreak comes in many forms. As a writer, I was so passionate about my books. I fell in love with the process of creating stories. I filled page after page with characters who exhibited very real feelings and aspirations. I became enamored with the art of composition.

Until doors were slammed in my face. Repeatedly.

I wasn't good enough, baby. So I decided that loving something meant I had a hell of a lot more to lose.

You tore down all my walls.

I love you. Really, I do.

I wasn't going to keep you, but that doesn't matter. I love you for the wild surprise you were. I love you for the innocence you represented and the hope you inspired.

Thank you for being you. Small human, I sincerely wish to see you in the hereafter. Until then, please remember you were the best gift I never expected.

Love,

Your mommy

I close the laptop and sit perfectly still. Silver Fox glances up at me, watching the tears stream down my face. I remain like this, completely motionless, as I utter my last goodbyes to the creature I once carried in my belly.

****

Andrew sets a plate of eggs and bacon in front of me. He places his hand on my shoulder, assuring me it's okay if I can't finish the whole thing.

"Thank you for cooking breakfast," I say, pushing the eggs around with my fork. Thankfully, they don't make me nauseous the way they did a few weeks ago. But my appetite is virtually nonexistent. I bite into the bacon and chew slowly.

Andrew sits down at the kitchen table. "Let me know how to help, Cal. Anything you need, anything at all...you got it."

"I think I just want to rest today," I tell him. "On second thought, can we go to the beach for a little while, maybe?"

"Sure," he says with a smile. He reaches for my hand. "I'd love to."

I clear my throat. "Um, Andrew? Look, I didn't sleep much last night, so I had a lot of time to think about things. You have been amazing throughout this whole ordeal. Start to finish, you've been supportive and considerate. But, uh, since the baby's gone now, you don't have to keep taking care of me. I don't want to burden you. We can part ways, if you want. No hard feelings."

He shakes his head. "That's crazy. I wasn't staying with you just because of the baby, Callie. In fact, the child would've been the biggest obstacle in our relationship. I like you for who you are, not because we accidentally got pregnant."

"But won't you resent me, down the road?" I ask. "You want kids. You've been ready for a long time. I'm nowhere *near* ready...and I'm not sure I ever will be. Being with me might mean giving up your dream."

Andrew frowns. "I've been ready for kids for a while, yes. If it had happened, I would've been fine. But I'm also fine without children. I have my nephew, and my sister is going to adopt a second child. I love being an uncle."

"You'll want kids of your own someday," I predict. "I can't guarantee I'll ever share your desire. How could I deprive you of being a dad?"

"You wouldn't be taking away from my life; you'd only be adding to it," he assures me, scooting his chair closer to mine. He places both hands on my knees, looking me squarely in the eye. "If I go to my grave without having children, I'll be okay. I am honestly fine either way. I can lead an amazing life, really enjoy it, and make a difference. With or without kids. But if I don't follow this through with you, if I don't fight for us with everything I've got, I will regret it sincerely. You are the best thing in my life."

"I'm not really that great," I argue, my voice frail. I focus on my hands, afraid to look up at Andrew.

He tilts my chin upward until I'm staring into those big brown eyes of his. "My job is to remind you that you are, in fact, *that* great. I've only known you since November, but I have never felt this way about anyone. Even with my ex-wife, there wasn't this kind of connection. You are all I want, Callie Schneider."

"I want you, too," I say. He wraps me in a hug, firm enough to remind me I'm safe yet gentle enough to prove I am cherished.

****

The waves lap at my toes, slightly cooler than I expected. I let the chilly water wash over my feet, enjoying the sharp contrast of the ocean below me and the piercing sun above me.

"You'll still move to Florida, right?" Andrew asks, his hand on the small of my back.

I nod. "Yes. I thought about it a lot last night. I adore California, but this feels like the right decision. With my letters being published, and the way everything has just fallen into place...well, I need to give South Florida a shot. I want to take a step back, evaluate my goals, and give myself a fresh start."

"Selfishly, I'm happy to hear that," he says with a smile.

I stand on my tippy toes and kiss him. "Selfishly, I'm happy you're happy."

Chapter Twenty-Nine

February 14, 2020

Dear small human,
This is my final note to you. Nobody else will see it; it won't be in the Clarity Books anthology. This one is just between me and you, kid.

Today is Valentine's Day. Your father planned an elaborate evening, but he won't share any details, except I'm supposed to wear a dress. Karina offered to do my hair and makeup, which was nice of her. She's a really fun roommate. Silver Fox approves of her, too. It's the best living situation I could've asked for, to be honest. Florida is starting to feel like home.

A lot has changed since I lost you last month.

Mackie asked me to be her child's godmother. It's an old Catholic tradition. I know nothing about Catholicism, but Mack promised it's more symbolic than religious. She wants me to be a role model for her kid. I never considered myself much of a role model, but I'd like to become one. I'm growing and learning every day, constantly striving to be a better version of me.

Andrew helps with that; he's a genuinely good guy. When I get stressed or overwhelmed, he reminds me I've carved my own path over the years, despite many daunting obstacles. Your daddy assures me I am stronger than even my worst, most intense fears. I would have doubted that statement six months ago. These days, however, I embody it.

I miss you when I glance in Andrew's eyes, little one. You were the first thing he and I created together. You were our first achievement, and one of our best. Your brief existence taught me to be selfless, generous, and kind...by looking past my own small bubble.

I miss you when I spend time with Andrew's nephew, Cameron. He doesn't know about the cousin he almost had. Your grandparents don't know, either. They would've loved you so much. They are as thoughtful and generous as their son. Your dad. The man who has stolen my heart.

When I meet you someday, in the mystery that is the afterlife, I will hold you in my arms and tell you about all the people who would've adored you. Maybe you already know. If so, I'll simply refresh your memory.

Your letters are currently being edited and revised by Justin's team of experts at Clarity Books. In a few short months, the world will hear your story. People all over the globe will appreciate you as much as I do. I truly believe those strangers will learn to love again, better and stronger than before. In your honor.

Thank you, sweet child.

Love always,

Mom

(official pen name: Mia Tesora, which means my treasure)

A word about the author...

A flight attendant for nearly a decade, Lisa Wilkes derives inspiration from her intercontinental excursions. *Flight Path* is Lisa's first novel about a romance made possible by one woman's glamorous traveling gig.
http://lisamichellewilkes.com

Thank you for purchasing
this publication of The Wild Rose Press, Inc.

For questions or more information
contact us at
info@thewildrosepress.com.

The Wild Rose Press, Inc.
www.thewildrosepress.com

To visit with authors of
The Wild Rose Press, Inc.
join our yahoo loop at
http://groups.yahoo.com/group/thewildrosepress/